Nothing Holds Back the Night

NOTHING HOLDS BACK THE NIGHT

A Novel

DELPHINE DE VIGAN

Translated from the French by George Miller

BLOOMSBURY

NEW YORK · LONDON · NEW DELHI · SYDNEY

Published by Bloomsbury USA, New York

All papers used by Bloomsbury USA are natural, recyclable products made from
wood grown in well-managed forests. The manufacturing processes conform
to the environmental regulations of the country of origin.

LIBRARY OF CONGRESS CATALOGING-IN-PUBLICATION DATA

Vigan, Delphine de.
[Rien ne s'oppose à la nuit. English]
Nothing holds back the night / Delphine de Vigan ; Translated from the French by George
Miller. — First U.S. Edition.
pages cm
"Originally published in France in 2011 as Rien ne s'oppose à la nuit."
ISBN: 978-1-62040-485-0 (alk. paper)
1. Vigan, Delphine de. —Family—Fiction. 2. Vigan, Delphine de. —Translation into
English. I. Miller, George, 1965- translator. II. Title.
PQ2722.I43R5413 2014
843'.92—dc23
2013021065

Originally published in France in 2011 as *Rien ne s'oppose à la nuit*
First published in Great Britain in 2013
First U.S. Edition 2014

1 3 5 7 9 10 8 6 4 2

Typeset by Hewer Text UK Ltd, Edinburgh
Printed and bound in the U.S.A. by Thomson-Shore Inc., Dexter, Michigan

For Margot

One day as I was painting, black invaded the whole canvas, without shape or contrast or transparency.

In that extreme I saw a kind of negation of black.

The differences in texture reflected more or less faintly the light, and a light emanated from the darkness, a pictorial light the emotional power of which stimulated my desire to paint.

My instrument was no longer the dark, but that secret light that came from the dark.

Pierre Soulages

PART ONE

My mother was blue, a pale blue mixed with the colour of ashes. Strangely, when I found her at home that January morning, her hands were darker than her face. Her knuckles looked as though they had been splashed with ink.

My mother had been dead for several days.

I don't know how many seconds or possibly minutes I needed to take this in, despite how obvious it was (my mother was lying on her bed, unresponsive to all entreaties); it was a very long time, a clumsy, frantic time, until a cry came from my lungs, as though I had been holding my breath for several minutes. Today, more than two years later, that still puzzles me: how did my brain manage to keep the perception of my mother's body at such a distance, especially its smell? How could it take so long to accept the information that lay before it? That's not the only question her death left me with.

★

3

Four or five weeks later, in an unusually impenetrable state of numbness, I received the Booksellers' Prize for a novel which featured a mother walled up in herself and withdrawn from everything, who regains her ability to speak after years of silence. I gave my own mother a copy of the book before it came out, probably feeling proud of having completed a new novel, but also conscious, even through fiction, of turning the knife in the wound.

I have no memory of where the prize-giving took place nor of the ceremony itself. I don't think the terror had left me; and yet I smiled. A few years earlier, when the father of my children reproached me for *rushing headlong into the future* (he mentioned my annoying ability to put on a brave face, whatever the circumstances), I had self-importantly told him that I was *in life*.

I kept smiling at the dinner in my honour; my only concern was to remain upright, then seated, not to suddenly collapse into my plate, or plunge head-first as I had done at the age of twelve into an empty swimming pool. I remember the physical, indeed athletic dimension this effort to hold on required, even if no one was taken in. It seemed to me better to contain the sadness, to bottle it up, muffle it, silence it until I was finally alone, rather than give in to what could only have been a long howl or, even worse, a deep moan, and would undoubtedly have prostrated me on the floor. Over the past few months, events in my life had sped up markedly and life had once again set the bar too high. And so, it seemed to me, there was nothing else to do except put a brave face on it or else face up to it (even if it meant pretending).

And as far as that is concerned, I have known for a long time that it's better to remain upright than lie down, and better to avoid looking down.

In the months that followed I wrote another book I had been planning for several months. In hindsight I don't know how I managed it, except that there was nothing else to do once the children had gone to school and I was in the void, nothing apart from that chair waiting in front of the computer, nowhere else for me to sit, I mean, nowhere to put myself. After eleven years with the same company – and a long confrontation which had left me feeling drained – I had just been sacked; I was conscious of feeling a kind of dizziness when I found Lucile at home, so blue and still, and then the dizziness turned into terror and the terror to a kind of fog. I wrote every day and no one but me knows how much that book, which has nothing to do with my mother, nonetheless bears the imprint of her death and the state of mind it left me in. And then that book came out and there was no mother to leave hilarious messages on my answering machine about my TV appearances.

One evening that same winter on our way back from an appointment at the dentist's, as we walked side by side on the narrow pavement on the rue de la Folie-Méricourt, my son asked me, without warning or anything in our preceding conversation which could have led him to it: 'Did Grandma . . . commit suicide, in a sense?'

Even today when I think of this question, I feel overwhelmed; not for its meaning but its form, that 'in a sense' from the lips of a nine-year-old child, a precaution for my sake, a way of testing the water, of tiptoeing. But maybe he was genuinely asking a question: given the circumstances, should Lucile's death be considered suicide?

The day I found my mother at home I was unable to pick up my children. They stayed at their father's. The following day I told them about their grandmother's death; I think I said something like, 'Grandma's dead', and in reply to their questions: 'She decided to go to sleep' (and yet I have read Françoise Dolto). A few weeks later, my son was calling me back to order: a spade is a spade. Grandma committed suicide, yes, she did herself in, rang down the curtain, gave up, called it a day, said stop, enough, *basta*, and she had good reasons for coming to that conclusion.

I don't know when the idea came to me to write about my mother, *around* her, *starting from* her. I know how strongly I resisted the idea, kept it at a distance for as long as possible, making a list of the countless authors who have written about their mothers, from the earliest to the most recent, as a way of proving how thoroughly the seam had been mined and the subject overworked. I banished phrases which came to me in the early hours or prompted by a memory, and so many openings of novels in all possible forms whose first words I didn't want to hear. I listed obstacles which would inevitably arise and the incalculable risks I would run in undertaking such a task.

My mother represented too vast a field, too dark, too desperate; in short, too risky.

I let my sister collect Lucile's letters, papers and writings and put them in a special trunk which soon after she took down to her cellar.

I had neither the space nor the strength.

And then I learned to think of Lucile without it taking my breath away: the way she walked, her upper body leaning forward, her bag resting on her hip with the strap across her body; the way she held her cigarette, crushed between her fingers; of how she pushed her way into a metro carriage with her head down; the way her hands shook; the care with which she chose her words, her short laugh, which seemed to take her by surprise; the way her voice changed under the influence of an emotion, though her face sometimes showed no sign of it.

I thought I ought never to forget anything of her bizarre, dry sense of humour, of her unique capacity for fantasy.

I remembered that Lucile had successively been the lover of Marcello Mastroianni (she clarified: 'I could go for half a dozen like him'), of Joshka Schidlow (a theatre critic on *Télérama* magazine whom she had never met but whose intelligence and writing style she admired), of a businessman called Édouard, whose true identity we never discovered, of Graham, a genuine tramp and sometime violinist in the fourteenth *arrondissement* who was murdered. I shan't speak of the men who really shared her life. I remembered my mother enjoyed a chicken stew with Claude Monet and Immanuel Kant one evening in a distant suburb from which she returned on the RER, and that she was refused a cheque book for years as a result of giving away her money in the street. I remembered that my mother ran the IT system of the company she worked for, as well as for the whole of the Paris public transport network, and that she danced on café tables.

I don't know when I gave in; perhaps the day I realised how much writing, my writing, was linked to her, to her fictions, those moments of madness in which her life had become so burdensome that she had to escape it, moments in which her pain could only find expression in stories.

And so I asked her brothers and sisters to talk to me about her, to tell their stories. I recorded them, along with others who had known Lucile and our joyful but ravaged family. I accumulated hours of digital words on my computer, hours full of memories, silences, tears and sighs, of laughter and secrets.

I asked my sister to bring the letters, writings and drawings out of the cellar; I searched, ferreted, scratched around, unearthed, exhumed. I spent hours reading and rereading, watching films, looking at photos, repeating the same questions and asking others too.

And then, like dozens of authors before me, I attempted to write my mother.

For over an hour, Lucile had been watching her brothers as they leapt from the ground to the stone, from the stone to the tree, and from the tree back to the ground, in a jerky dance she had trouble following. They were now huddled round what she imagined must be an insect, but she couldn't see it. Soon their sisters joined them, feverish and impatient, trying to push their way in to the middle of the group. When they saw the creature, the girls screamed; *as though they're being strangled*, thought Lucile, so shrill were their cries, especially Lisbeth's, who was capering around like a goat, while Justine called to Lucile in her shrillest tone to come and look at once. In her light crêpe silk dress, with her legs crossed so that nothing would get crumpled and her socks pulled up without a wrinkle over her ankles, Lucile had no intention of moving. Sitting on her bench, she didn't miss a second of the scene being played out before her, but nothing in the world would have made her reduce the distance between her and her brothers and sisters, who had by now been joined by other children attracted by their shrieks. Every Thursday, absolutely without exception, their mother Liane sent her unruly brood to the square; the older ones were entrusted with looking after the little ones, their only instruction not to come back before two hours were up. With great commotion, the siblings left the apartment on the rue de Maubeuge, went down the five flights of stairs, crossed the rue Lamartine then the rue Rochechouart before reaching the square, triumphant and remarkable, for no one could ignore these children who were only a few months apart in age, with their blond almost white hair, their bright eyes and their noisy games. Meanwhile, Liane would lie down on the nearest bed and sleep like a log; two hours of silence to recover from the round of pregnancies, childbirth and breast-feeding, the nights interrupted by crying and nightmares, the washing and the dirty nappies, the endless round of meals.

Lucile always sat on the same bench, a little apart, but sufficiently close to the trapezes and swings, a strategic vantage point which was ideal for seeing everything. Sometimes she agreed to play with the others; sometimes she stayed where she was, *sorting things in my head*, she explained, though she never said exactly what, or only made a vague gesture with her hands. Lucile sorted through the shouts, laughter, tears, comings and goings, the perpetual noise and commotion in which she lived. However, Liane was pregnant again; there would soon be seven of them, then probably eight and maybe more. Sometimes Lucile wondered if there was a limit to her mother's ability to bear children, if her belly could fill up and empty like this for ever, producing smooth pink babies that Liane devoured with her laughter and kisses. Or perhaps women were limited to a certain number of children, which Liane would soon reach, and then at last her body would be left unoccupied. With her feet swinging freely, sitting exactly in the middle of the bench, Lucile was thinking about the baby that was on its way and whose birth was expected in November. A black baby. For every night, before she fell asleep in the girls' bedroom, which already contained three beds, Lucile dreamed about a little sister who was entirely, irreversibly black, plump and shiny like a black pudding, whom her brothers and sisters would not dare go near, a little sister whose tears no one would understand, who would howl ceaselessly and whom her parents would eventually entrust to her. Lucile would take the baby under her wing and into her bed, and, even though she hated dolls, she would be the only one who could look after her. The black baby would be called Max, like the husband of Mme Estoquet, her teacher. He was a truck driver. The black baby would belong exclusively to her, would obey her in every situation, and would protect her.

Justine's cries roused Lucile from her thoughts. Milo had set fire to the insect, which had burnt up in an instant. Justine came running up and hid between Lucile's legs, her little body racked with sobs and her head resting on her knees. As Lucile stroked her sister's hair, she noticed the trickle of green snot on her dress. It was not the day for this. Firmly she raised Justine's head and ordered her to blow her nose. Her little sister wanted to show her the dead insect and eventually Lucile got up. All that remained of the creature were some ashes and the hardened shell of its carapace. Lucile kicked sand over it, then raised her leg and spat on her hand to rub her sandal. Then she took a tissue from her pocket, dried Justine's tears and wiped her nose, before taking her face in her hands and kissing her, a proper kiss like one of Liane's, with her lips pressed to her sister's round cheeks.

Justine, whose nappy had come undone, ran off to join the others. They had already thrown themselves into a new game and were all clustered around Barthélémy. He was loudly telling them what to do. Lucile returned to her place on the bench. She watched as her brothers and sisters first scattered, then ran together again before separating once more. She felt as though she were watching an octopus or a jellyfish or, now that she thought about it, a squishy animal with several heads, which didn't exist. There was something about this nameless protean being – which she was certain she was part of, just as each segment is part of the worm even when it is separated from it – something that covered her entirely, which submerged her.

Of all of them, Lucile had always been the quietest. If Barthélémy or Lisbeth knocked on the toilet door when she had taken refuge there to read or escape the noise, she would command in a voice firm enough to discourage any repeat attempt: leave me alone.

Lucile's mother appeared on the sandy path at the entrance to the square, waving, looking radiant and beautiful. Liane caught the light in an inexplicable way. Perhaps because her hair was so light and her smile so broad. Perhaps because of her confidence in life, her way of wagering everything, holding nothing back. The children ran towards her. Milo threw himself into her arms and clung on to her clothes. Liane began to laugh her musical laugh and said over and over: my little kings!

She had come to fetch Lucile for her photo shoot. When she announced this, there were mingled cries of enthusiasm and protest – the shoot had been arranged for several days after all – a complete hubbub during which Liane praised Lucile for keeping her clothes spotless and managed to give her eldest daughter a few instructions. Lisbeth was to put the four little ones in the bath, get the potatoes on and wait for their father to come home.

★

Lucile took her mother's hand and they headed towards the metro. Lucile had been a model for several months. She had trod the catwalk for the Virginie and L'Empereur collections, two upmarket children's clothes labels, posed for several ads and appeared in the fashion pages of various newspapers. The previous year, Liane had admitted to Lisbeth that the Christmas dinner and all the presents had been paid for by the photos which appeared in *Marie-Claire* and *Mon Tricot*, two series in which Lucile had starred. Her brothers and sisters sometimes went to photo shoots too, but Lucile was the most in demand of them all. Lucile loved the photos. A few months earlier, huge posters for a textile brand had covered the walls of the metro, featuring a close-up of her face with her hair tied back. She was wearing a red pullover and giving the thumbs-up. The accompanying slogan was: 'Intexa – it's like this!' At the same time, all the children in her class and in every class in Paris had received a blotter with Lucile's face on it.

Lucile loved the photos, but what she loved best of all was the time she spent with her mother. The trips there and back on the metro, the waiting between shoots, the *pain au chocolat* they bought in the first baker's they came to; it was stolen time devoted to her alone, when no other child could insist on taking Liane's hand. Lucile knew that these moments would soon cease, because Liane reckoned that at the start of the next school year Lisbeth would be old enough to take Lucile to these sessions or perhaps she could go by herself.

Lucile had put on the first outfit, a fitted dress with fine blue and white stripes and a white flounce underneath which was a couple of inches longer than the dress. When she spun around the dress opened like a flower, revealing her knees. The hairstylist had combed her hair carefully and then pinned it up at the side with a heart-shaped hairclip. Lucile looked at the shiny black sandals she had just put on; they had a perfect brilliance without any scratches, sandals such as she had dreamed of that would make her sisters pale with envy. With a bit of luck she would be allowed to keep them. For the first session, Lucile had to pose sitting down with a little birdcage in her arms. Once Lucile had adopted the pose, the assistant came over to arrange the flounce on the dress around her. Lucile couldn't stop looking at the bird.

'When did it die?' she asked.

The photographer, absorbed with his equipment, didn't seem to have heard. Lucile looked around, determined to catch the eye of someone who could answer her. A young trainee came over to her.

'Probably a long time ago.'

'How long?'

'I don't know. A year, maybe two . . .'

'Did it die in that position?'

'No, not necessarily. There was the man whose job it was to put it the way he wanted.'

'The taxidermist?'

'Yes, that's right.'

'What does he put inside?'

'Straw, I think, and probably other stuff.'

★

The photographer requested silence, the session was about to begin. But Lucile kept looking at the bird from below, searching for an orifice.

'Where do they put the stuffing in?'

Liane told Lucile to be quiet.

Then, when the stylist asked her to, Lucile put on a knitted woollen ski suit (she posed, sticks in her hands, against a cardboard background), a tennis outfit with a pleated white skirt which would have made any of her friends swoon, and finally a swimming suit consisting of a crop top, high pants and a thick plastic bathing cap which she thought was ridiculous. But nothing could detract from Lucile's beauty. Wherever she went, people looked at Lucile admiringly. They praised the regularity of her features, the length of her eyelashes, the colour of her eyes, which went from green to blue, passing through every metallic shade, her smile, which could be shy or relaxed, her light hair. For a long time, the attention she attracted had made Lucile ill at ease and gave her a feeling that something sticky was attached to her body, but at the age of seven, Lucile had built the walls of a hidden territory which belonged to her alone, a territory where the noise and the gaze of others did not exist.

One pose followed another in silent concentration as the backdrop and lighting changed. Lucile went back and forth between the dressing room and the set, adopted poses, pretended to be moving, repeated the same gesture ten, twenty times with no sign of tiredness or impatience. Lucile was a good girl, a model of good behaviour.

When the session was over and Lucile was getting changed, the stylist offered Liane another photo shoot for *Jardin des Modes* at the end of the summer. Liane accepted.

'And your little boy, the one who came with Lucile once and is a bit younger than her?'

'Antonin? He's just turned six.'

'He looks very like her, doesn't he?'

'That's what people say, yes.'

'Bring him along. We'll do a series with the two of them.'

In the metro, Lucile took her mother's hand and didn't let go the whole way back.

When they came into the room, the tablecloth was on the table. Georges, Lucile's father, had just got back and was reading the paper. The children burst in like a single being, Lisbeth, Barthélémy, Antonin, Milo and Justine, dressed in the same towelling pyjamas – Liane had bought six pairs on special offer at the start of the winter – and wearing identical luxury slippers with triple soles, a gift from Dr Baramian. A few months earlier, exhausted by the noise which came from the floor above during his consultations and convinced that Georges and Liane's children were walking around in clogs, Dr Baramian had sent his secretary to collect a note of their shoe sizes. Very soon after, he had a pair of slippers delivered for each of them. Apart from the general commotion, it turned out that Milo, who moved around on his potty at high speed – alternating between potty and legs, potty and legs – was in fact the noisiest of them all. Touched by the doctor's kindness, Liane had tried to mute the noise her son made by putting him

– still on his potty – on top of a chest of drawers. Milo broke his clavicle and the din continued.

Liane sent Lucile to have a shower while the others set the table.

Recently Liane had given up making her children say a prayer before dinner. Barthélémy's clowning had got the better of her patience – he repeated his mother's prayer in a stage whisper, beginning every evening with 'Our Father, who fart in heaven', and causing general hilarity.

They were finishing their soup when Lucile came to the table, with bare feet and wet hair.

'Well, my beauty, have you been having your picture taken?'

The way Georges looked at his daughter seemed full of surprise. Lucile possessed a sombre quality that he had too. Lucile had intrigued him since she was very young. Her way of withdrawing, absenting herself, of standing to one side of a chair as though she were waiting for someone, of using language sparingly, her way, he had sometimes thought, of not compromising herself. But Lucile, he knew, missed nothing, not a sound or an image. She took everything in. Absorbed it all. Like his other children, Lucile wanted to please him, watched for his smile, his approval, his praise. Like the others, she waited for her father to come home and sometimes, with Liane's encouragement, told him about her day. But Lucile, more than all the others, had a connection with him.

And Georges could not stop looking at her in fascination.

★

Years later, her mother would talk about this attraction that Lucile exerted on people, her combination of beauty and absence, the way she had of meeting your gaze while lost in thought.

Years later, when Lucile herself was dead long before she could become an old lady, we would find among her things the advertisements showing a little girl, smiling and natural.

Years later, when we came to clear Lucile's apartment, we would find a whole roll of film at the back of a drawer, containing shots she had taken from every angle of her father's dead body in a beige or ochre suit, the colour of vomit.

The possibility of death (or rather the awareness that death could strike at any moment) came into Lucile's life during the summer of 1954, just before she turned eight. From then on, the idea of death would be part of Lucile, a fault line, or rather an indelible imprint, like the round, crudely drawn watch that she would later have tattooed on her wrist.

At the end of July, Liane and the children had gone to L., a little village in the Ardèche where Georges's parents lived. Some of their cousins had joined them. Only Barthélémy was absent; he had been so troublesome in the weeks leading up to the holidays that his parents had decided to send him to a summer camp. Liane was seven months pregnant. Lucile was missing her elder brother, who had always filled the space with his commotion, his teasing and his sudden bold acts. However annoying he might be, Barthélémy made things more interesting, she thought.

The days flowed by in the August heat, sweet and full; the children played in the garden, swam in the Auzon, made things with clay from the river. In the big schoolteacher's house in the middle of the village, Liane, with help from her in-laws, was able to rest. Georges had stayed behind in Paris to work.

One afternoon when Lucile was practising the piano, cries filled the garden. Not the cries of games or squabbles, which she no longer noticed, but much shriller cries, cries of terror that she didn't recognise. Lucile stopped, her hands poised above the keyboard, trying to distinguish words, but she couldn't make them out. Then Milo's little voice – or was it one of the others? – eventually reached her, perfectly clearly: 'They've fallen in! They've fallen in!' Lucile could feel the pounding of her heart reach her stomach and then in the palms of her hands. She waited a few more seconds before getting up. Something had happened, she realised, something that could not be fixed. Then she heard Liane's shouts and rushed out of the house. She found the children clustered around the well, Justine crouching by her mother's skirts, while Liane, leaning over the black hole whose bottom she could not see, was shouting her son's name.

Antonin and his cousin Tommy had been playing on the planks that covered the well when the wood had given way. The other children had seen the two boys fall in. Tommy had bobbed to the surface at once; they could see him and speak to him. The water was icy but he seemed to be holding on. Antonin did not reappear. By the time the firemen arrived, Liane had to be restrained from jumping in. It took both her parents-in-law to hold her back. After a few minutes, Tommy had begun to cry, his voice echoing in a strange way, both near and far at the same time. Lucile thought that perhaps a monster was eyeing him up from under the water or nibbling at his feet, ready to drag him down into the abyss.

During all this she had stood back, three feet behind her mother, who was struggling with a strength she had never seen before. For the first time, Lucile said her prayers silently, every one that she knew, the Our Father and Hail Mary, without any hesitation or mistakes. The firemen arrived with their equipment and the children were sent to the neighbours. They searched for Antonin's body for a long time before they found him. The well was linked to an underground tank. Antonin had died of hypothermia.

Georges hurried back from Paris. Antonin was dressed in white and laid out in the bedroom on the top floor and Liane explained to the children that Antonin had become an angel. Now he would live in the sky, way up high, and would be able to look down on them.

During the wake, only the older ones were allowed to see him. While they prayed, Liane stroked the dead child's plump hands. They were cold and soft, but as the hours went by, Antonin's hands became stiff and Lucile began to doubt that he would be resurrected soon. She looked at his smooth face, his arms by his sides, his mouth half-open, as though he had just fallen asleep and was still breathing.

The burial took place a few days later. Lisbeth and Lucile wore identical dresses (something improvised from what they had in their luggage) and, standing close together, they gave off an air of importance that befitted their status as the eldest. When the coffin had been lowered into the ground, they stood beside their parents, holding themselves very erect, while people expressed their condolences. Family and neighbours filed past in their dark clothes. Lisbeth and Lucile observed the ritual: hands were shaken, shoulders patted; there were hugs, restrained sobs, things whispered in their ears, words of consolation and encouragement repeated ten, twenty times, but all they could catch was a whistling sound or a tickle of compassion breathed in their ear. Soon they no longer heard anything but that; they exchanged glances at each new whisper and little by little an irrepressible fit of the giggles bubbled up. Georges sent them off to calm down.

Antonin had become an angel and was watching them. Lucile imagined his little body with outstretched arms suspended weightlessly in the air.

For a few more days she believed that he would come back and they would look after the goats together above the village. They would go to see Mrs Lethac's baby rabbits and would wander along the dried-up river bed looking for clay.

At the end of the month a family friend went to fetch Barthélémy from the south. When Barthélémy returned from summer camp, his brother was dead and buried. He cried for three days and nothing could soothe him. He cried noisily until he was exhausted.

From now on, Antonin's death would just be a seismic wave underground, which would continue to make itself felt, but in silence.

Lucile and Lisbeth were keeping watch from the window of the girls' pink bedroom, craning forward on tiptoe, waiting for the entry buzzer to crackle. Despite the cold, Lucile felt hot, even suffocated. Liane had wondered if her daughter might have a fever when she returned from school, but as she went to fetch the thermometer, the baby started to cry. A few weeks earlier, a little pink girl called Violette had come out of Liane's stomach, beautiful and plump like a bather. She burst out laughing when you tickled her. Lucile was disappointed at first; the baby looked just like any other. But Violette's smiles, the interest she showed in her older siblings (she waved her arms whenever one of them came into the room), and her fine hair, which Lucile liked to blow on so that it fluttered on the top of her head, had got the better of her disappointment. It was true that Violette was not black and would not be given over exclusively to her, but Liane, now entirely absorbed with the baby, no longer spent long periods sitting in the kitchen staring into space. Violette demanded to be held and fed, she wanted attention. Along with her the sweet smell of talcum had returned, and the sharper one of nappy cream. Yet the atmosphere in the apartment was still suffused with bitterness, as though steeped in it. When Georges returned in the evening, he sometimes sat without uttering a word, exhausted, his features frozen.

Neither Lucile nor any of her brothers or sisters had seen their parents cry.

★

Lucile breathed out and watched the mist her breath made. The courtyard was silent. Lisbeth was stamping her feet with impatience. Beside them, Justine was playing on the bed with an old doll whose nappy she was changing for the umpteenth time. The boys had withdrawn to their bedroom, Barthélémy having ordered a retreat in anticipation, which Milo, frowning petulantly, had obediently followed.

He was about to arrive. Any minute now. They would hear footsteps on the stairs, a key in the door, and then he would be there, in the living room. He would be there for ever. What would he look like? Would he have clothes and shoes, or would he walk in naked apart from a rough habit like a beggar? Would he be dirty? Would he know how to play hide and seek, and statues, would he know how to hang upside down?

Unable to wait any longer, Lisbeth left the room in search of news. She returned empty-handed. Liane didn't know any more than they did, they would have to wait. Their father had gone to fetch him, it was quite a distance, perhaps there were traffic jams.

He was about to arrive. Any minute now. Would he be tall, taller than Antonin, or would he be small and thin? Did he like spinach, white pudding? Did he have scars on his body, or on his face? Would he have a bag, a suitcase or a bundle on the end of a stick like in Hans Andersen's fairy tales?

They didn't know much about him. He was called Jean-Marc, he was seven, his mother had hit him, he'd been taken away. He was called Jean-Marc and they had to be nice to him. He was a little martyr. That word passed between the siblings during the night; a martyr like Jesus Christ, like Oliver Twist, like Saint Étienne and Saint Laurence and Saint Paul. Jean-Marc was going to live under their roof. He would sleep in Antonin's bed and probably wear his clothes. He would go to mass and school, get into the car to go on holiday and he would be their brother. When this word came into her head, Lucile felt her heart beat faster in a fit of anger. Just at that moment, the doorbell rang.

The girls rushed to meet their father. Lucile saw Georges's face, his drawn, tired features. He must have had to go a long way. And just for a second, a split second, Lucile got the feeling that her father had had second thoughts. What if Georges regretted going to fetch the child? What if her father, who had told them that the boy was coming several weeks ago and insisted on how important it was to welcome him as though he were part of the family, didn't want him any more?

Jean-Marc was standing behind Georges, hidden by the large figure he had been hesitantly following. Georges took hold of the child and encouraged him to show himself. Lucile looked at Jean-Marc, a quick glance at first, from top to toe and back again, and then tried to catch his eye. The boy's face was pale, extremely pale, he had black hair, and he was wearing a pullover that was threadbare and too short for him. He was trembling. His eyes were fixed on the floor and his body shrank away as though he feared being slapped. One by one, Lisbeth, Lucile and Justine came forward to kiss him. Barthélémy and Milo eventually emerged from their room, both displaying the same air of scepticism, and looked the child over. Milo couldn't help smiling at him. Jean-Marc was the same height as him. His bag looked almost empty. Milo thought he could give him some things; the lead soldiers he had doubles of, for example, or the pack of cards he no longer played with. Milo wanted to take Jean-Marc by the hand and pull him after him, but when he saw how hostile Barthélémy was looking, he abandoned that idea.

Like the others, Lucile couldn't stop staring at the boy. She searched for the traces of blows on his face, infected wounds, scars that hadn't completely healed. Jean-Marc didn't look such a martyr after all. There were no plasters or bandages that she could see, he wasn't limping and his nose wasn't bleeding. What if he were just an imposter? An urchin like you encounter in books or on country roads, his face grey and dirty with mud, who seeks refuge in families in order to relieve them of their possessions? The child eventually looked up and his eyes came to rest on Lucile, as though astounded. His dark eyes, now wider, returned at once to the ground. Lucile noticed his dirty nails, the white, bald patches of scalp visible under his hair, the dark rings round his eyes, as though he had been crying. She felt overcome by a great sadness and suddenly torn between the desire to chase the child away and the desire to hug him.

Liane asked Jean-Marc if he had had a good journey. Was he tired? Was he hungry? No sound came from his mouth and it seemed only with the greatest difficulty that he nodded or shook his head. Georges suggested to Lisbeth that she show him the apartment. Lisbeth motioned Jean-Marc to follow her. She began in the boys' blue bedroom, with the rest of the children following them, elbowing each other. There was whispering and the sound of laughter: Jean-Marc's socks were a funny colour. Barthélémy remained at the back. He was observing the boy from a distance and there was nothing, nothing at all that could bear comparison. Jean-Marc was small, had a dark complexion and was dirty; with any luck he would be mute. How could his father have believed that he could replace Antonin with someone like this, an oaf, as Georges himself would say, Georges who railed against oafs the world over and who had just unwittingly brought one into his own home? Barthélémy felt a brutal sadness well up inside him, as though he had swallowed a foreign body, a pebble covered in earth or the end of an earthworm. He would never be able to love Jean-Marc, nor even become his friend, nor go out in the street with him, let alone play in the park or on the beach. He could never tell him a secret or have a pact with him. The boy with the scrawny arms could look at him all he liked with his hangdog expression, he wouldn't give in. His brother was dead and his brother was irreplaceable.

I stopped there. A week went by, and then another, without me being able to add a line or even so much as a word to the text, as though it were frozen in a temporary state, destined to remain a sketch for ever, an abortive attempt. Each day I sat down in front of my computer, opened the file called *Nothing*, and reread it. I deleted one or two sentences, moved a few commas, and then indeed nothing more, nothing at all. It wasn't working, it wasn't right, it had nothing to do with what I wanted or had imagined. I had run out of steam.

Yet the obsession remained. It continued to wake me in the night as every new book does, so that over several months I am writing in my head all the time: in the shower, in the metro, in the street. I had already experienced this state of possession. But for the first time, when it came to taking notes or typing at my keyboard, there was nothing but an immense feeling of exhaustion or boundless discouragement.

I reorganised my workspace, bought a new chair, burned candles, incense. I went out, walked the streets, reread the notes I had made in recent months. The photos of Lucile as a child were still spread out on the table, along with pages torn from magazines, contact sheets from ad campaigns and the famous blotter distributed in schools.

In order to feel I was making progress, I decided to transcribe the interviews I had recorded, word for word transcriptions like they do in the career I had for so many years, with the aim of carrying out a content analysis, according to a interpretative grid generally worked out in advance, to which themes spontaneously brought up by the interviewees can be added. I began and spent whole days with headphones on, eyes burning in front of the screen out of a crazy desire to miss nothing, to get everything down.

I listened to changes in voices, the click of lighters, cigarette smoke being exhaled, Kleenexes being fumbled for in vain and noses being blown noisily, the silences, the words which prove elusive and those which come unbidden and unwanted. My mother's brothers and sisters, Lisbeth, Barthélémy, Justine, Violette, my own sister, Manon, and everyone I had seen during the previous weeks had let me into their trust. They gave me their memories, their stories, the idea they had constructed for themselves of their history, they had opened up as far as they could to the limits of what they could bear. Now they were waiting, probably wondering what I was going to do with all this, what shape it would take, what sort of blow they would be dealt.

And that suddenly struck me as insurmountable.

Amid the flood of words and silences was a sentence Barthélémy uttered about Antonin's death, a sentence which, coming from a man who is now sixty-five, I found overwhelming: 'If I'd been there, he wouldn't have died.'

And there were others here and there, highlighted in yellow, which spoke of regret, fear, bafflement, pain, guilt, anger and sometimes peace.

And there were the words Justine spoke as I walked her to the metro at the end of the afternoon she had spent at my place talking about Lucile: 'You will end your novel on a positive note, won't you? Because, you know, we all come from that place.'

As I was completing my transcriptions and still unable to write, I heard myself tell a friend I was having lunch with: 'My mother is dead but the material I'm working with is alive.'

I wrote about Antonin's death – which is considered in family mythology as *the* inaugural drama (there were to be others). To do so, I had to choose the versions which struck me as the most probable from those I had been given, the closest at any rate to what Liane, my grandmother, recounted, sitting on a stool in that improbable mustard-yellow kitchen which marked my childhood and no longer exists. In another version, my grandparents Liane and Georges are both on holiday at L. with the children, whom they have left alone while they have lunch with the neighbours, who live 300 yards away. Antonin and Tommy fall in the well, my grandparents come running when they are told, but it's too late. In yet another version, my grandmother with her big stomach, alerted by the children, dives into the well and they see her reappear as she periodically comes up for air. According to some people, the two boys had been jumping on the planks until they cracked, and according to others, they were quietly making things with clay when the wood, which was rotten and eaten away by insects, collapsed under their weight. And in yet another version, only Antonin fell in, while Tommy escaped.

★

What had I imagined? That I could tell the story of Lucile's child-hood through an objective, omniscient and omnipotent narrative? That all I would need to do was dip into the material I had been given and make my choice, like going shopping? By what right?

I had probably been hoping that a truth would emerge from this strange material. But the truth didn't exist. I had only scattered fragments and the very fact of arranging them already constituted a fiction. Whatever I wrote, I would be in the realm of fables. How could I have imagined for a moment that I could do justice to Lucile's life? What was I searching for ultimately if not to get closer to my mother's pain, explore its contours, its secret recesses, the shadow it cast?

Lucile's pain was part of our childhood and later part of our adult life, Lucile's pain probably formed my sister and me. Yet every attempt to explain it is doomed to failure. And so I am forced to content myself with writing scraps, fragments and conjecture.

Writing can do nothing. At very best it allows you to ask questions and interrogate memory.

Lucile's family – our family therefore – has given rise to numerous commentaries and hypotheses throughout its history. The people I met during my research spoke of fascination; I often heard it mentioned during my childhood. My family embodies the noisiest, most spec-tacular kind of joy, the unrelenting echo of the dead, and the repercussions of disaster. Today I know that, like so many other fami-lies, it also illustrates the destructive power of words, and of silence.

★

Today, Lucile's brothers and sisters (those who remain) are scattered to the four corners of France. Liane died a month and a half before my mother and I believe I am right in saying that the death of Liane, who had already lost three children, gave Lucile the green light she was waiting for to put an end to her own life. Each of us has kept our own vision of our family's foundational events. These different visions sometimes contradict one another; they are so many scattered fragments and bringing them together in a compilation serves no purpose.

One morning I got up and decided that I had to write, even if I had to tie myself to my chair, and I had to go on searching, even though I was sure I would never find an answer. The book would perhaps be no more than that: the account of that quest, containing within it its own genesis, its narrative meanders, its unfinished attempts. But it would be that impulse – hesitant and incomplete – from me to her.

My grandmother Liane was a wonderful storyteller. When I think of her, apart from her legendary talent for doing the splits and her many sporting exploits, I see her sitting in the kitchen, wrapped up in an unlikely pair of red woollen hand-knitted pyjamas (up to the age of eighty, Liane wore various prototypes of nightwear that she made herself in bright colours, with or without hoods), like a mischievous imp or elf, telling the same story for the hundredth time, with a twinkle in her eye and a musical laugh. Liane liked telling stories. For example, how at the age of twenty-two she had broken off her engagement after her mother explained to her a few days before the fateful event what her future role as wife entailed. Liane, like many young women of her age and background, knew almost nothing about sex. A few months earlier she had agreed to an engagement to a young man from a good family who seemed to match her idea of what a good husband should be. Liane was delighted at the prospect of becoming a lady. But it was a far cry from that to lying naked beside that man and allowing him to do *those things* to her which her mother had mentioned so late in the day. On reflection, it was out of the question. Liane liked to talk about the strict middle-class education she had received, being forbidden to speak at table, the demands made by her father, who was a well-known lawyer in Giens, but who in the end agreed to her breaking off her engagement, even though the wedding breakfast was already ordered and paid for. A few months later, Liane met my grandfather at a party while she was visiting one of her older sisters who lived in Paris. At the time Liane was a gymnastics teacher in the same girls' school she had attended as a pupil. Georges told Liane that she was a ravishing little blue fairy; she was wearing a green dress. Georges wasn't colour-blind, he just knew how to surprise women. It didn't take Liane long to fall in love with him. This time, the idea of being naked in bed with a man seemed not only possible but desirable.

Georges came from a family of industrialists ruined by a grandfather with a taste for gambling. His father, after having worked on the railway for a long time, had become a journalist on *La Croix du Nord*. When the paper ceased publication during the German occupation, Georges's family experienced serious hardship. Despite being from a much less middle-class background than Liane, Georges was accepted by my grandmother's parents and they were married in 1943. Lisbeth was born a few months later.

I have no doubt that my grandparents loved each other. Liane admired Georges for his intelligence, his humour and his natural authority. Georges loved Liane for her exceptional vitality, her musical laugh and eternal candour. They made a strange couple: him so apparently cerebral yet totally ruled by his emotions and her, so emotional on the surface, but solid as a rock and absolutely convinced that she was stupid.

In the kitchen of the house they lived in from the seventies till the end of their lives, inside the doors of a huge cupboard which long did duty as a serving surface, were written the dates of birth – and death, where appropriate – of all their descendants. When I was a child, these dates were written in chalk on a blackboard, then, after the kitchen was repainted yellow (I don't know when this happened), the blackboard disappeared and was replaced by a big piece of paper on to which the dates were copied in blue marker.

Lucile, my mother, was the third of a family of nine children. As I write these lines, she would have been sixty-three. When I began my research, Lisbeth emailed me a scanned photo of those cupboard doors taken two years before, when the house had to be cleared. I printed out the photo in colour and stuck it on the first page of the notebook I always have with me. I reproduce here the contents of the photo of the left door, which shows just the first two generations:

GEORGES	06.09.1917–2000
LIANE	07.12.1919
LISBETH	19.07.1944
BARTHELEMY	15.11.1945
LUCILE	17.11.1946
ANTONIN	10.05.1948–1954
JEAN-MARC	07.07.1948–1963
MILO	07.07.1950–1978
JUSTINE	18.03.1952
VIOLETTE	06.11.1954
TOM	10.07.1962

Now no one will be able to complete these lists. Neither the date of Liane's death (November 2007) nor Lucile's (a few weeks later, 25 January 2008) appears. Nor will the children to come appear. The death of my grandmother spelled the end of the house in Pierremont, a little town in the Yonne through which the Burgundy canal passes, which was her family's fiefdom and then ours. The town council acquired the house by compulsory purchase and by now it has probably been knocked down so that the *route nationale* can be extended. The fight against this project was one of the great battles waged by my grandfather Georges, who saved the house from demolition several times.

I look at this photo and its strange geometry. Exactly in the middle of the list of siblings, as though at its heart, are the deaths of my mother's three brothers: three consecutive lines which are longer by virtue of the second date, long like their inexhaustible resonance within flesh and blood.

The last time I visited Violette, Lucile's youngest sister, we searched her cellar for various things I wanted to see. Violette collected up most of the papers when the Pierremont house was cleared. In envelopes stuffed with old photos, arranged by child, we found a picture of Jean-Marc which neither of us had seen before, taken shortly before he became part of the family. Jean-Marc is looking into the lens; his arms are thin, his stomach seems swollen like an undernourished child's, his head is shaved. You can tell he's worried from his eyes. He's a child who is scared. We looked at the photo in silence, struck by the infinite sadness it exuded, then I put it back with the others. We didn't say a word.

That same day, Violette gave me an enlargement of another photo, taken in the summer of '55, a year after Antonin's death and a few months after Jean-Marc arrived. The whole family is sitting in a

Peugeot 202 convertible with the top down which my grandfather had at the time; they have stopped in the middle of what looks like a tree-lined country road. In her arms Liane is holding Violette, who must be nine or ten months old; both of them are looking at the photographer. Georges appears in profile, his head turned towards his children. Barthélémy and Jean-Marc stand side by side between the back and front seats, while behind them Milo, Justine, Lisbeth and Lucile are sitting on top of the back seat, looking at the camera. In the summer light they are all smiling, not the fixed smiles of posed photos but genuine smiles of amusement. Jean-Marc's hair has grown, his cheeks filled out. Lucile is leaning against the door, her hair is tied back in a pony-tail; she's beautiful, laughing. As though in spite of themselves, the children are bunched up in the right-hand side of the photo; beside Milo there's an empty place.

Sometimes, for no reason, Jean-Marc would protect his head with a sudden movement, as though threatened with an invisible blow. Then Liane would go to him, remove his arms from above his head, reveal his face and stroke his cheek. You had to be kind to him, help him with his homework, show him how to tie his laces, sit at the table, teach him his prayers for mass. You had to lend him books and toys, speak kindly to him. Lucile didn't like Jean-Marc. She didn't love him the way she loved Lisbeth or Barthélémy, or the way she had loved Antonin – instinctively. She tried to have kind feelings towards him and sometimes succeeded, when Jean-Marc looked at her with that expression *that could melt your heart*, as her mother said, but the feeling of helplessness always returned. Lucile felt guilty for keeping her distance, for observing him like a foreign body, something different, for finding it so hard to touch him. She didn't want to sit next to him at table, or in the car or on the metro. Jean-Marc was peculiar, he spoke a different language, stood in a different way. Lucile didn't like Jean-Marc but she had got used to him. Jean-Marc was part of the background, he had found his place. She would not have dreamed of questioning his presence. He was there, protected from his own family and trying to fit in with theirs, to adopt its codes, its timetable and its vocabulary. In addition, Lucile shared something with him which the others didn't know about. Lucile was also afraid. Afraid of noise, of silence, of cars, afraid of child-snatchers, of falling over, of tearing her dress, of losing something important. She didn't know when the fear had begun. The fear had always been there. Lucile needed Lisbeth to turn on the light in the corridor and cross the courtyard of their apartment building with her when it got dark. She needed Lisbeth to tell her stories when she couldn't get to sleep and to stand behind her when she went up a ladder. Barthélémy made fun of her. He didn't understand. Barthélémy disobeyed their mother, he was always coming up with new exploits, climbing walls, sneaking off, disappearing. Nothing scared him or could curb his enthusiasm. One day when he had been sent to stand in the corner, he methodically peeled off the wallpaper, watched by his astonished parents. And when Liane, exhausted and at the end of her tether, locked him in the toilet, he would get out through the window and make his way round the courtyard on the window ledges until he reached his room or made his escape via the stairwell. Neighbours watched the child suspended above the void and cried in alarm. But Barthélémy liked heights; he extended his territory from gutter to drainpipe and from drainpipe to cornice, and was soon able to go over the rooftops from number 15A as far as 25.

When she had to make a wish to mark the first occurrence of something – first strawberries, first snow, first butterflies – Lucile always made the same wish. She longed to be invisible: to see and hear everything without giving any sign of her physical presence. She would just be a wave, a breath of air, a perfume maybe, nothing that could be touched or caught. For as long as she could remember, Lucile had captured people's attention. No sooner did she come into a room or stop on the pavement, than adults would bend down, go into raptures, take her hand, stroke her hair, ask her questions: what a delightful little girl, she's so pretty, how beautiful she is, she looks so well-behaved, are you working hard at school? Since the Intexa textile campaign, Lucile had become a child star. She had taken part in the TV show *La Piste aux étoiles* with Pierre Tchernia, then in the extravaganza organised by Georges Cravenne at the Eiffel Tower, where she had her photo taken sitting on Brigitte Bardot's knee. All the big clothing brands wanted her. Georges and Liane only accepted certain offers of work. Some months, the money from the photos helped pay the rent, but Lucile had to keep going to school.

In class, since the blotters had been handed out, Lucile no longer had any prospect of blending into the background. She had experienced admiration, envy, jealousy, converging on her in a concentrated form which made her feel awkward. Lucile could see the desire that some girls had to get close to her, to claim the place by her side, but also their eagerness to find some shameful flaw or ridiculous defect in her which would tarnish her image and enable them to crush her. In spite of everything, Lucile was proud. Proud of earning money, proud of being chosen over others, proud because Georges was proud of her and praised her success.

When she managed to be by herself, Lucile listened to Charles Trenet songs on the record player. Smiling into the mirror, with her hair nicely brushed, she would sing 'Boum', 'La Java du diable' or 'J'ai ta main'. She knew them all by heart.

★

Sunday morning had long been devoted to cuddles: in the warmth of the sheets, in twenty-minute sessions two by two (Lisbeth and Barthélémy; Lucile and Antonin; Milo and Justine), the children would get into Liane and Georges's bed, their small bodies clinging to those of their parents. But after Antonin's death, when they got back from holiday in L., the ritual ceased.

Georges had set up his own advertising agency two years earlier and was prospecting tirelessly for clients. During the week, the children rarely saw him. He came back at night after dinner, kissed them one by one in the same distant fashion and every day Antonin's absence came back to him in the same insidious way as they walked away in their patterned pyjamas: the fact was, one of them was missing. Georges had changed. Not in a sudden, radical way, but quietly, little by little, as though he had allowed himself to be overcome by a hidden resentment whose victory he refused to admit. Georges had lost none of his verve, his wit or his critical turn of mind. His acerbic glances and taste for mockery were still intact. On the contrary, Georges had gained in acuteness what he had lost in tenderness. At dinners and parties he made people laugh and continued to be centre of attention. Words were how he expressed his power, his mastery. Georges's speech was arrogant, precise and pedantic. He castigated others for incorrect agreements, errors of syntax, semantic sloppiness. Georges had a perfect mastery of French grammar and knew every slang term. During a party, a conversation or a bad film, a bitter taste would sometimes assail him and soon a knot of anger would start forming in his throat, which grew and grew.

★

One day when Georges had been staring into the void for several minutes, indifferent to the noise all around him, Lisbeth became worried and went to find her mother in the kitchen.

'That's not papa in there.'

'What do you mean?'

'It's a man wearing a mask that looks like papa. But I'm sure it's not him.'

In the evening, Georges would observe the children, and the little boy he had brought into their midst, as brown as the others were blond, this gentle, fearful boy who for weeks would not meet his eye. Georges observed his family and thought about the choices he had made. He had married a woman whose main wish was to bring children into the world and raise them. Lots of children. He wasn't one of those men who quibble and dither and skimp, one of those unambitious, petty, timorous men. He didn't have enough money – so what? He would find it. He didn't have enough room? Well, he would *make* them all fit, he'd build beds from cupboards. Life simply had to yield to his desires. His desires were immense. Space was filled with noise, cries, arguments. He needed this many children, this profusion. The same went for women, even if he loved only one. So far, none had resisted him. And there were so many bodies to discover. But deep down – and this is probably what Georges was thinking about in the evening, staring vacantly at the strips of parquet – wherever he was, in the arms of women, at the centre of long tables surrounded by friends, behind the wheel of the car on country roads, his children crammed in the back, wherever he was, yes, deep down, he was alone.

★

Liane had begun to laugh and sing again. As a girl, she had learned a whole repertoire of rhymes and songs which she now hummed to her children, *brave little soldier, back from the war, one shoe off and one shoe on, brave little soldier, where are you from?* Sometimes, something burning pierced her stomach which no pregnancy could fill. But Liane believed in heaven and in a merciful God and eternal rest. One day, in humanity's idea of heaven or some unknown place, amid a mixture of cotton wool and warmth, she would be with her son again. When Violette was born, a few weeks after Antonin's burial, even plumper and more vigorous than all the others, Liane had thought that God was sending her a sign. Or a gift. Violette's birth shrouded her sorrow in a veil of tiredness and plenitude. Violette absorbed all her energy and at the same time kept her alive. Liane loved newborn babies, the smell in the folds of their necks, their tiny fingers, and the milk which leaked from her breasts in the middle of the night. Liane was completely absorbed by the baby, her waking up in the night, her voracious demands. Violette bestowed her babbling, her smiles, her glances on her. But when Justine, her little daughter who was not yet three, came to her with her outstretched arms and grabbed hold of her skirt, Liane pushed her away. Justine wanted her mother and was claiming the share which was her due. But Liane didn't have the strength. She had nothing left to give.

The others were older. They coped. Lisbeth played her role of eldest, helping her mother make the meals, wash the dishes, keeping an eye on the little ones. Barthélémy spent most of his time outdoors, mocked God and always found a way to avoid mass. Milo played with Jean-Marc, collected cars and jacks. Lucile watched the adults, never missing a word of their conversations, taking it all in.

More than any of them, Lucile was Georges's daughter. She looked like her father, had his sense of humour, his look, his intonation. Liane wished she could have loved her better, reassured her, broken down the fortress of her silence. Instead, Lucile remained the mysterious child who grew up too fast and whom she no longer hugged.

Lucile would soon be more vivacious than her, more intelligent and wittier. Liane didn't know when she had realised this. And Lucile continued to observe her, with that air of knowing everything without having learned anything, that way of being there without being there, of having a parallel existence to the others', and sometimes of judging her.

The coins were below the surface, only just buried in the sand. All you had to do was comb through it gently with your fingers or a toy rake. Lucile exclaimed and held up what she had found, watching her brother's reaction. Barthélémy whistled admiringly. She added the coin to her haul for the week: fifteen francs in small change. Every evening when the beach was empty, they returned to the climbing apparatus and went over the sand with a fine-tooth comb. Throughout the day, holidaymakers had climbed on the bars, hung by their feet, defied gravity on the swings and scattered their riches. Every evening the children gathered lost hairclips, coins and keyrings, enough to buy a bag or two of chips or even, when the catch had been good, to go to the cinema. This time, Lucile had been lucky. She put the money in her pocket. Barthélémy meanwhile was counting his takings. Including the coins he had stolen that morning from Liane's purse, he was as rich as Croesus.

'My treat!' he said to Lucile.

She followed her brother without knowing where they were going. They walked along the promenade, then Barthélémy stopped at the terrace of an ice-cream parlour. Lucile looked around. It struck her as a very smart place.

'You sure you've got enough?'

'Don't worry . . .'

★

Barthélémy's hair was combed back, revealing the amazing regularity of his features. He was sitting up straight, with his chair tipped back slightly, one arm on the arm-rest, a relaxed, nonchalant pose; the way a young man would sit, he reckoned. When he ordered two banana splits, the waitress gave him a quizzical look and asked if he had enough money. When he showed her his coins, she asked about their parents: did they know they were here? Lucile flashed her her advertising smile, her head slightly cocked to the side, her hands lying flat on her legs, with that sweet look that she could feign to perfection, and the waitress went off reassured. Lucile was now drumming her heels with impatience. There they both were, just like grown-ups, far from all the commotion that characterised the house in the hours after their return from the beach; far from the wet, sandy bathing costumes dropped on the tiles on the bathroom floor; far from the arguments over whose turn it was in the shower and who would hang up the towels. This year Georges had enough money to rent a house for the whole of August and send his family to the seaside. In any case, there was no question of going back to L. They had been to Nozan two years before and the children had loved the big beach, the ice-cream seller and the walks in the forest. In addition to their tribe, Liane and Georges had brought along the concierge's son. That had been decided a few days before they left; Georges had bumped into the child on the stairs, thought he looked pale, *peelywally*, he pronounced and then decided that the child needed a change of air. Georges was like that. He invited tramps to his table, took in refugees of all sorts, invited other people's children to come on holiday, as if he didn't have enough of his own. Then Liane would prepare the meals, make and strip the beds, do the washing, adopt his enthusiasms out of solidarity with her husband.

Lucile saw the enormous ice-cream goblet piled high with smooth, whipped cream arrive at the table. She began methodically on the left side: cream, ice cream and fruit in equal proportions, and closed her eyes to savour it. After ten days of sunshine, her hair had become almost white, as had the fine down on her arms, which she liked brushing the wrong way or trying to pull out with her fingers. Given the choice, she would rather have been a hairy monster with proper long thick hair, or tough and spiky like a hedgehog's. She had put on her sandals without drying her feet and sand was sticking to her ankles. She could also feel the salt on her skin; she loved that sensation. It was like a protective layer covering her body, which was almost invisible to the naked eye. Lucile was scared in the water, but she loved the beach. On the beach under the open sky, the noise level that accompanied her family wherever it went and the space it took up became almost imperceptible. Voices, laughter and shouts were less loud there. Amid the vast expanse of sand, between the dunes and the shore, the Poiriers were just a group of tiny shapes, bright and moving, which mingled with others and eventually blended into them. Liane set up the parasol, put the ice box in the shade, then lay down on her towel, offering her skin to the sun. Liane was born for sunbathing. Around midday, she would split open the baguettes and everyone would make their own sandwich. The children spent the day in the water, inventing games, piling on to the little inflatable dinghy, sharing the masks and snorkels. In the evening, they would return exhausted, with tangled hair and skin a little more tanned than the day before.

★

Lucile had not yet attacked the second half of her ice cream, when they saw Jean-Marc coming towards them. Barthélémy sighed.

'Shit, here comes the scrum-half!'

During the year, Jean-Marc had been given this nickname, both as a reference to Georges's beloved rugby, and especially because he was at the intersection of two camps, between the older and the younger children, accepted with condescension by the former and acclaimed by the latter. The scrum-half was neither fish nor fowl, or maybe both at once.

Jean-Marc had now reached them.

'Mum's looking for you. She's worried.'

Barthélémy quickly looked him up and down. He didn't want to see him. In any case, he didn't have enough money to buy him an ice cream. And they were in decent company. Jean-Marc would show them up with that strange accent he couldn't get rid of, though it wasn't for want of correcting him or making him repeat what he said. Jean-Marc couldn't stop himself glancing at the ice creams out of the corner of his eye. A look of desire crossed his face.

Lucile looked at him. With his tan, the scars on his legs seemed whiter, almost phosphorescent. For a long time, Jean-Marc's real mother had forced him to kneel down in the embers in the fireplace. The doctor told Liane that he would bear the scars all his life; there was nothing that could be done. Jean-Marc looked surreptitiously at Lucile with a worried expression. She had a sudden access of tenderness towards him and felt that she might almost give him a hug.

'Do you want one?'

Jean-Marc nodded. Lucile got the coins out of her pocket. Barthélémy magnanimously called the waitress over.

'Miss, the same for the young man, please.'

Self-confident and just a little overbearing, Barthélémy was imitating his father. Jean-Marc couldn't hold back a smile of pride. Much more than the prospect of tasting a banana split, which he wasn't even sure he'd be able to finish, he was overjoyed at being allowed on the terrace of the ice-cream parlour with Barthélémy and Lucile.

Lucile smiled.

'I saw you swimming today. You're fast.'

Jean-Marc didn't say anything. Barthélémy added, in spite of a little twinge of jealousy: 'You could go in for competitions.'

This prospect delighted Lucile: 'You'll be world champion and your mother will see you in the paper with your smart swimming costume, and she'll rub her eyes and be mad with rage!'

'And what's more, you'll become rich – rich as Croesus!' added Barthélémy, who had learned the expression from his father and thought it terribly witty.

'Imagine your picture on the front page and you with huge muscles, and your mother quaking with fear in case you come and take your revenge!'

As Lucile said this, Barthélémy stood up and spread his legs to demonstrate the weightlifting stance, with his chest puffed out and his arm muscles bulging. All three of them burst out laughing.

The waitress put an ice cream down in front of Jean-Marc. It looked even bigger than the others. He glanced at Lucile, seeking her approval, then dug in to the dessert, cream first, savouring it in silence.

Autumn had come and it seemed to Lucile that, even if things had not gone back to how they used to be, they were calming down: the visible portion of sadness had dissolved in the dirty washing-up water, and Liane's belly had remained empty for several months. Jean-Marc had found his place at table and in the boys' room. He no longer screamed in the middle of the night or looked down when someone spoke to him. Jean-Marc had entered the frame, he smiled in photos and blended in as though he had always been there. They had almost forgotten he had come from elsewhere. Lucile thought that her family had perhaps assumed its final form – three boys and four girls – a configuration which struck her as amply sufficient for the space they were allotted and which gave her an honourable place among the older children. Whatever happened, she remained her father's favourite, the one he looked at first, the one who always benefited from his encouragement, his smiles and his indulgence, despite how little appetite she showed for school and her poor results. Better than anyone else, Georges could perceive his daughter's unique mind, her carefully chosen words, the acuteness with which she looked at things. Lucile hoped that life would go on like this, in this invisible geometry that linked them one to another, which had now stabilised, and to which each of them seemed to have adapted. She felt a strange need for permanence; she dreaded departures, exits, separations.

★

When her parents told them they had been invited to London by one of Georges's clients and that they would be away for the weekend, Lucile greeted the news like the announcement of an imminent earthquake. A whole weekend! That seemed to her like an eternity, and the idea that a serious accident might happen when Liane and Georges were away made her breathless. For several minutes, Lucile stared into space, absorbed by horrible visions she could not banish – shocks, falls, burns affecting each of her brothers and sisters in turn, and then she saw herself slip under a metro train. Suddenly she realised how vulnerable they were, how their lives ultimately might hang by a thread, turn on a careless step, one second more or one second less. Anything – especially something bad – could happen. The apartment, the street, the city contained an infinite number of dangers, of possible accidents, of irreparable dramas. Liane and Georges had no right to do this. She felt the tears run down her cheeks and took a step back to hide behind Lisbeth, who was listening attentively to her father.

Georges was still explaining how the weekend would be organised; it was all to proceed under their oldest sister's supervision and it would give them an ideal opportunity to prove how mature they were. The older ones were to look after the youngsters, make the meals, take them to the square for fresh air, make sure everything ran smoothly and follow the programme Liane had detailed on a notepad alongside menus for each meal and suggestions for what to do with the leftovers. Marie-Noëlle, a colleague of Georges's, would visit them at least once over the weekend and they could phone her at any time. Was everything clear?

Their geographical limits remained the same: rue Clauzel, rue

Milton, rue Buffault, place de Montholon. Anvers Square was out of bounds.

Lisbeth nodded and Barthélémy adopted his most serious expression and did the same. Lucile looked at her brother's face and thought she could discern just how excited he was at the prospect of a weekend without their parents. She wiped her cheeks with the back of her hand, but her whole body now felt shivery. She was scared. She was the only one who was scared. She was the only one who realised how much their existence was subject to planks that cracked, careering cars, dizzying falls. From afar, her cousins' shouts grew louder without anyone being able to hear them: 'They've fallen in! They've fallen in!'

When the day came, Liane and Georges distributed instructions for each of them along with their kisses. Barthélémy was told to obey his sister and not to go out of any windows. Lucile, they suggested, should put her books down and help with the chores, and the little ones were told to be good and to play quietly. The instructions for Violette's feeds had been written out and given to Lisbeth.

Lucile didn't cry when they closed the door behind them. She waved from the window and watched her parents get into the car that would take them to the station. When the car disappeared from sight, she thought that she might never see them again. Their train might crash into another, their ferry vanish in a shipwreck in the middle of the Channel, the place where they were staying in London might catch fire. Lucile closed her eyes to try to escape the vortex of catastrophe into which her imagination was dragging her. What if the seven of them were left on their own, like Tom Thumb abandoned in the middle of the forest with his brothers and sisters? Lucile had time to see their thin bodies and torn clothes before she reopened her eyes. She was alone in the room. She found Lisbeth and Barthélémy at a loose end in the kitchen. She watched their faces for a few minutes. They were paler than normal, their movements hesitant. They felt no sense of victory. Like her, they were prey to a vast and confused sense of fear. A very unusual silence had taken over the apartment.

Saturday passed without mishap; everyone followed their instructions to the letter. Jean-Marc organised games with Justine and Milo, who were so obedient they might have been taking part in a national competition for well-behaved children. Barthélémy had never been so calm nor so unadventurous. At the end of the day, Marie-Noëlle visited them to make sure there wasn't anything they needed. She found them in the best of spirits and went home reassured.

In the night, Violette began to cry. In the girls' small bedroom, Lisbeth turned on the light and cradled her in her arms. Violette cried twice as loud, her little body racked with sobs. She looked all around in terror. Lucile took her turn at trying to calm her, stroked her hair, kissed her cheeks. Violette screamed louder and louder, her face growing ever redder and her forehead burning. Soon the boys, woken by the sound of crying, joined the three girls. They prepared a bottle, sang songs to her, turned on the transistor. But an inconsolable Violette screamed ever louder. Lucile felt fear swell within her, Violette's crying resonated in her head and was getting louder by the second. Violette's crying contained a message which Lucile couldn't decipher; probably she ought to be crying with her, crying about things that would never be spoken, about the children's sadness, about the noisy world that spun ever faster, a world full of dangers in which they might disappear without warning. She was sure Violette had a serious illness, she was going to die before their eyes and it would be their fault; they should take her temperature again, call the emergency services, take her to hospital. Tears were streaming down Lucile's cheeks, tears which no one noticed amid all the commotion.

At 3 a.m., Lisbeth, exhausted and distressed, rang the neighbours' doorbell. They took the child in, eventually calmed her down and, when Violette had gone back to sleep, returned her to her cot.

After the Christmas holidays, Lucile and Lisbeth moved in to a maid's room on the sixth floor. Georges had managed to persuade the owner to clear the room and rent it to him for a modest additional charge, promising that he could raise the rent a little later when his agency had found its feet. Since Violette had joined her sisters in the girls' bedroom, taking their number to four, it had become impossible to work there. Lisbeth needed peace. Upstairs she could study. It didn't change much for Lucile, who consistently avoided doing her homework or learning her lessons, but Liane thought that being further away might help her concentration.

The room was tiny and lacked a washbasin and plumbing. Gilberte Pasquier lived on the same floor; she was a young woman who had been French shorthand champion and Lucile admired her greatly. Gilberte Pasquier wore grey suits and dizzyingly high heels; her lips were painted with a different shade of pink every day.

After tea in the kitchen – bread and butter and dark chocolate – Lucile and Lisbeth would rush up the stairs, proud to be returning to their den, aware of the privilege it represented to be so far away from the rest of the family (four floors), and able to lock the door. It was a place of their own, a place where Barthélémy couldn't rummage through their things, where the noise would only reach them distantly and in bursts (for example, Justine's cries; her rages could reach an exceptional level of decibels); here the mess was theirs alone. Lisbeth described her day, her friends and teachers, while Lucile wouldn't describe anything, but would sometimes agree to show her sister the love letters she received, the most recent being from a girl in her class, whose literary demeanour and poetic style had caught her attention. Georges had fitted bunk beds and a folding desk that he had made himself, which enabled Lisbeth to sit on the lower bed and do her homework. Meanwhile, Lucile would listen for Gilberte Pasquier's resolute footsteps, which were easy to recognise, and just as the young woman reached her door, she would go out on to the landing to say hello. In a few seconds, she would take everything in: colours, outfits, stockings and make-up. One day she would be like Gilberte Pasquier, a woman whom men scarcely dared look at, whom they admired from afar in petrified silence.

The two sisters then joined the rest of the family, had their showers and helped Liane with the meal. In the evening, when bedtime came, Lucile couldn't go up to her room alone. Lisbeth had to cross the landing to turn the light on, go upstairs with her and tell her stories until she fell asleep. At first, Lucile had demanded the top bunk, but her bedwetting soon exhausted her sister's patience. So Lucile took the bottom bunk, and was instructed to urinate in the china chamberpot, which one of them – more often than not Lisbeth – emptied every morning in the toilet on the landing.

Since the start of the new school year, Barthélémy had been entrusted with taking Lucile to the dentist. Lucile, born just after the war, had bad teeth. But instead of going there, they took back streets, hung around for hours or went to the cinema, window-shopped or stole sweets from the local sweetshop. Lucile admired her brother – his growing insolence and self-assurance. She was proud he chose her as his partner in crime, confided his plans and his secrets to her rather than Lisbeth, because Lisbeth became upset at his misdemeanours and had no hestitation in reporting them. When Liane wasn't there, one of his favourite games was catching his elder sister, pinning her to the ground and, on pain of dreadful torture, making her say his name ten times over: Who's the handsomest? Who's the bravest? The most intelligent? The funniest? The wittiest? The most articulate?

He never did it to Lucile. Lucile impressed him. Lucile could deter him from hand to hand combat with one look. Lucile was a bastion of silence amid all the noise. Because of the sad expression on her face, Barthélémy nicknamed her Blue, or, on particularly melancholic days, Blue-Blue. Sometimes he wanted to protect her, or to take her far away where they would be free to do nothing but wander about and never set foot in school.

Sometimes Liane sent Lucile shopping in the rue des Martyrs. For every item she bought, she kept a tiny sum, almost nothing really, just a little delivery charge. In that way Lucile practised a type of mental arithmetic less unappealing than the calculations taught at school. At the end of the month, she generally had about twenty francs, which were soon converted into sweets.

In Saint-Pierre Square, witches were said to bundle children up in white sheets and make them disappear for ever. Lucile climbed the steps which led to the basilica several times and came down them two at a time, fear in her stomach. At the bottom, trinket-sellers sold small bags of sand attached to a little bit of string decorated with crêpe paper, which she would make spin in the air and watch fall back to earth like multi-coloured butterflies. This was her favourite game of all.

Lucile spent hours in the bookshop on rue de Maubeuge in front of the shelf of girls' books. Eventually she would choose a book, which she slipped under her arm. She'd button up her coat and say goodbye to the lady with a broad smile, saying that sadly she'd found nothing to tempt her. Years later, Lucile found out that the woman with the kind expression had been a silent accomplice in her introduction to reading.

One afternoon, Dr Baramian, who had not yet been driven out by the noise, invited Lucile and Lisbeth to his office to show them his tape recorder. Neither of them had known that such a gadget existed. Dr Baramian had them recite a poem into the microphone, in the middle of which they made a mistake. For a few seconds they stumbled, trying to restart the same verse in unison and eventually got back on track. Then Dr Baramian rewound the tape and let them listen to the recording. Lucile thought the doctor was playing a trick on them. She couldn't believe it: it wasn't possible, those weren't their voices. And then came the moment when they made a mistake, Lisbeth's laughter, their difficulty getting started again at the right place and there could be no further doubt. Dr Baramian was a magician.

Since the end of the holidays, a local woman had been coming once or twice a week to help Liane darn socks, sew hems and repair holes. Nicknamed Mrs Stitch, she ate lunch with the Poirier family every Thursday. Lucile observed Mrs Stitch carefully, her soft wrinkled skin, pitted with tiny craters, her sparse hair. Lucile wondered if, after looking like Gilberte Pasquier, she too would be transformed like this and would become an old lady, shrivelled and stooped, whom no one noticed. Then she would be free at last to come and go, infinitely light and almost transparent. Then she would no longer be afraid, not of anything.

Mrs Stitch had a small moustache and fine down on her chin. When she chewed, it was not uncommon for a breadcrumb or some other piece of food to escape from her mouth and remain somewhere in the vicinity. One Thursday, when a grain of rice had been trembling for several minutes above her top lip, Barthélémy, with an explanatory gesture, said: 'Schmoulz, Mrs Stitch!'

Lucile smiled. She liked new words. This one was a notable success with the children and was instantly destined for posterity. (Even today, *schmoulz* designates for all Liane and Georges's descendants, and by extension for many of their friends, any more or less chewed particle of food which is stuck to a corner of the mouth or chin.)

Georges, who was increasingly preoccupied with his work, saw little of his children. He got back late in the evening when the noise had ceased and it was time to send them to bed. He kissed their foreheads tenderly, while Liane told him about the events of their day. On Sundays he woke them up early and made them get in to the Peugeot one by one in a pre-established order which enabled the car to hold them all, and set off for pastures new. Lucile watched the trees go by along the roadside, the names of towns on the signs on the main roads. She liked the sensation of flight. In the forest of Rambouillet or Fontainebleau, the Poiriers met other families for ever larger games. Georges was not lacking in partners in crime or imagination. He loved treasure hunts, mystery tours and wild goose chases. After their picnic, while her brothers and sisters scattered with a single shout of joy, Lucile would make her way slowly along a path, walking carefully, listening to every sound, her feet barely touching the carpet of dead leaves, looking behind her at every step.

The man I love, whose love sometimes has to contend with my distraction, became worried some time ago about me embarking on this project. At least that was how I interpreted the question he asked rather tentatively: Did I need to write *this*? To which I replied, without hesitation, No. I needed to write, and there was nothing else I *could* write apart from this. The subtle distinction was significant.

My books have always been like this; they have ultimately made their presence felt of their own accord, for obscure reasons which I only discover long after the text is complete. To those who expressed fears about the dangers that such a project might hold so soon after my mother's death, I always answered confidently, No, not at all, the very idea. I know now – though I am not even halfway through the vast project in which I'm embroiled (I almost wrote 'the vast dunghill I'm knee-deep in') – how much I have overestimated my strength. I know now the particular state of tension which writing this plunges me into, how demanding, disturbing, exhausting it is – in short, how much it is costing me physically. I probably set out to pay homage to Lucile, to give her a coffin made of paper – for those seem the most beautiful of all to me – and a destiny as a character. But I know too that I am using my writing as a way of looking for the origin of her suffering, as though there were a precise moment when the core of her self was breached in a definitive, irreparable way, and I cannot ignore the extent to which this quest – as if its difficulty were not enough – is in vain. It is through this prism that I interviewed her brothers and sisters, whose pain in some cases was at least as visible as my mother's, that I questioned them with the same determination, eager for details, alert to the possibility of an objective cause that eluded me as I thought I was getting close to it. That was how I interviewed them, without ever asking the question which they nonetheless answered: was the pain already there?

In the Word document containing transcripts of most of my interviews, 'rue de Maubeuge' crops up as a theme in its own right. Liane and Georges moved there in 1950 (from a tiny apartment on the rue de Presles which none of my mother's brothers or sisters really remembered) and they left in 1960. So Lucile lived there between the ages of four and fourteen. As is the case in many families, periods can be summed up by the places which contained them. So 'rue de Maubeuge' brings together the beginning of Georges's first advertising agency, its closure, Justine's birth, the creation of the second agency, Antonin's death, Violette's birth, and the arrival of Jean-Marc.

Even today, 'rue de Maubeuge' can't be mentioned without its mythological dimension: Lisbeth's dedication, Barthélémy's escapades on the window sill on the second floor, the success of Lucile's photos, Justine's seismic fits of temper, Violette's exemplary appetite, Mrs Stitch's *schmoulz*, Sunday picnics, Liane's perpetual smile.

Behind the myth are the death of one child and the arrival of another: 'a piece of jigsaw puzzle that was forced into place', as

62

Violette put it during one of our interviews. In the notes that Lucile wrote about her childhood, which we found in a cardboard box in her apartment, I came upon this sentence about Jean-Marc's arrival: 'In this way I was discovering confusedly, despite the explanations and denials, that we were interchangeable. I was never able to convince myself otherwise after that, neither with lovers nor with friends.'

Behind the myth were Liane's great exhaustion, her inability to take care of Justine after Antonin disappeared, and a sort of lack of differentiation common in large families; there were allegiances, rivalries, collusions which linked the children secretly, their words, their fantasies, the invisible traffic between them that the adults were unaware of.

Behind the myth there was Milo, whom no one said much about, apart from comments about still waters, smooth and apparently without ripples. And Barthélémy, who was under psychiatric observation in Necker hospital for reasons that no one is very clear about today, probably because he had been extremely disruptive and was still wetting the bed. Two years after Antonin's death, Liane took him to the children's hospital. When he had settled in to his little white room, she left, saying that she was going to buy some magazines, and didn't come back. He spent several days there in a state of great distress, convinced that his parents had abandoned him, until they came to fetch him, after being alerted by a family friend who was alarmed by the state she found him in when she visited.

Marie-Noëlle worked with Georges for twenty years and was one of our family's closest friends. Linked with the family's private as well as public life, she was the privileged witness of its vitality, but also knew all about the dramas and disasters that befell it. It was Marie-Noëlle who went to fetch Barthélémy and brought him back to the Ardèche after Antonin's death, and Marie-Noëlle who took Justine in for a while when Liane couldn't look after her, and Marie-Noëlle whom Liane called the day she found Jean-Marc dead in his bedroom. Of Lucile, she said to me – as others did – 'She was a mysterious child. Completely mysterious.'

At the suggestion of Lucile's brothers and sisters, I spent a whole afternoon interviewing Marie-Noëlle at home. Today she's an old lady of over eighty. I'm not sure the word 'old' is appropriate given how mischievous her mind is, and I have a feeling that this is what captivated Georges the first time he saw her, the gentle irony hinted at behind her words, her air of being nobody's fool, of knowing exactly what to believe. Afterwards, Marie-Noëlle emailed me some details and dates I had requested. Later still, I listened to the several hours of memories she had provided in order to transcribe them. At the mention of the rue de Maubeuge, there was still emotion in her voice and when Marie-Noëlle described the first time she saw my grandmother, it was clear that the image in her memory was intact: Liane, who was pregnant with Justine at the time and wrapped up in an awful woolly dressing gown, opened the door to her, with her blonde plait and unmistakable bump. Throughout the apartment a smell of pee predominated, though no one seemed to notice it any more (almost all of Lucile's brothers and sisters wet the bed until an advanced age). Marie-Noëlle had come to visit Georges, then a journalist on *Radio-Cinéma*, the magazine which would become *Télérama* a few years later. She had heard through a mutual friend that he was planning to set up an advertising agency.

Amid the jumble of the storeroom which served as their office, Marie-Noëlle and Georges drew up the articles of association for the agency before they found premises. A few months later, Georges finally cashed their first cheque: the agency had designed and printed business cards for Le Soulier de Ninon, a shop whose clientele were mainly Pigalle prostitutes. On leaving the building, he dragged Marie-Noëlle to the local Italian delicatessen and spent half the money buying enough food to last the family for several days. The feast, to which she was invited, was devoured that evening.

Marie-Noëlle is one of those who remember the weekend Liane and Georges spent in London and her visit to the children. Though this weekend was mentioned several times by different people, there was no hint of reproach against my grandparents, at least not explicitly. How could Liane and Georges, who had lost a child in an accident a few months earlier, have gone so far away and left such young children unsupervised? What lack of concern or recklessness led them to undertake the journey? It staggers me. Of course, I view this episode through the lens of my own time. And of course I have a rather hazy notion of what the Paris of the 1950s was like, and how mature a child of eleven, the eldest of seven, might be. I look at the facts from my own vantage point, with a fear that something might happen to my own children, which I struggle with all the time (a fear which I must admit is greater than average and which I know is related to my family history).

Rather than an act of thoughtlessness, I see their departure as a sort of headlong rush towards the future, proof of the blind, unshakeable confidence which Liane and Georges still had in life at that point, and in themselves as a couple and the family they had built.

Violette and Justine were ready and waiting in the hall, with their hats on and their coats buttoned up. Liane called again to Lucile, who had been in the bathroom for nearly an hour, more loudly this time: Mrs Richard had said ten o'clock on the dot, they were going to be late. Lucile was looking at her face in the mirror, her plump cheeks, her bobbed hair, her skin, which was no longer as smooth as it had been, the horrible spot on her chin. She took a step backwards. Her body had changed, her breasts showed beneath her blouse, while Lisbeth, though two years older, was still waiting in vain for her transformation. She forced a smile to check that she could still manage one, looking at herself as she would soon look into the lens, from the front, then three-quarters, slightly turned to the side. Yes, she could still smile, and even laugh and make faces, though she had no desire to.

The younger girls were growing impatient in the hall. They were eager to get there, to put on the dresses, tights and hats. Violette in particular loved being photographed, posing, trying on new shoes. Perhaps they would get to keep one or two of the outfits again this time, if Mrs Richard let them. Eventually Lucile came out of the bathroom, dragging her heels, and put her coat on with calculated slowness.

'If you don't want to go again, my princess, you don't need to. But this time you have an appointment and Mrs Richard is counting on you and your sisters. You've done the Pingouin catalogue before and the pictures were wonderful.'

Liane handed her daughter some metro tickets, which Lucile stuck in her pocket without looking at them.

'If it isn't raining, walk back and that'll save on tickets.'

Lucile nodded and opened the door. Liane kissed the two little ones and made them promise to be good for Mrs Richard, whose instructions they must follow to the letter without complaining or getting their hair messed up.

Standing outside the building, Lucile looked at her reflection in a window. She was fat, it was as simple as that. Fat and ugly. She didn't want to go up, or see Mrs Richard, or try on clothes. She took a deep breath and pressed the buzzer. The door opened and the little ones rushed inside towards the lift.

Mrs Richard opened the door and greeted Lucile warmly. What a young lady she had become in just a few months! And still as pretty! Then she bent down to kiss the little ones and asked them to take off their coats. She congratulated Violette on the Germalyne campaign she had fronted, which was displayed in chemists all over Paris and on posters and billboards.

'Your mummy must be proud . . .'

Violette gave a confident little nod that melted Mrs Richard's heart.

'We'll start with Lucile and then take some pictures of you two. Nadine will give you the clothes to put on, but go and wash your hands first!'

Lucile went into the changing room. She felt cold and held off getting undressed. From where she was, she could see the studio. The lights had been put in place and the set was ready. Mrs Richard asked her to hurry up, they had a lot of shots to get through, she couldn't dilly-dally. She handed Lucile a black roll-neck sweater, which Lucile unfolded carefully, and then a pleated skirt on a hanger. Mrs Richard lingered for a moment until she realised that Lucile didn't want to undress in front of her. She left the room with a laugh. 'You only needed to say, my dear. You *have* grown up, haven't you!'

Lucile put the outfit on. As there was no mirror, she couldn't look at herself from the front, but looking down, she hated what she saw. The clothes were hideous and made her body bulge. The skirt in particular, which was ridiculous on someone of her age, made her look like a nun. She went into the studio and stood in front of the grey background so that the photographer could adjust his camera. When he had done so, she followed his instructions, changed angle and position several times, put on different clothes, played with a hoop in front of the camera. She had never felt so numb in her life, as though she were naked in the white light, trapped in clothes that didn't suit her. Later she was joined by her two sisters, wearing a variety of sweaters and cardigans for some group shots, then in a whole series of gorgeous woollen dresses. Then her sisters posed separately and together. Lucile disappeared into the changing room to put her own clothes back on. That was when she realised that a tear had rolled down her cheek, a tear that she had not felt well up or slide out, which had not been preceded or followed by another. She didn't want to be photographed any more, that was all. She would tell her mother. She wasn't the girl in the pleated skirt, she didn't play with balls or hoops any more; she had nothing to do with this image of sweetness they wanted her to portray. She couldn't do it any more. From now on that was behind her, it was already drifting into the distance; it would gradually disappear from her memory or leave only fragments, something which she would probably miss some day, which belonged to childhood and came to an end with it.

Mrs Richard gave Justine and Violette two dresses, which they greeted with cries of joy. She made Lucile promise to pass on her best wishes to Liane. The little ones put their coats on again, said goodbye nicely and went down the stairs murmuring contentedly. Outside it wasn't raining. Lucile decided they would walk back to the rue de Maubeuge. The two little ones held her hand, one on either side, striking the ground with their sandals more and more noisily, watching for Lucile's reaction.

Lucile's fingers felt the warmth of their palms and she smiled.

When they opened the front door, Barthélémy was sitting in the armchair in the living room, casually leafing through a magazine. Lisbeth was washing towels in the bathroom; Milo and Jean-Marc were fighting in the bedroom, to judge by the noise which was leaking out in spite of the closed door. Dirty washing, used dish-towels and exercise books were strewn all over the floor. The whole apartment was a mess. Liane had gone to the cinema, just like that.

Liane disappeared all of a sudden, when the noise level or the mess became more than she could bear. Liane had always had this need to get away in the middle of the afternoon, to sit in a darkened cinema or collapse into bed. It didn't matter whether dinner time was approaching or the dishes were piled up in the sink or the earth was shaking. From when they were very little, she had left her children alone in the apartment on the rue de Presles to meet Georges, haughtily ignoring her neighbour's indignant comments.

The pattern had been the same for weeks, but that didn't lessen the shame. Lucile would grab the rope with both hands, jump off the ground so that it coiled once round her feet, pull her body upright, then freeze in that position, incapable of going any higher. It was beyond her to grasp the rope higher up, free her feet from the bottom or wind it round them again. The rope was smooth, hopelessly so, and so Lucile remained a foot off the ground, gently swinging back and forth. The best she could do was hold that position for a few minutes before giving up. Mrs Mareuil, her gymnastics teacher, at first thought that she was concerned about her looks, then that she was trying to provoke her, then she realised the truth: Lucile didn't know how to climb a smooth rope, nor for that matter, as she was soon to discover, a knotted one. While most of her classmates managed to get to the top in three or four perfectly coordinated movements, Lucile remained at the bottom, unconvincingly mimicking an effort to reach the top, unable to get further than a couple of feet even for the sake of appearances. Mrs Mareuil was unsparing with her sarcasm, which each week became a little more biting. Didn't pretty little Lucile look ridiculous hanging like a ham from a string? You had to agree that she didn't have much strength in her arms or legs. Like an insect balancing in the wind, and just as vulnerable. Mrs Mareuil waited for the sniggers and stifled laughter from the class. But there were none – neither whispers nor muttering. No smiles on their faces. Usually girls were so cruel to each other. Why did Lucile Poirier benefit from this immunity? Neither Mrs Mareuil nor the girls who witnessed this scene each week could have said. And Lucile swung at the end of her rope in deathly silence.

Lucile didn't like sport. She was afraid of balls, rackets and the vaulting horse. She wasn't a fast runner, couldn't put the shot more than a few feet in front of her, never caught the ball, closed her eyes as soon as things started to get too hectic. Lucile couldn't touch her toes standing up or sitting down, or do the crab. She had never been able to do cartwheels, or stag leaps or handstands. Lucile's body was knotted, recalcitrant, impossible to untie. She was only just able to do a forward roll and even then only when she was on top form.

Mrs Mareuil took this absence of sporting ability as a personal slight, a quietly uttered insult repeated each Friday. She hated Lucile and did not conceal her contempt in the appropriate box in her school report.

It grieved Liane to see her daughter was so unsporty: always the last to run, to jump into the water, to agree to a game of table tennis. She was the last to get out of bed, quite simply, as though all of life were contained in the pages of books, as though it was enough to stay there, sheltered, contemplating life from a distance. In spite of her succession of pregnancies, Liane had kept her athletic, sculpted shape, her bearing was erect, her head held high. A few years earlier she had declared in front of witnesses that she would still be able to do the splits at the age of seventy. The bet had been accepted.

Among her brothers and sisters, Lucile was the exception. Lisbeth did all sorts of leaps and pirouettes; Barthélémy, in addition to his legendary acrobatics, was a remarkable tennis player; Jean-Marc spent his weekends at swimming competitions; Milo was a talented runner. As for the little ones, you only needed to see them jump, dance or simply wave their arms about to realise how relaxed and supple they were.

As the weeks went by, the gymnastics class at the lycée Lamartine became a torture for Lucile. The thought of it kept her awake. At the start of the year, she claimed she had a headache, period pains, stomachache. But Liane didn't fall for that for long. So Lucile would go off to school every Friday morning with a knot in her stomach and sweaty palms, having taken a spoonful of milk of magnesia or an aspirin.

In the second term, lacking any legitimate reason, Lucile began bunking off gymnastics. She hung around the street or sat on a bench in the square letting the hours go by. And then she cut other equally boring classes. She forged Liane's signature; that had become easy. She needed to be able to breathe.

During the school holidays, Liane regularly went to her family home in Pierremont with the children. Georges joined them at weekends. Lucile and her brothers and sisters loved this place near the river and the canal, with its smell of chalk and dust and damp, and the sound of crows cawing. They made friends with local children of their own age. Gradually, Lucile, Lisbeth and Barthélémy created a little gang and now that they had become adolescents, they met up every evening after they had all sneaked out. In the Poirier house all they had to do was drop down from the first-floor balcony, which overlooked the deserted street. The operation was discreet and without much danger except when Lucile, seeking a foothold, had pressed the doorbell. After checking that the coast was clear, they ran to the village square, which had a dark corner that made an excellent meeting place. When everyone was present, they made their way to a little beach they had created on the riverbank, where they drank sodas or beer and the older ones smoked cigarettes.

One evening when they were all there, the conversation turned to the loathsome Pichet, the local tobacconist, who was known for his drunken moods and the unscrupulous way he exploited a girl whom social services placed in his care during the school holidays. Lucile believed he '*touched her up*'. What's more, for several months, in an effort to prevent any attempts at theft, Pichet had forbidden them to enter his grocery-bar-tobacconist's in a group. Lucile proposed punitive action, and Barthélémy worked out the plan. They would kidnap the giant metal carrot which served as a sign for tobacconists in those days. The following evening, the expedition was set up. Getting the carrot down took ages. It hung much higher up than they had imagined, measured a good six feet and weighed more than forty pounds. Lucile directed the operation. After several attempts, punctuated with chuckles and stifled laughter, Barthélémy, aided by another boy in the gang, managed to get it off. They then carried it to the other end of the village where they hid it in a little shed. Lucile hadn't felt so happy for a long time.

Two days later, a paragraph in *L'Yonne républicaine* mentioned the mysterious disappearance. The gang decided to repeat their exploit and attack the other tobacconist's in Pierremont that very evening; its proprietor, though less unpleasant, was just as sinister. Two days after that, a lengthier paragraph put forward the theory that there was a quarrel between bar owners. Drunk with their latest success, the teenagers decided to expand their zone of activity to neighbouring parishes. And so, after a few days, they marched back with the carrot from a nearby village in a wheelbarrow. This feat meant they were promoted from the local news page to page two of the paper: 'Another carrot vanishes'.

Lucile was delighted. She liked the absurdity of the act, its pointlessness. This anonymous glory without a picture. They spent the final days of the holidays collecting more carrots, which were piled up in the disused shed. Each time, their misdemeanour appeared in the local press, accompanied by different theories. Until the day when Lucile discovered in the newsagent's that they had made the front page of *L'Yonne républicaine*: 'Yonne's carrot gang strikes again!' She bought the paper and took it home. Different theories were considered: the manic activity of a collector, the recycling of particular materials, the first sign of a regional mafia, a commando operation by the anti-tobacco league. The gang of seven decided to abandon its activities when the Auxerre police initiated an investigation.

A few days later, Lucile and her gang decided to get rid of the evidence of their crime and in the middle of the night flung about ten metal carrots into the Burgundy canal.

The following summer, when the canal was drained, the carrots were discovered at the bottom. Ten 'bodies' silently pointed to the nearest house, where two active members of the gang lived. The children felt scared, but there was no evidence to corroborate the suspicions.

Lucile and her brothers and sisters continued to holiday in Pierremont and get into trouble.

The next year Georges decided to buy the house in Pierremont from his parents-in-law, who were no longer able to keep it up. The building work was about to begin, and would never entirely end.

I had got to this point, that is, page 75 of the Word document I was working on, when, just before an autumn weekend for which I had no particular plans, I finally decided to listen to the cassettes my grandfather recorded about fifteen years before he died.

Between 1984 and 1986, amid the curls of smoke from his pipe, Georges sat at his desk and recounted part of his life on to cassettes, which today number thirty-seven. This monologue lasting over fifty hours was originally intended for Violette, who was then about thirty. Violette had asked her father to describe his child-hood, which he rarely spoke of. Georges agreed, got hooked and took his story far beyond the initial request. When Georges had finished, he decided to make a copy for the rest of the family. Violette today has one of two sets.

I shall come back in more detail later to how I retrieved those cassettes, after a deeply distressing scene which haunted me for weeks. That scene also explains why I hadn't managed to listen to them until then, though they had been in my possession for some time and I had got hold of a prehistoric machine to play them on.

Haltingly, I wrote about the rue de Maubeuge in a desire to give an account of both the era and the milieu in which my mother had grown up; meanwhile the cassettes lay around somewhere at the bottom of a bookcase, stuffed in the old plastic bag I had brought them home in.

When I was preparing to write about the move that took my grandparents from Paris to Versailles, it struck me that I had overlooked them. I couldn't go on without listening to the cassettes, continuing to write as though they didn't exist. I had the cassettes at home; they had been copied by Georges himself and, beyond my reluctance to hear the voice of my grandfather, who had died more than ten years ago, I owed it to myself at very least to have a listen.

When I got the boxes out of the bag to sort them, I realised that three were missing (18, 19 and 20). It occurred to me to call Violette, but I thought better of it. Shortly before her death, after the point when I believe she decided to put an end to her life, Lucile had borrowed all the cassettes to listen to them. If I mentioned to Violette that three were missing, she would probably think that Lucile had destroyed them or spirited them away. It is true that Lucile, in other circumstances, had demonstrated a radical attitude to objects symbolically or actually relating to her family. But it was entirely possible that in searching in Violette's cellar, I had accidentally left some of the cassettes behind or maybe they were in another box.

On the Saturday morning, I slipped cassette 17 into the player to find out where the break occurred. That tape ends in June 1942 with Georges losing his job on *Toute la France* (a paper for prisoners' families, whose editor had recently been arrested) and looking for a new post.

Cassette 21 begins a few weeks later when Georges meets Liane at a party. Georges is twenty-five, affects the style of a seducer, which he has been perfecting since he arrived in Paris, and is mastering different strategies for approaching the female sex, the effectiveness of which is once again confirmed this evening. Georges loves dancing, holding his partner close with rather adventurous hands, and making women laugh. Liane, whom he's never met before and whom he calls his 'little blue fairy' (an allusion to a song by Charles Trenet, a singer he greatly admires), accepts his invitation to dance, although she considers him, at first regard and in view of the reputation which precedes him, to be a handsome cad. Moreover, she doesn't take long to lay her cards on the table: her dress is green, not blue, and there is no question of him engaging in any sort of flirtation with her. Georges takes that as read. They dance a bit then Georges flits again from woman to woman before going home with six or seven telephone numbers, a personal record, he adds. In the weeks that follow, the image of this young woman from the provinces, whose smile, freshness and blonde curls he describes, comes back to his memory. They see each other again a few months later at a party at the home of Barbara, one of Liane's sisters, who is already married and living in Paris. Caught out by the curfew, Georges spends the rest of the night talking with the little blue fairy. Next morning he agrees to accompany her to Sunday mass. They are in love. And that is how Georges, who had been intimate with many women, chose Liane, who was ignorant of just about every aspect of life. I think he could see in her a woman who would never betray him, who would be devoted to him body and soul, a soul which was large and generous, and who would see in him throughout her life only the brilliant, unconventional man she married.

When she returned to Giens, Liane asked her parents' permission to write to Georges. She met him several times during her visits to Paris, where she went regularly for violin lessons. They were married in Pierremont in 1943. The reception was held in Liane's parents' house, which by this time the Germans had vacated. As Georges didn't have a penny to his name, a neighbour lent him a morning coat that was a little too big for the religious ceremony, and his future mother-in-law gave him a suit for the civil one. And so Georges married – not without some concern – a woman with whom he had never made love and, he added, whose breasts he had not even seen. Their short honeymoon (a few days in a French province) was a relief: Liane proved to be 'hot-blooded'. Georges next describes them moving in to a little two-room apartment in Paris and starting their life together.

I listened to all of cassette 21, captivated by Georges's account, his way of alternating between detail, anecdote and analysis, and of handling the suspense between digressions. Georges's way of speaking was like his writing: clear, precise and well-constructed. I could simply have skipped five or six tapes and gone straight to the period I wanted, Lucile's childhood. Instead, I spent more than ten days listening to the cassettes, a notebook on my knees or by my side, turning them over one after the other until I reached the end.

Later, the day before a dinner at which I would see her, I eventually mentioned the three missing cassettes to Violette. Whatever the reason, it wasn't too serious as she had the original set. I asked her for the missing tapes, which she agreed to give me. The idea that Lucile might have destroyed or removed them intrigued me.

Cassette 18 begins with Georges losing his job when *Toute la France* is closed down. He looks for another paper that will take him on. He completes an article on Parisian youth, which he considers brilliant, and takes it to *Révolution nationale*, a collaborationist weekly which published Drieu la Rochelle and Brasillach. The article appealed to Lucien Combelle, who ran the paper, and he decided to publish it in two instalments. Then Combelle asked Georges to write a regular column on Parisian life. He agreed and entitled it 'Loving, drinking, singing'. He now spent a good number of his evenings in music halls and bars. A few weeks later, at Combelle's invitation, Georges became the sub-editor on *Révolution nationale*. It was at this period that he met Liane.

The three missing cassettes mainly concern Georges's life during the Occupation: his work at *Révolution nationale*, his feelings of respect bordering on fascination for Combelle, whose boldness and honesty he praises, the numerous encounters which the paper affords him, including with Robert Brasillach. At the Liberation, Georges describes how Combelle, who refused to flee France, was arrested and condemned to fifteen years' hard labour, then pardoned in 1951.

Georges's work at *Révolution nationale* is not strictly speaking a family secret. Everyone knows about it, though everyone has half-forgotten it. Some of them have wondered about the significance they should accord to Georges's attitude and have sought answers.

None of Lucile's brothers or sisters seem to have discussed the subject with him as he didn't like to talk about it, but none of them today seem to have come to a definitive judgement about Georges's presence at *Révolution nationale.*

As far as I'm aware, most of Georges's children (whose political views were in some cases radically opposed to his) saw him as a reactionary. By the time I was old enough to start taking an interest in the world, Georges had become embittered and world-weary; with the same bitterness he lambasted the press, the TV, the revolutionary left, champagne socialists, right-wing hypocrites, the proliferation of roundabouts on local roads, national education, singers with weedy voices, TV presenters with sloppy vocabulary, the 'sort of's and 'at the level of's and other linguistic tics, adolescents of all epochs and types. But for as long as I can remember, the two subjects to avoid at all costs during family lunches were French politics and cinema (to which list pasteurised Camembert would later be added).

And yet, however disillusioned he became, Georges continued till the end of his life to fight for unlikely or desperate causes.

On the cassettes which follow the missing ones, Georges returns to his position during the war and – whatever he says – tries to justify himself.

He doesn't mention the discussions he may have had with his own father who, after losing his job on *La Croix du Nord* when that paper closed, refused to write for the *Journal de Roubaix*, which was under the control of the German censors, and instead visited the soup kitchens for several months.

After the Liberation, suffering a malaise he does not name and arguing that those who didn't work during the Occupation should take priority, Georges took more than a year to present himself before the Purification Committee to get his professional identity card. This was granted after examination of his file, enabling him to resume his profession. Georges mentions the possibility of having received the support of François Chalais. Later still, on another cassette, when he is telling the story of the post-war period, Georges returns for the last time to his activities during the Occupation and asks himself astonishingly euphemistically: 'Was it opportunistic to work for a paper which was called *Révolution nationale* and which wasn't a Resistance paper? Of course . . .'

For several weeks, I pondered whether I should mention these things somehow, or consider them irrelevant to my subject. Could Georges's position during the war be a factor in Lucile's suffering? The possibility occurred to me on account of the missing cassettes (Lucile always had a flair for symbolic disappearances, as well as for coded messages which were more or less comprehensible for other people), but I was also influenced by the book *L'Intranquille* by the painter Gérard Garouste. Lucile has a number of things in common with Garouste, starting with the illness both of them suffered, long called manic depression and now known as bipolar disorder. I felt overwhelmed when I read his book a few months ago while I was considering writing about my mother but couldn't make up my mind. In the book, Garouste talks about his father, whose anti-Semitism was visceral and pathological, and who made a fortune from robbing the Jews. The murky horror and the shame which his father inspired in Garouste played a large part in his suffering and seems to have haunted him for a long time.

As far as I know, Georges was neither anti-Semitic nor a fascist. I never heard him say anything which would have allowed the least ambiguity on this; moreover, Georges spoke loudly and clearly and was not in the habit of hiding his opinions. As I see it today, Georges's collaboration with *Révolution nationale* was the act of an opportunistic young man who was eager for recognition and lacking in judgement.

Ultimately, even if like some of her brothers and sisters Lucile wondered about her father's past, and even if she was surprised by how many contradictions he contained, I think that as far as his time during the Occupation is concerned, she gave him the benefit of the doubt at least.

She hated him for other reasons.

Georges recorded over fifty hours of memories in all. They begin in the north with his earliest childhood and end in 1954, the year that Antonin died, as though Georges was unable to go beyond that sorrow. Thirty years after that accident, I am listening to my grandfather's voice on that tape, his slow account of the Saturday when their life collapsed around them, the words he struggles to find, the theories he expresses about his son's death, the description of his train journey to L., his hoarse account of his pain. Georges gives his own version of the event (he was in Paris), which differs from all the others I heard.

Georges's recordings contain an incredible number of names, faces, conversations and quips, as though it had all happened the day before. His memory is impressive for the amount of detail it contains. Sometimes on the same cassette or a few cassettes later, Georges remembers a fact, clarifies, corrects, adds an anecdote that Liane has reminded him about over lunch. I imagine them both in the kitchen at Pierremont in the solitude of winter. Georges emerges from his office, where he has spent the morning with his tape recorder, joins her for a bowl of piping hot soup, asks her what so-and-so's wife was called, the name of the Saint-Palais ice-cream maker, what age Lucile was when they had to shave her head to stop her pulling her hair out. Together, they reconstruct their little world of the fifties, their carefree glory days.

As I expected, Georges's recordings are a precious record of my grandparents' state of mind. When she married Georges, Liane told him that she wanted twelve children. He could take it or leave it. Georges agreed. Until Milo was born, he played along, felt pleased at his wife's successive pregnancies, took delight in seeing her bloom through her maternities. After that, anxiety caught up with him: the agency was slow to take off, they had had five children in six years, had no money put aside, and even if he still had freelance work from *Radio-Cinéma*, Georges was never sure that their money would last to the end of the month. He judged that it would be more sensible to have a break. So Georges spoke solemnly to Liane and Liane reluctantly agreed. She would use the rhythm method.

A few months later, Liane was pregnant with Justine. Georges thought that she had tricked him, then made the best of it. When the baby was born, in response to the gossips who claimed that they were having children non-stop for the family allowance, Georges, by way of announcement, reproduced a railway discount card on which he had written: 'The Poiriers are delighted to announce that they qualify for a 75 per cent reduction at last!'

In addition, as he didn't have a photo of Justine to hand, he used one of Milo as a baby. No one would be able to tell the difference between them.

A few months later, Liane was pregnant with Violette. Georges protests weakly, and concluded that Liane was taking no heed at all of his speeches, but didn't hold it against her.

★

The rue de Maubeuge years were a period of perpetual money worries, even if Georges's relationship with money was always based on denial. Georges lived beyond his means, whereas Liane kept scrupulous accounts (at Violette's house I saw school exercise books from the house in Pierremont in which she recorded her smallest expenses), anxiously watched out for the family allowance official and called Marie-Noëlle when one of the children urgently needed a new pair of shoes.

The rue de Maubeuge years were a mix of insouciance and insecurity, of hearty meals conjured out of nothing and later recalled nostalgically, of nappies washed by hand, of bedsheets stained with pee, a table that welcomed old friends and new (wherever he was, Georges only had to go into a station or a restaurant to meet people whom he would invite to dinner), discussions late into the night and hasty plans. Among this perpetual procession, you would encounter the neighbours from upstairs and down, friends from here and there, young au pairs, new and established journalists, artists from the bar, Georges's younger brother, Liane's sisters and brothers-in-law, Gilberte Pasquier, who married an air traffic controller, Pierre Dac and Francis Blanche (Georges worked with them for several months after the Liberation).

Whatever happened during the day, Liane always collapsed for an hour or two and slept like a log. It was a matter of survival, those who knew her explained later.

When I try to imagine them, it seems to me that my grandparents formed a couple who were at one and the same time unlikely and natural, whose vitality and energy commanded respect. Liane claimed to anyone who would listen that marriage gave her happiness and freedom. Her gaiety, laughter and vitality were irresistible.

Georges worshipped his wife and showered her with gifts. Repurposing an old trunk, which he insulated with cork and sheets of zinc, he made her a giant ice box, which enabled them to discover the joys of cold food. But it had to be fed ice and the container that held the water needed emptying. A few months later, Georges yielded to temptation and took out a loan to buy Liane a real refrigerator; then he bought her a little Hoover washing machine, which still had a manual spin.

Liane never questioned Georges's choices and closed her eyes to anything that might tarnish her love for him.

They shared for different reasons a sort of headlong rush towards the future, a Bohemian way of life – boho before boho was invented.

On an impulse, Liane and Georges left the rue de Maubeuge in April 1960. Mutual friends had put them in touch with a couple who were renting a huge house in Versailles, in one of the middle-class districts in the centre. All but one of the couple's nine children had left home. Lucile's family dreamed of having space, and the A. family wanted to return to Paris. After a few visits on either side, they decided to swap houses. Georges's new agency was developing rapidly and he decided he could afford a higher rent. The house had three storeys and was set in a respectable walled garden. Lucile's family therefore took possession of fourteen rooms, all except a little office in which the A. family had stored some of their possessions which would not fit in the Paris apartment, an office to which Lucile soon found the key and which she visited regularly in order to appropriate various half-useful or tempting objects.

When he saw Lucile for the first time, the A. family's youngest, a boy of around twenty, fell madly in love with her. She was fourteen. The young man expended a spectacular amount of energy to remain in contact with the Poirier family, came up with pretexts to visit Georges, offered his help with various tasks and before long asked for Lucile's hand in the most solemn and serious way imaginable. Georges roared with laughter.

All of the children from oldest to youngest chose their own room. Lucile, Justine, Violette and their parents took over the first floor;

Milo, Jean-Marc and Lisbeth the second; and Barthélémy, claiming his personal fiefdom, began a reign over the top floor which would last several years. For the first time, Lucile had a space of her own which no one else could enter. She moved in her mess, a tangle of clothes and books which she alone could make sense of, and shut the door behind her. Lucile spent hours daydreaming, lying on her bed, inventing her future, a future which she imagined as being above all without constraints, without anything that could stop her or hold her back. When she thought of the future, it wasn't a man or a job that came to Lucile's mind. No prince, no success filled her dreams: only time spread out before her to spend as she chose, a time of contemplation which offered her refuge.

Like the older children, Lucile continued to go to school in Paris. But that summer, her persistent truancy got her expelled. The next year, she started at Blanche-de-Castille, a Catholic school in Versailles, where she didn't work any harder and got dreadful results in everything except French. Lucile, who could not be shifted from her silence, occupied space and made her boredom plain. There was an insolence in the way she looked at her teachers which most of them could not tolerate. Not to mention the little notes she exchanged with her friends, mocking the ridiculous clothes the teachers wore or suggesting that some sister was having a lustful relationship with some other. Liane and Georges received a first warning. This time Georges was categorical with his daughter. This was her last chance. Liane was tired of going to plead her case in various educational establishments and had plenty to do with her other children. If

Lucile was expelled from Blanche-de-Castille, she would go to secretarial college. She would become a secretary, it was as simple as that, a shorthand secretary, and would remain one all her life. The way Georges described it, there was no occupation less enviable. But Lucile had not forgotten the tall and graceful Gilberte Pasquier.

Lucile was lying with her head supported on her hand, her body aligned with the edge of the bed, as near as possible to the bedside lamp, whose yellow light projected a sharp-edged circle onto the pages she had been turning for several hours, unaware of the time and indifferent to the calls from downstairs.

Suddenly her mother's voice became sharper.

'Lucile, our guests are here!'

Lucile jumped up, dropping her book. She put on her shoes, ran her fingers through her hair without bothering to look in the mirror, smoothed her shirt, then went downstairs to the living room. Her brother and sister were already there, smiling politely. Lisbeth had put on a bit of lipstick and was wearing a dress she had made herself, which was gathered at the waist and fitted her perfectly. Barthélémy, with his hands in his pockets, was trying to conceal his awkwardness. Lucile came into the room and Georges introduced his second daughter. She sat down beside him, taking care to sit up straight while everyone was looking at her. She was asked what class she was in, what job she would like to do later, what things in life interested her. Lucile replied in a tone devoid of arrogance that she didn't have the faintest idea. They persisted: there must be some activity she did outside school? Lucile hadn't yet responded when one of the guests commented in a stage whisper: 'She won't have any trouble finding a husband, anyway!' Lucile didn't respond, and nor did Georges, who teased her, however, about the state of her bedroom, which he began describing in abundant detail: the heaps of dirty laundry left on the floor, the piles of scrap paper and inaccessible notebooks, not to mention the areas which no one could get near, where you would probably discover, if you dared look, copious sweet wrappers and one or two women's novels. If she was going to find a husband, she would have to learn to create a bit of order around her. Georges next launched into one of his favourite tirades on the profound inertia and propensity to laziness of the youth of today. Not content with having captured the attention of his listeners, he moved on to the inability of teachers not only to engage their pupils' interest but also to impose their authority. What's more, those same teachers were unable to formulate a sentence of more than three words in correct French! Georges followed this with a diatribe about how teaching in France had evolved, a diatribe which he had perfected through having repeated it so often, to which he added variations and details to suit his audience. One of the guests, a Swedish client of the agency with plans to market refrigeration equipment, took the opportunity to complain about the difficulties of the language of Descartes. The imperfect subjunctive always caught out anyone who claimed to have mastered it in the end. Georges promised him some private lessons and went on with his speech. By way of example he offered the fact that Lucile had been expelled from every school she had attended. His audience gave an astonished gasp. French schools had no room for critical minds. Moreover, he and his wife were beginning to wonder about the potential suitability of their children for the school system, given that none of the seven of them thus far had distinguished themselves by their results. This, despite their aptitude.

'Milo's doing well at school,' Liane corrected. 'And Violette's desperate to go. My darling always exaggerates.'

'Seven?' said the astonished wife of the commercial director of a major orange juice brand.

She asked to see the others. Were they as beautiful as the older ones? Liane called the rest of the siblings. Milo appeared at the head of the little troupe, which soon stood in a line in the middle of the living room. Somewhat shyly, the children said hello one after the other. The guests were enraptured. What a splendid family! Justine took advantage of the comments provoked by their appearance to slip back out to the kitchen, quickly followed by Violette, who never let her out of her sight. Milo and Jean-Marc lingered a while longer with the adults, sitting close together on the arm-rest of the sofa. When Liane took them back to join their sisters, Milo asked when he would be old enough to stay and talk to the adults. Liane whispered in his ear: 'Soon, my angel, soon.'

Since moving house, Liane and Georges had organised many dinner parties. Liane took on someone to help with preparing the meal, serving it and clearing up. At the start of the evening, the three eldest would come down to say hello, 'make an effort', and answer questions about their studies or talk about the last play they had seen at the Théâtre-Français, for which all three had season tickets. Sometimes Georges asked them to stay for the aperitif. He thought it useful for his children to listen to adults and learn to join in their conversations. Little by little, through these interactions before dinner, Lucile discovered her father's limitations. Georges didn't know everything. Surrounded by other characters who were as strong, brilliant and erudite as he was, Georges didn't always get the last word. He sometimes clashed with opinions contrary to his own and arguments that he had difficulty besting, though that never stopped him concluding in a tone that brooked no appeal that he was right. Lucile observed her father and glimpsed his intolerance and his contradictions. Georges had long decreed Proust to be a minor writer, a page-pisser, an incontinent copyboy. His style? Cheap embroidery for Presbyterian spinsters. You might as well take a sleeping pill. Georges made people laugh; no one dared contradict him. But one day, at one of those parties where he always hung onto the starring role, Georges came across a Proust specialist, who was capable of parrying his attacks and defending the writer's prose, whole pages of which he knew by heart. Lucile listened to the two men engaged in verbal jousting, hanging on every word. So, she realised, her father could be wrong and even make himself look ridiculous. Barthélémy, who also heard the discussion, took the side of his father's opponent. Georges ordered him to be quiet. The next day, Lucile stole enough from Liane's purse to buy the first volume of *À la recherche du temps perdu* and hid it deep in her famous pile.

In the living room at Versailles on evenings when they had guests, Lucile remained within herself, silent and observant. It was rare to hear her voice, but impossible to ignore her presence. The three older ones would then join the younger children, who were eating in the kitchen, while Liane and her husband led their guests into the dining room. Georges had a talent for mixing his clients – business leaders, sales and commercial directors – with his closest friends. The regulars from the rue de Maubeuge had tagged along, and were soon joined by new acquaintances Georges made wherever he went. Talk about work didn't last long. There was laughter, anecdotes, observations on the ways of the world. Once the adults were at table, Barthélémy would return to the living room to down the dregs of glasses, then take himself off to the hall, where the coats and bags were. He collected a few coins, but rarely took notes. This money-spinner didn't last long; Lisbeth soon gave the game away.

After not having had a baby for seven years, by which time she had long given up pretending to use the rhythm method, Liane fell pregnant. The news at first caused a strange sort of agitation, tinged with worry. They had got out of practice. But Liane remained serene as her body became rounder and her skin stretched; before long she went and fetched the cot, the baby blankets, the music boxes and the clothes that had been put away in the attic long ago. Now that Violette had started school, she took to having an afternoon nap again, making the most of those few hours of silence which were hers alone. With her hands on her belly, under the thick warmth of the eiderdown, Liane was happy. The older children were getting on with their lives, starting to have boyfriends and girlfriends, being invited to dances and parties. Before long they would be leaving home. The little ones were no longer so little, and even Violette, her beloved little girl, had learned to read and write. Liane would soon be forty-three. She had given birth to seven children, not counting Jean-Marc, and knew no feelings richer and more intense than the sensation of a little being moving inside her stomach, and then holding it against her as it eagerly sought her breast.

Liane experienced this pregnancy like none of her previous ones. She enjoyed how her condition made her slow down, and watched her breasts swell. She didn't feel ill or tired; nothing seemed easier to her or more natural. No worries spoiled these few months of bliss; the children helped her and Georges was in an excellent mood. Of course, he did come home late in the evening, sometimes went on business trips, and had special relationships with women. Should she complain? He saw these women one to one, lavished advice on them, introduced them to people, showed them Paris. Sometimes he even invited them to dinner. They were young and looked at him admiringly.

There was one thing Liane had understood from the outset: if she began to imagine for a second, even a fraction of a second, the caresses that Georges might indulge in with other women, if she gave in to that image, just once, she was done for. She was lucky, very lucky: she loved her husband and her husband loved her. She should be glad and not let anything tarnish her joy. Georges wanted women, every woman, but was none the less her husband, her darling, as she called him, including when she spoke to someone else about him. Life in Versailles was infinitely better than it had been in the rue de Maubeuge. She now had help at home, a washing machine with automatic spin dryer, and a food processor from the United States. The days of minute calculations and lists of outgoings with no income to balance the books were behind her. The prospect of another child didn't scare her. Liane, in spite of her many pregnancies, had kept her slender waist and athletic figure. When she went out in the evening with Georges, she put on a bit of make-up, smoked a few menthol cigarettes, ran her fingers through her hair, laughed.

She had thought her body was no longer fertile and here she was pregnant again: she was the happiest of women. Justine, Milo and

Jean-Marc were beside themselves with impatience for the baby to be born. Violette, a little worried about losing her place, clung on to her mother.

This child, unexpected and unhoped for, would be the last: a gift from God.

When summer came, Liane and Georges sent their tribe to the house in Pierremont under the supervision of the older children. Lisbeth was eighteen, Barthélémy seventeen, Lucile sixteen. Liane stayed in Versailles with her big belly, waiting for the birth. In August they were all going to Alicante in Spain, where Georges had again rented a large apartment.

Late one afternoon in early July, Liane's waters broke. She called Georges at the agency and, accompanied by a neighbour, rushed off to the Parisian clinic where she was registered. She gave birth to a magnificent little boy with hair that was almost white less than two hours later. Georges arrived just after the battle was over.

In Pierremont, they heard the news that evening by phone. Tom was born! Lisbeth and Lucile bought cider to celebrate and invited some friends over to continue the party. According to Georges, the baby was magnificent and sturdier than any of the rest of them. The older children raised their glasses and drank to Tom's arrival. Someone had brought a guitar; cigarettes were plentiful and the party went on late into the night.

Early next morning Milo, Justine and Violette (then aged respectively twelve, ten and eight) took advantage of the torpor following the party to meet up with their own friends and set off on an expedition, after raiding the fridge for a picnic. They walked along the river and decided to go as far as the dam. When they got there, they climbed on to a footbridge to take a look. It was never clear if Violette went under or over the guardrail. She fell eight feet head-first onto a concrete slab. It was a few seconds before the other children realised that she was no longer there. Violette was lying face down in a foot of water. When Neneuil, the oldest of the children, spotted her, he jumped down and instinctively turned her over.

Lucile was woken by shouts. Lucile, who normally took so long to get up, leapt out of bed, her throat tight as though someone were strangling her. She put on her trousers and ran after the children towards the dam. When she saw Violette lying on the ground, she was almost sick from fear. Her legs and hands were shaking as she went towards her and she thought for a moment she was going to faint. Violette was pale, her eyes barely open. Lucile wanted to take her sister in her arms, but she remembered what she had been taught: you mustn't move someone who has had an accident. Lisbeth had called for help. It would be here soon. Lucile took Violette's hand, trying to find the words to reassure her, but no words came into her mind, only cries, muffled shouts which collided with one another without a single sound coming out of her mouth. In the ambulance, Lucile sat beside her sister, her stomach knotted with anxiety, hypnotised by the blood coming from Violette's ears, which soaked into her towelling pyjamas, a red spot at first, and then the whole top. Violette was delirious.

They had to call Georges at the agency. Lisbeth faced her father's questions and his blank, devastated voice. The medical team had taken charge of Violette, she was conscious, she was hurt, yes, badly hurt, they hadn't said anything, no. Nothing.

While Georges was on his way to Joigny from Paris, the doctor who had delivered Liane's baby appeared at her bedside. Choosing his words carefully, he told her that she was going to have to be very brave. The child she had brought into the world wasn't like other children. Tom had Down's syndrome, a condition which they were beginning to understand better and which was now called Trisomy 21. Because Liane didn't react, the doctor added, taking care to enunciate each syllable: 'Your son is a mongol, Mrs Poirier.'

The doctor advised Liane to give the baby to social services. A child like that, especially in a large family, could only spell disaster. His intellectual development would be extremely limited and care services were lacking. Tom would be a permanent worry. It was best to face the truth: all their lives they would be dragging him around like a ball and chain. Liane was stunned. She said she would speak to her husband. She looked at Tom in the crib beside her, his tiny curled fingers, the soft down on his head, his incredibly fine, well-defined mouth. The baby was looking for his thumb and making a sucking sound. It seemed to her that he was just like all the others: unable to survive alone.

The following days were marked by great confusion. Violette, who had suffered a fractured skull, had narrowly escaped something much worse; she needed to stay in hospital for three weeks. Liane, stuck in the clinic, had to wait ten days before she could see her daughter.

Georges shuttled between Paris, the hospital in Joigny and the house in Pierremont.

In early August, the whole family left for Alicante, apart from Violette, whose convalescence required her to remain lying down for several hours a day and whose condition was unsuited to the heat. She was entrusted to Georges's sister and spent the rest of the summer with her cousins.

In September, when the whole family was back in Paris, Georges picked Tom up and took him round all the hospitals. His son was not going to stay handicapped. Georges sought out many tests, supplementary examinations, opinions and second opinions. He got hold of all the research that had been published on the subject in the past twenty years, attended conferences and met all sorts of gurus. He would find a solution even if he had to cross oceans to do so. This wasn't necessary. The additional chromosome in the twenty-first pair had been discovered two years previously in France by Professor Lejeune, who was the first person in the world to establish the link between the state of mental retardation and chromosomal abnormalities and he had given it the name Trisomy 21 syndrome. After weeks of initiatives, bold attempts and outraged correspondence, Georges eventually got to meet Professor Lejeune. If Tom had one chromosome too many, it simply had to be removed. The doctor met him in his office and spent over an hour with him. Destroying the extra chromosome wasn't conceivable, but one day it might be possible to neutralise it. Trisomy 21 should be considered an illness, not a handicap. In the distant future, medicine might be able to cure or reduce the intellectual retardation. But not now.

Georges left in a state of great sadness. He took a decision that would significantly alter the course of his life: he would devote all his energy to this child and would develop his abilities to the full.

Not for an instant did Georges or Liane consider putting Tom in an institution.

Tom was lying in his cot, his eyes wide open. For several minutes he had been making sharp noises to summon his sisters. Violette was doing her homework while Justine was playing with Solange, a classmate she had invited to tea. Justine went over to the cot and picked the baby up. Tom waved his arms and legs in delight. Justine noticed the sharp smell coming from his nappy and with an expert air announced that she was going to change her brother. She suggested that Solange come with her, spread out a hand towel on her parents' bed and put Tom down. She cleaned his bottom, the folds of his thighs and his willy, then dried him carefully. Between two little bursts of singing, Tom began laughing. Justine kissed his cheeks, stomach and little arms, as she had so often seen her mother do, proud of being able to show Solange that she knew how to look after the baby. She often gave him his bottle too, and when her parents weren't there, he slept with her. Tom grabbed her hair and tried to pull it, but Justine gave him a look. The child hesitated for a moment, then let go and began kicking his legs in the air again in delight. Solange was staring at Tom in puzzlement. Justine had turned round to look at her several times, seeking a smile on her friend's face, a sign of tenderness, but Solange was avoiding Tom's eye, though he was devoting all his energy to getting her attention.

Finally, Solange turned to Justine and announced her verdict: 'Your brother's a mongol.'

Justine looked at her friend, Little Miss Know-It-All with her chin raised and her stuck-up nose. Tom was waving his limbs more than ever; he caught his feet with his hands and took them to his mouth. Justine held him still to fasten the clean nappy, put his trousers and bootees back on and sat him up again. Tom stayed like that for a few seconds, trying to keep his balance, then fell backwards with a little squeal of joy.

Justine shrugged. 'Whatever.'

She picked up the child and left the room without a word. She didn't want to play with Solange any more; she wanted Solange to go home. Solange wasn't her friend anyway. Solange wore terrible dresses and was *bird-brained*, that's what her father had said the last time she came to play at the house one Sunday.

That evening after Solange had gone, Justine knocked on Milo's door and went in without waiting. Milo was lying on his bed, absorbed in a magazine. Justine sat down beside him. Milo smiled at her, then went back to reading.

'Is it true that Tom's a mongol?'

Milo looked up at his sister, clearly torn between the instructions he had been given and the truth he reckoned he owed her.

'Yeah, it's true.'

'How do you know?'

'Mum told Lisbeth. She told Lucile, who told me.'

Justine felt overcome by a great sadness. It wasn't possible. Tom was an angel, a little prince, not a mongol. She rushed downstairs. Georges was reading the paper in the living room, Liane was busy preparing dinner. Justine hesitated for a moment, then chose the kitchen, where Violette was sitting beside her mother. They were both peeling vegetables.

Justine stood in front of the table.

'Is it true that Tom's a mongol?'

There was silence for a moment, then Liane answered in her gentlest voice: 'It's true, my darling girl. But we don't say "mongol". Tom has Down's syndrome. That means he's handicapped and won't ever be like other children. But we can teach him lots of things and we'll try to make him happy.'

Liane's voice had changed. Violette noticed its low, pained tone at once. She dropped the peeler and put her arms round her mother's neck.

'Can't he be fixed?'

How could Liane stay so calm? Justine wanted to grab the plates and throw them around the room, to knock everything over, the table, chairs, pots, knives and forks, to knock it all over and scream. She didn't want Tom to have Down's syndrome. She wanted him to be strong and normal and able to defend himself. Because Tom was going to grow up and become a little boy. In the street, on the metro, people would look at him, would turn round and whisper behind his back. She couldn't bear the thought of people laughing at him.

Justine picked up the fruit basket and suddenly dropped it. She looked defiantly at her mother. The oranges rolled as far as the fridge but the apples scattered further, almost as far as the hall. She wasn't going to pick them up. Liane would just have to do it herself.

★

Justine left the kitchen and went up the stairs in tears, where she bumped into Lucile. Lucile took her by the shoulders and steered her into her room. She sat her sister down on her bed and asked what had made her so sad. Justine didn't answer. Her body was shaking with anger, her breathing seemed to be seeking an anchor point which would enable her to calm her panic. Lucile stroked her hair and stayed silent long enough for Justine's breathing to settle down and her sobs to cease. Justine had long legs and astonishingly regular features. She was beautiful. Justine had always been an angry child. She would never clear her plate, couldn't bear opposition and would fly into mad rages, the cause of which was generally unclear. Justine battled against her mother, and in the confrontation angled for her attention. She was said to be a difficult child. The rest was almost forgotten.

Lucile had gone to fetch a glass of water and gradually Justine calmed down. She was now sitting on the edge of the bed, like a good little girl with her hands on her thighs, which wasn't like her. Lucile was still watching her.

'It's because of Tom,' Justine said eventually. 'He's a mongol.'

Lucile put her hand on top of her sister's.

'So what? It's not that bad.'

'What if people make fun of him?'

'No one will make fun of him. Mum and Dad will protect him. So will we.'

★

Justine seemed reassured and left the room.

For several months Justine and Violette had been looking after

Tom, just as Lucile and Lisbeth had looked after them when they were little.

Lucile had adored Violette, her chubby cheeks, her blonde curls, teaching her nursery rhymes and songs and even some of the times tables. But Justine had always seemed more distant to her. Even though sometimes Lucile imagined that, as a result of the secret geometry which exists among siblings, they were linked by something. Something they all silently shared, which probably had no name and far from bringing them closer together, actually drove them apart.

Now Justine and Violette watched over Tom and delighted in his progress. Things perpetuated themselves, were passed on; that's the way large families were. Tom was a darling child, a little king, a prince. He slept well, ate well, never cried. He was so easy. As soon as you went near him, he held out his arms and squealed with delight. Sometimes Lucile held him, stroking the blond down on his head and kissing his little hands. Like her brothers and sisters, she had become attached to Tom, couldn't imagine him different, wouldn't have swapped him for any other child. And yet, from the first months, it seemed to her as though in this family awash with children, Tom was an additional factor of dilution. Tom was a sorrow which her parents had managed to turn into a gift. A gift that took up a lot of space.

One day Lucile would go. She would leave the noise, the commotion, the movement. That day she would be one and one only, distinct from the others, would no longer be part of a group. She often wondered what the world would be like that day – would it be more brutal or on the contrary gentler?

Jean-Marc hadn't come down for his breakfast, nor did he come down for ten o'clock mass. Liane had kept an eye on her watch, unable to believe it. She considered waking him up at one point, but thought better of it. Jean-Marc had had a long training session the day before in preparation for a regional swimming competition. He probably needed the rest. She could let him sleep. She would wait for him; they could go to midday mass. Jean-Marc would be up before long. She liked this weekly appointment, a moment which belonged to just the two of them. Jean-Marc was the only one of her children who believed in God. Milo and the older ones had long refused to go to mass; Georges hadn't set foot in a church since Antonin's death; Justine and Violette took part in the catechism without complaint, but they were too young to truly share her faith. Only Jean-Marc went with her entirely of his own free will, and even went without her when she couldn't go. Jean-Marc liked praying, he had told her, praying on his knees with his hands together, his whispered words ascending to heaven. One day perhaps, borne up by his fervour, they might reach the Lord. Jean-Marc didn't pray for himself but for others, those who he knew were worried or unhappy, for Jean-Marc had always perceived the distress of those around him better than anyone else.

To Liane, faith was a gift from God which she had been fortunate to receive, just as she had been fortunate to take in Jean-Marc nine years earlier – even if he was not her son, she had become

linked to him by a strange attachment which was just as organic –
and just as she had been fortunate to bring into the world this baby
who was different from all the others, and who brought her nothing
but joy and wonder. Tom was beginning to stand up and soon he
would be walking.

Jean-Marc still hadn't come down for midday mass and Liane felt a
knot of anxiety grow within her, which she banished with a cup of
scalding tea that she drank standing in the kitchen. His swimming
must have exhausted him. He could skip mass this once. Jean-Marc
would soon be fifteen. He was preparing to start at the Academy
of Visual Art, where Barthélémy had been studying for the past
two years. He had been so happy when he heard he'd got in. Liane
had seen his face when he came back from the open day and how
proud he was at the thought of following in his brother's footsteps,
studying at the same place as him. Before the school year started,
he deserved to sleep.

Lucile was dozing in bed, woken from time to time by a shout, or the
noise of a chair, a voice. In the damp sheets, she lost consciousness of
her body, as though she were floating on the surface of stagnant water
that was at exactly the same temperature as her skin. She had no
desire to get up or even to open the curtains. They had come home
from holiday a few days before and she was enjoying prolonging this
state of suspension, of numbness, of not making plans, letting things
come and go, welcoming time stretching out. Soon she'd have to face
the new school year, begin afresh. For as far back as she could remember, Lucile had hated this time of year. Each year, you had to reinvent

your timetable, redefine itineraries, start everything anew. And this time, having been expelled from Blanche-de-Castille without leave to appeal, her name was down for secretarial college.

Liane had put her coat on. She would wake Jean-Marc when she got back. He could rest. Georges had gone to Pierremont for the weekend in order to advance the building work, so he couldn't make remarks about it. For according to Georges, lie-ins had been invented for the indolent and feeble. To lead a healthy life, you had to be up with the lark, Sundays included. However unappealing that was to idle youths and lazy girls.

Just as she was leaving the house, Liane knocked on Lucile's door. After a few seconds, her daughter replied with a groggy yes.

'I'm going to mass, darling.'

Lucile got up and opened the door to her mother.

'You need to put the chicken in the oven at about quarter past twelve. I've got it all prepared.'

Lucile nodded and closed her door.

Liane set off towards the church. She felt the little ball swell in her stomach, but refused to pay attention to it and hurried on. Suddenly she stopped. It wasn't normal. Something was wrong. Jean-Marc never slept so late. He never missed mass. Liane turned around and began to run back towards the house. She took the stairs two at a time. The closer she got to her son's room, the more her anxiety grew.

Lucile heard her mother return and rush upstairs, then knock on

Jean-Marc's door, calling him several times. Lucile heard her mother open the door, and then she heard nothing.

Liane discovered the boy lying on his bed with a plastic bag over his head. She flung herself on him, tore off the bag and uncovered his face. His mouth remained open, as though searching for air.

After the laying out, Jean-Marc, dressed in a dark suit, remained in the house for three days. His body lay on his bed, surrounded with candles. All the children were able to see him. A few weeks earlier, Barthélémy had strongly objected to the idea that Jean-Marc would soon be joining him at his school. Since when had Jean-Marc been any good at art? He didn't want him on his back, he was ashamed of him. But now that his brother was dead, Barthélémy, who didn't believe in God, prayed with all his strength that he would come back to life. He would have given anything to go back in time, for Jean-Marc's death never to have taken place, for his family not to be devastated yet again by something like this.

The press got hold of the story. Journalists came. They rang the doorbell and telephoned constantly. One after the other they encountered Georges's aggression and insults. Some of them waited near the house in the hope of getting a few words from the brothers and sisters of the dead boy, or anyone who put their head outside the door. Like the others, Lucile left the house with her scarf round her face, ignoring the calls and haranguing, looking straight ahead.

Jean-Marc's death had been explained calmly to Lucile and her brothers and sisters. Because he was a battered child, Jean-Marc was in the habit of protecting his head as he went to sleep. That evening, exhausted by his swimming training, he had covered his head in a plastic bag and hadn't woken up. Jean-Marc had died in his sleep of asphyxia. He hadn't suffered. That was all they said.

From then on the atmosphere in the house, vast as it was, became heavy and oppressive. Georges was distraught and jumped at any ringing sound. The newspaper headlines that fuelled his anger were hidden from the children. Nothing must be said to other people. Jean-Marc was dead; there was nothing more to add.

Can you fall asleep at the age of almost fifteen with a plastic bag on your head without intending to, without having chosen to? That was the question Lucile asked herself, along with most of her brothers and sisters probably. And if Jean-Marc had chosen to put an end to his life, what unhappiness, what abandonment was the cause of his distress? No one had noticed anything; Jean-Marc seemed happy. What were they guilty of, those of them who were still alive, those who had seen nothing?

Initially, once I had finally accepted that I would write this book after a long, silent negotiation with myself, I thought I would have no difficulty introducing fiction and no qualms about filling in gaps. By which I mean I thought in a sense I would remain in charge. I thought I would be capable of constructing a story that was fluid and controlled, or at least a text that would develop in a regular, confident form and would take on meaning as it went. I believed I could invent, give it life, direction, create tension, get from one end to the other avoiding fault lines and breaks. I hoped I'd be able to handle the material as I wished, and the image that occurred to me was the traditional one of pastry-making: like Liane taught me when I was a child, shortcrust or flaky, which I would make by hand, using various ingredients, then roll out under my palms, flattening it with force, or even fling it at the ceiling to see how it would stick.

Instead of which, I am unable to alter anything. Instead of which, I feel as though I spend hours with my hands in the air and my sleeves rolled up to the elbow, tied in a horrible butcher's apron, terrified by the thought of betraying history, getting dates or places or ages wrong; instead of which, I fear I shall fail to construct the story as I had imagined it.

Unable to free myself completely from reality, I am involuntarily producing fiction; I'm looking for the angle which will allow me to come closer and closer still; I'm looking for a place which is neither truth nor fable, but both at once.

Every day that passes I see how difficult it is to write about my mother, to define her in words, how much her voice is missing. Lucile talked to us very little about her childhood. She didn't tell stories. Now I tell myself that that was her way of escaping the mythology, of refusing to take part in the fabrication and narrative reconstruction which all families indulge in.

I have no memory of my mother telling me herself about the events which marked her childhood, by which I mean a first-person account which would have given us access, at least in part, to how she saw things. What I'm ultimately lacking is her own point of view, the words she would have chosen, what importance she would have accorded to certain facts, the details that would have struck her. She sometimes mentioned these things, Antonin and Jean-Marc's deaths, the photos of the child star she had been, Liane's personality and her father's; she spoke of them with a certain aggression, but divorced from any story or narrative context, as though they were stones she was throwing to hit us full on or in order to rid herself of the worst memories.

I am trying all the same to reconstruct her viewpoint from the fragments she gave to different people; to Violette shortly before her death, to my sister Manon, and sometimes to me. I recompose, certainly, fill the blanks, arrange things as I think best. I grow a little further from Lucile in wanting to get closer to her.

★

I don't know what Lucile felt when Tom was born. I imagined it. I know she adored this late, vulnerable child who had to be protected from the world. I know how much Tom meant to her when he was an adult, how much it mattered to her that he felt comfortable when he stayed with her for a few days. Some people pointed out to me that Tom, because of the instant affection he inspired, the attention he demanded, and the resolve my grandparents had to develop his abilities to the full, probably took up a lot of space. Hopes, affection and disappointed impulses gradually came to be lodged in this funny, kind child who was so devoid of malice. As the years went by, Tom became the focus for Georges and was idolised by the whole family. Today, he's its mascot and in my view what holds it together.

When I was a child, I used to play with Tom in the garden in Versailles. We would chase Enzyme, Justine's dachshund, and whisper endearments in his long ears and watch him shake his head. Tom is just a few years older than me.

When I was a child, there were photos of Antonin and Jean-Marc, the sons who had disappeared, side by side on the bookcase in the living room at Pierremont. Later, a black and white portrait of Milo was added to them. During the school holidays, my sister and I, along with my many cousins, spent whole weeks in the mysterious shadow of those deaths. Given the attraction that morbid things hold for children, we continually circled around those photos, observing the tiniest details, exploring the mystery. We asked Liane to repeat the anecdotes and memories dozens of times. Sitting on her little stool in the legendary yellow kitchen, my grandmother told us about her sons in her light, melodious voice, sometimes with her unique emotional laugh, and those deep sighs, full of anguish, which were all that conveyed the state of distress that those deaths had left her in.

I discovered much later from Violette that Jean-Marc had died of hypoxyphilia, also known as autoerotic asphyxiation, in other words, during a masturbation session in which he was trying to enhance his orgasm through suffocation. Jean-Marc apparently engaged in masochism and fetishistic practices. During the interviews I conducted to write this book, Lisbeth told me that a few weeks before his death, she had burst into his room without knocking to get back some knickers he had stolen from her and surprised him sticking pins into his penis, around which he had tied a scarf.

Today I try to reconstruct how events happen, the scale of their impact. It seems to me that Jean-Marc's death and the official version the children were given of it (one can imagine how hard the truth would have been to explain to children) introduced them to the notion of suicide for the first time. For a long time, Lucile considered her brother's strange death from this angle. Without any additional explanation, the official version, though it seemed less brutal, gave rise to an element of doubt and probably of guilt, in particular among the older children, who had always felt ambivalent towards Jean-Marc.

Accounts of Jean-Marc's death diverge on a number of minor points, notably who was with Georges for the building work in Pierremont at the time (apparently Lisbeth and Barthélémy) and who had stayed in Versailles with Liane (Lucile and the little ones).

As far as press harassment is concerned, one version has Georges appealing to his brother-in-law, who was then editor of *Ici Paris*, to use his influence to put a stop to it, and in another it's Claude, Liane's brother-in-law, who puts the story in his paper, earning him Georges's undying resentment. But I heard this version denied several times.

Everyone agrees that it was Liane who discovered the body and telephoned Georges to tell him to come home at once. Liane also called Marie-Noëlle, their longtime friend, who arrived at once to deal with the most urgent matters. Milo, who was thirteen, wept noisily for hours over the brother who was closest to him in age, his brother who had disappeared. Milo was inconsolable and cried as Barthélémy had cried a few years earlier over Antonin. Today, both deaths are mentioned in the same way in the same language: an invisible, deadly thread links them.

I don't know anything about Lucile beyond the fact that she was there, in a nearby bedroom, and that she was seventeen. I don't know what she did, if she shouted, if she wept, what mark these events left on her.

Lisbeth, who now lives in the south of France, told me that she kept the front page of a newspaper that appeared at the time of Jean-Marc's death, whose headline ('The battered child who didn't outlive his past') enraged Georges. I asked to see the article. After searching for several days, Lisbeth rang to say she hadn't found it. Now that she thought about it, she had probably thrown it away.

A few years ago, Lisbeth decided to 'get rid of all the bad memories'. It was in this state of having jettisoned the worst that Lisbeth spent several hours telling me the story of our family. I called several times in the weeks following those meetings to ask for details which only she would know. It was in this state that she gave me details and anecdotes in a panoramic Technicolor version from which the out-takes and alternate angles are missing, and in which suffering colours every sentence without ever being named. Lisbeth is not alone. Everyone does the best they can and I respect her line of defence, her survival strategy, which is very similar to Barthélémy's. Perhaps it is because they were the eldest. Perhaps because they were the most exposed. Today Lisbeth and Barthélémy have opted to keep the best, the most whimsical, the most luminous memories. They have thrown the rest away. They may be right. Like the others, they welcomed my project enthusiastically and like the others they are now wondering what I am going to do with all this. They are *fretting*, as we say in our family. Now as I write, I often think of them – Lisbeth, Barthélémy, Justine and Violette – with the infinite affection I feel for them, but also the certainty of offending them, or disappointing them.

I don't include Tom, whom we all adore, in this; he is forty-eight and for several years has been living in a home for the mentally disabled: he is the only one who I know will not read this.

Barthélémy's hair had sprouted almost overnight, as though he had drunk a magic potion. It fell in a clump over his eyes, divided into thick curls, with two unruly tufts on top, which he allowed to grow out and then down. Georges saw red. Barthélémy's hair was the epitome of the age of stupidity. What's more, Barthélémy thought stupidly, dressed stupidly, moved stupidly. Georges believed he had behaved tolerantly towards his children; he had given them a liberal education and respected their personalities and their opinions as much as possible, but this was too much. There were limits. In life, first impressions count. Turning up anywhere with hair that was long, and, worse, of dubious cleanliness, amounted to social suicide: automatic dismissal, self-sabotage. Georges could not bear Barthélémy's hair or the way his son now contradicted him in public, his airs and graces, his invitations to dances, and his success with clucking, cackling females, his empty-eyed friends who affected to be literary aficionados. Barthélémy no longer played tennis (Georges had long hoped that his son would make the national rankings), he hung around with people older than him and put on artistic airs. Since growing his hair, every time Barthélémy entered a room or came into his field of vision, Georges drew attention to his appearance with a cutting remark or a pained sigh. Barthélémy was giving himself airs, which is what you have to do when you have no content to offer; it was all packaging, and God knows Georges knew all about showing off and empty packages from all his years in advertising. Georges was on the look-out, would pounce upon a detail, a silence, a hesitation, would jump at the slightest chance to launch into one of his acerbic monologues, which he was perfecting as time went by and which always reached this rueful conclusion, which he bleated to Liane: 'What can I say, my dear, it's the aaaage of stupiiiiiidity.'

Georges didn't like Lisbeth's squawking, her noisy ebullience or her preoccupation with clothes either. He couldn't bear Lucile spending time out of the house without saying where she was or who she was with, her tight trousers, her lipstick, her eye-rolling or her disapproving silences. When his children began going out in the evenings and started taking hours to get ready; when they started mixing with other teenagers, whom they talked about at table and late into the evening; when they started getting invited here, there and everywhere, Georges felt the full force of their growing distance. The whole thing was outright treason.

As his children grew up, Georges gave in to ever harsher mockery. Acne, blushing and not meeting his eye fuelled his diatribes. Georges was a master of the devastating simile; nothing escaped his attention. Clothes, attitudes, accessories were gone over with a fine-tooth comb, analysed and decried. Some evenings the mockery resembled a lynching. Because Georges always enjoyed striking the final blow, having the last word.

Lucile was no exception to the rule, but her father never went so far as to humiliate her. Lucile kept out of his way, avoided his eye. Silence gave him no purchase. As time went by, she seemed to be leading a secret parallel life to which he had no access. Georges took it out instead on Barthélémy's friends, who were interested in his daughter; he loudly deplored their lack of culture, their puny physiques, their meagre ambitions. Above all, he detested Forrest, a boy with an angelic face, who only had eyes for Lucile.

Lucile hated her father's refusal to brook opposition, his lack of indulgence, his boundless ferocity. She observed his face, deformed by silent pain, his nostrils pinched in disgust, the bitter pursing of his lips. She didn't recognise him. She couldn't have said when Georges became this bitter creature. Or maybe she was now discovering him in his true light and getting the measure of his aggression? He, who always boasted his children's intelligence was well above average, was now the first to mock them when they hesitated, the first to become irritated by their wishes and to laugh at their tastes. Milo, Justine and Violette, too, would one day wear fashionable clothes, sport provocative hairstyles and foment revolution. They too would one day escape him.

Helplessly, Liane would listen to her husband and sometimes try to temper his language. For her, the children's adolescence was a strange, enclosed territory within the family she had created, a place whose demands and displays she had stopped trying to understand; they were too remote from the memories of her own provincial childhood and late puberty, which she had experienced under the control of a father whose authority was beyond question. She would have preferred her children to remain small, to simply stop growing up. In fact, thinking about it, Liane loved nothing so much as babies' delicate new flesh, which she devoured with endless kisses. Of course, she remained close to Lisbeth, who had always been her right hand. And of course, she was proud of Barthélémy, who had turned into a splendid young man. For the moment, Milo was doing well at school; he read the papers and was taking an interest in the world. The girls were still little and she could still smother Violette in kisses. But Lucile, when she got back from secretarial college, would smoke cigarettes in her room, and display a polite detachment that gave none of her thoughts or feelings away.

Lucile had escaped her long ago.

Twice in recent weeks Lucile and Lisbeth had got home long after the time their father had stipulated. And so, when they were invited to a big party organised by their cousins in Chaville, Georges forbade them to go. There was no appeal. It made no difference that they had spent weeks making their dresses. What was more, Georges demanded their presence at a dinner he was organising that same evening to which he had invited the commercial director of the agency, a young humorist he had just met, and the producer of TV serials in which the little ones had appeared. During the dinner, Lucile and Lisbeth forced themselves to join in the conversation and answer the questions they were asked. As soon as the dessert was over, they asked to go up to bed.

When the guests had gone, Georges, who was annoyed that the girls had disappeared so early, went up to see them with the firm intention of telling them a thing or two about good manners. Both their rooms were empty and Lucile's window was open. Georges and Liane jumped in the car and made it to Chaville in under half an hour.

Georges parked outside the house. Music spilled into the street, though the shutters were closed. Liane rang the doorbell while Georges waited in the car. She appeared on the threshold of the room where they were dancing and looked for her daughters. Without a word being spoken, Lisbeth and Lucile were sitting on the back seat in less than two minutes. In the rear-view mirror, Lucile caught Georges's eye and shrank down. When they got back to Versailles, he launched into a strangled fit of rage and before their eyes angrily tore the dresses they had carefully sewn. In the night, Lucile decided to run away. The following morning she told Lisbeth her plan; Lisbeth didn't have to be asked twice. Lisbeth dreamed of travel, distant countries and men with melodious accents. She wasn't afraid of leaving. They would start out living incognito in Pierremont, long enough to find work and put some money aside. Then, if Lucile was up for it, they could run far away, much further away.

They pretended to leave for school at the usual time. But instead of going to class they took the first train from Versailles to the Gare Saint-Lazare, then went to the bank to withdraw Lisbeth's savings. Lisbeth had always been the only one able to put money aside. For a short while, she had been babysitting to fund her future travels. The two sisters next went to the Gare de Lyon, where a few hours later, they caught the first train to Pierremont.

Lucile had never noticed how dark and run-down the house was. How damp and icy the atmosphere was. When evening came, they heard all sorts of strange noises coming from the attic. In terror she asked Lisbeth to sleep with her. Early next morning, they saw Georges arrive with a bag of croissants in his hand, relieved and smiling. He made them a big breakfast, then got them into the car. In less than two hours, they were in Paris.

L ucile would hang around the boulevards with Barthélémy's friend Forrest or seek refuge in a cinema. He had fallen in love with her the first day he saw her. He used to come to Versailles or Pierremont, and never took his eyes off her. Forrest had become her confidant, the chaste lover who bided his time. Lucile didn't want to sleep with him. She had her hair short like a flapper, wore roll-neck sweaters, with ski-pants and flat shoes, and put on a Jean Seberg air. Forrest wanted to be a photographer. In Pierremont he took several series of shots, one of which shows Lucile, Lisbeth and Barthélémy dancing along a railway track. That same day, Lucile had stolen the heavy enamelled plaque, weathered by wind and rain, from the station's main signpost:

Do not cross without looking in both directions. Another train may be coming.

In Paris he and Lucile photographed themselves in front of a mirror, Lucile close to him. But Forrest was just a first flirtation for Lucile, a sweet, tender memory.

Lucile had met Gabriel some time before, when she was on holiday with her family in Alicante. They had seen each other over several summers, had lain side by side on the beach, gone out in a group in the evening. Gabriel was the younger brother of Georges's colleague, Marie-Noëlle. Marie-Noëlle had asked Georges to take him with them several times; he needed a change of air. Gabriel was a fluent talker, as dark as Lucile was fair, with a slim, athletic body, at ease in all situations and seemingly very self-confident. Gabriel stayed several times in the huge apartment that Liane and Georges rented in Franco's Spain in the scorching July sun. The last summer that Lucile spent with her parents in Alicante, she and Gabriel made love for the first time.

A few weeks later, Liane noticed her daughter's breasts; the fine skin was tightly stretched and each day they became a little fuller. Lucile was pregnant. In the living room at Versailles, there was a council of war. Given her condition, it was desirable for Lucile to get married. She was eighteen, still a minor; Gabriel was twenty-one. Liane and Georges refused to force her, though. It was up to her to make the choice. Lucile didn't hesitate. She was in love. The time had come for her to leave her family, to start her own, to live the life of a lady. Far from the turmoil, she would be able to create her own space and operate in silence. Until then, she had never known how to imagine her future, or how to give it shape and colour. She had never known how to project herself into another life, invent new vistas. Sometimes she had come to the conclusion that her dreams were so large, so outsized, that they wouldn't fit inside her own head.

In the turmoil of the preparations which now took up almost all her mental space – engagement, wedding, apartment to rent – Lucile sometimes stopped, stared into space, and allowed a feeling of sweetness and freedom to overwhelm her. She would be the first of all her brothers and sisters to leave home. She was opening the path on to the future. For the first time, this appeared to her distinctly: clear and luminous.

Lucile and Gabriel were married in October. Immediately after the wedding, she left the family home for a tiny studio where they awaited the arrival of the baby. In early March Lucile gave birth to a little girl in a clinic in Boulogne. Later, Lucile and Gabriel moved into an apartment in the thirteenth *arrondissement*.

As Lucile leaves her family, it seems to me that there is a missing dimension in this strange composition I have been working on for months which may become a book. I have got the colours or the décor wrong; I've mixed everything up, confusing red and black and losing the thread along the way. But ultimately nothing which I could have written would have fully satisfied me, nothing would have seemed close enough to her, to them.

I would like to have written about my family at their most joyful: their noisy, excessive vitality, their powerful way of fighting against their tragedy.

I would like to have written about the many summers Liane and Georges spent with their children on southern beaches, in France, Italy or Spain; about the ability that Georges had to live beyond his means, to find places that matched his taste for excess for the lowest price and drag his whole tribe along, always with some sickly cousin or anaemic neighbour. A record of these summer trips is provided by a whole series of super-8 films which I got hold of and transferred to video, in which you see Lucile and her siblings on the beach, hair bleached by the sun, wearing period bathing costumes, all together in the water around a dinghy or lying in a row on the sand. Lucile is beautiful. She's smiling, taking part in games, running with the others, staying beside them.

Nor have I said that Georges was probably one of the first fathers to introduce his children to waterskiing, pulling them proudly behind him on the Yonne on homemade wooden skis, at the steering wheel of an inflatable boat with a tiny two-horsepower engine. Over the years, Georges kitted himself out more and more seriously and waterskiing became the family sport.

Lucile's childhood disappeared with her and will always be opaque.

Lucile became the fragile, funny, strikingly beautiful woman who was silent and often subversive and who stood on the edge of the abyss for a long time without ever taking her eyes off it entirely; she became this woman who was admired and desired, who aroused passions; this woman who was bruised, wounded, humiliated, who lost everything in a day and had several spells in psychiatric hospitals; this inconsolable woman, under a life sentence, imprisoned in her solitude.

On the video labelled 'The Poiriers 1960–1970', I discovered a film I didn't know about. It shows Lucile and Gabriel, my father, shortly before their marriage on a visit to my grandparents at the house in Pierremont. In the pale light of an autumn weekend, they get out of a small 1960s car which I can't identify and look at the lens, a little intimidated. Liane greets them and puts her hand on Lucile's stomach, looking pleased, calling Georges, who's presumably behind the movie camera, to witness. I look at Lucile and Gabriel and I am stunned by how childlike both of them look, like two little tearaways who've been encouraged to pretend to be grownups. They are wearing Shetland pullovers in light colours, standing side by side; Gabriel puts his arm around Lucile's neck. She has the round cheeks of a young girl; neither her body nor her face seem to have emerged from adolescence and when I think about it, my fifteen-year-old daughter looks older than her.

From both Lisbeth and my father's sister I received copies of letters that Lucile wrote when she was pregnant with me, just after discovering she was expecting and in the months that followed. In them she talks about the prospect of marriage, the foetus which is moving in her stomach, the reports to Social Security, the problems of piped gas. She is 'so emotional, delighted, overwhelmed, in love' that she doesn't know where to begin. She listens to *Salut les copains* on the radio, munches apples and tries to organise things in the studio that she and Gabriel have moved into. At the foot of the page, Lucile has drawn herself in profile, with protruding stomach and bottom. By a little arrow, it says: 'This is me. It's no laughing matter.' In a letter to Lisbeth, she mentions her favourite names: Geraldine if it's a girl and Lucifer or Beelzebub if it's a boy. Clearly Lucile has no idea about the life that awaits her and none of this seems real.

There is a sadness about the super-8 film of my parents' marriage, which took place when Lucile was a few months pregnant. My mother is wearing a white dress with straps, slightly gathered at the waist, a tulle veil over her face. Gabriel is wearing a dark suit. They are beautiful, they look in love, but something in Lucile's eyes seems diluted; a sort of absence (or vulnerability) sets her at a remove from her surroundings.

It's a middle-class wedding of the most traditional kind. The wedding breakfast takes place after the religious ceremony in the public rooms of a mansion in Versailles. Everyone is chic and well dressed; Liane is radiant as the bride's mother, Justine and Violette (thirteen and eleven respectively), surrounded by a few cousins, are playing the part of bridesmaids with the utmost seriousness. Lucile's life beyond her family has scarcely begun; she is leaving the college where she has learned secretarial skills, she's expecting a child, her husband is working in the advertising agency that Georges runs.

On the face of it, they have all the ingredients for happiness.

I haven't yet mentioned the documentary that was made about my family in early 1968 – two years after Lucile's wedding – and broadcast on the first channel of ORTF in February 1969. I knew it existed: having been the subject of a TV report, even one that couldn't be found, was part of family mythology in the same way as the spectacular splits which my grandmother did in a bright leotard at the age of seventy or the DIY construction of the swimming pool at Pierremont. But no one had so far managed to find the programme, whose exact title had been forgotten and which wasn't available in the public archives of the National Audiovisual Institute. Thanks to help of various kinds, I managed to find it and transfer it to DVD. The programme is called *Forum* and is about the relations between parents and children. It all seems extraordinarily dated: the black and white images, which are a little faded, the clothes they are wearing, their way of speaking, the shape of their spectacles, the editing, the décor. The first part features different families and is followed by a debate during which parents, adolescents, psychologists and psychoanalysts, who have no connection with the families in the film, comment on what they have seen and express their views on the educational choices and quality of parent–child relations.

The report filmed at my grandparents' home concludes the programme. The narrator explains that the family isn't presented as an educational model in the strict sense 'for in matters of education there can be no prescriptions'. But they express the hope that this one – even if it ends the programme and therefore is not discussed – may give food for thought and extend the debate.

The film begins with the image of the first landing of the house in Versailles. Milo rushes into the frame to answer the phone and calls loudly to Lisbeth. She comes running to take the call, but her voice is immediately masked by the voice-over, which introduces the members of the family one by one in the rather affected tone of documentaries of the time, while the picture shows each of them in turn: 'Lisbeth, twenty-four. Barthélémy, twenty-three, married to Coline. They have a six-month-old baby. Lucile, twenty-one, married to Gabriel. Their little girl is two. Milo, eighteen, in his penultimate year of high school. Justine, sixteen, a pupil at the Lycée Estienne. Violette, fourteen, a high school student.' Then, after a pause: 'Georges, their father, set up his own advertising agency. Liane, their mother, has raised nine children and managed to keep smiling.' Then we see the Poiriers, including spouses, sitting round the big table in the dining room. The conversation is lively; everyone is laughing. The voice-over continues: 'To complete the family, we must mention Tom, aged six, who is in bed, and two boys who died in accidents. After years of hardship and discomfort, the family moved to a house in Versailles. Boredom is rare in a large family. But this one has received an upbringing which perhaps explains its character and its dreams.'

When I received the passwords that would allow me to watch this film for the first time, it was several days before I did so. I wanted to be alone in front of my computer. These images reveal something that Lucile lost a few years later, something that life shattered in a thousand pieces, like in fairy tales in which enraged witches with crooked fingers set upon princesses who are too pretty. Among the material I discovered during my research, this film is undoubtedly one of the things which upset me the most.

Lucile appears several times; the camera comes close to her face, capturing her expression, her smile in close-up, while she recounts memories of her adolescence. Of all Liane and Georges's children, she is the one we see most often. She describes her abortive attempt to run away with Lisbeth, her 'line parties' to which she secretly invited her friends when Georges gave them whole pages to copy out as a punishment. Everyone rolled up their sleeves and got down to it. She admits that she never did anything at school. It wasn't for lack of being lectured 'sadly but optimistically', she explains, about getting back on the right track.

'But that never happened for me.'

With her typical reserve, measuring the weight of each word she uttered, it is as if Lucile steps out of the screen. She is stunningly beautiful, dazzlingly intelligent; I think anyone would notice it if they watched the film. A few images show me as a child beside her, absorbed in a game.

A little later, Lucile says: 'I'm very anxious by nature.'

Later still: 'If there is something they've succeeded in, it's giving us confidence in the future.'

I believe that at the moment she was asked, that was exactly what she felt. She is afraid and she is confident. Life will settle the difference.

The film shows a happy, united family in which priority is given to the children's autonomy and the development of their personalities. Lisbeth, Barthélémy, Justine and Violette are interviewed one after the other and all attest to the freedom they are given: freedom to express themselves, to go to the cinema, to decorate their rooms as they wish, to drive and to travel. Violette explains that she has been taking the train to Paris since the age of ten; Lisbeth talks about her trips to the USA and Mexico. All of that is true. No one says that Tom has Down's syndrome (he remains in bed throughout the whole film …), nor do they linger over the two boys who died in accidents. Liane, with her irresistible smile, talks about how she abandoned her principles and how different the education her children received was from her own, while Georges turns fine phrases about the importance of knowing when to let his offspring leave the nest. Extracts from super-8 films of holidays in Spain are included in the report and reinforce the image of perfect happiness.

Justine hated this film and when I found it, she could scarcely bear to watch it. She told me later what a state of anxiety and confusion she had been in when it was filmed and how one of the few phrases we hear her utter had been suggested, not to say dictated, to her:

'Yes, my father is a dad and also a friend, a friend you can laugh with and talk to. You can tell him anything and when you've got something to say to him, you say "can I have lunch with you tomorrow?", and then it's like having lunch with a friend.'

It was also Justine who told me how much the film had hurt Milo, had enraged him; Milo, who had unrestrainedly displayed his revolt and anger against his father, of which there is no sign. You only see Milo for a few seconds, stubbing out a cigarette and trying to avoid the camera.

Here, we are at the heart of the myth. The film depicts the legend which Liane and Georges were writing as they created it, as we all do with our own lives. The film shows them as a couple and as parents; it probably reflects their own image of themselves, which they needed in order to carry on. It is how they perceive themselves and how they perceive their family. Their children are starting to leave home, they feel they didn't do too badly, particularly in terms of education, they are comfortably off, take holidays, have friends round. After the lean years of the rue de Maubeuge, and while Georges's agency is doing well (it didn't survive May '68), my grandparents play at being middle class. For the first time, Georges was able to give his wife a life befitting her background. And yet something in their way of being always escaped convention. It was their strength, I think, and it is that which predominates in my memory of them.

For example, long before it was an accepted lifestyle, Liane and Georges always went about naked in front of their children. Both of them had shed or never possessed any embarrassment of that sort. I, along with all their grandchildren, saw them naked almost till the end of their lives. Georges, at all ages, would change out of his wet bathing trunks into dry underpants and Liane long permitted me to be present when she got out of the shower, which was followed by a precisely timed ritual that fascinated me: a rub-down with an exfoliating glove, application of Nivea cream and the piling on of a dozen layers of clothes.

I am the product of this myth and in a way it falls to me to maintain and perpetuate it, so that my family lives on and our rather desperate and absurd fantasy with it. And yet, watching this film, and seeing them all so beautiful, so well-endowed, at once so different from each other and so similarly charismatic, the words which came to mind were: '*what a waste*'.

What happened? What disorder or silent poison caused it? Is the death of the children enough to explain the fault line, or fault lines? Because the years that followed cannot be described without mentioning 'drama', 'alcohol', 'madness' and 'suicide', which make up our family lexicon alongside 'celebration', 'doing the splits' and 'waterskiing'. During my interviews, some people spoke of '*disaster*', including those who were most closely involved, and it seems to me that this word is the most appropriate, if you consider that you can rebuild on top of any ruin – which all of us in our way have done.

Am I entitled to write that my mother and her siblings have all been at one moment or another of their lives (or all their lives) wounded, damaged, off-balance; that they all have experienced at some moment or another of their lives (or all their lives) a sense of despair at being alive, and that they bore the mark of their childhood, their history, their parents and their family as though it had been branded into them?

Am I entitled to write that Georges did them harm as a father, that he was destructive and humiliating, that he raised his children up to the skies, encouraged them, praised them, adulated them, and at the same time destroyed them? Do I have the right to say that the demands he made of his sons were equalled only by his intolerance, and that his relationship with some of his daughters was ambiguous to say the least?

Am I entitled to write that Liane never could, never knew *how* to counterbalance him, that she was devoted to him as she was to God, even if it meant sacrificing her own children?

I do not know.

Liane used to sing such sad songs in her gentle voice. Liane addressed her children and her grandchildren formally with a religious and respectful 'vous', which my friends thought sweet. She called us 'my little prince', 'my darling girl', 'sweetness', 'my little plum'. I addressed her as 'tu' and I adored her.

A few nights ago I had a dream which is still haunting me.

We are all together in the dining room at Pierremont around

the huge wooden table that can seat twenty people for celebrations. Everyone is there, nothing has changed: the collection of porcelain plates is hanging on the wall, little wicker baskets are scattered about the table, there's a smell of roast lamb in the air. Liane is opposite me. It's a family meal like the ones we had until the end of the nineties, when Georges was still alive. The atmosphere is a little tense; Georges is doing his usual routine, proffering some truths about the world as it is and as it used to be, while Liane is encouraging people to help themselves while it's hot. Thinking back on it, I don't see Lucile, I'm not sure she's in the dream; no, she isn't there, though her absence hasn't been remarked on. At one point, by one of those coincidences that mean that several conversations stop at the same time (an angel passing), silence falls. Liane's smile vanishes, she turns to me and says, from behind the sorry and grief-stricken veil that sometimes alters her gaze, without a hint of hostility: 'What you're doing is not nice, my darling girl. It's not nice.'

I wake suddenly soaked in sweat. The man I love, to whom I will describe this dream several hours later without being able to convey my terror, is asleep beside me. Everything around us is calm. It takes several minutes for my pulse to return to normal.

I don't go back to sleep. Not for a moment. I know where I'm going next.

PART TWO

My mother and father lived together for almost seven years, for most of that time in an apartment on the rue Auguste-Lançon in a part of the thirteenth *arrondissement* that I hardly know. I have never been back. When, as I was writing this book, I came to those seven years, I thought about leaving ten blank pages, numbered like the rest, but devoid of text. It then struck me that the artifice would clearly indicate a gap, but wouldn't make it any more acceptable, still less comprehensible.

During those years my father worked first for Georges's ad agency, then, when that closed, as administrative director in a bank. Lucile didn't work; she looked after her two daughters: first me, and then my sister Manon, who was born four years later. Seen from the outside, Lucile and Gabriel made what you would call a fine couple. They ate with friends, went for weekends with their respective parents, took their children to Montsouris Park. They loved each other, they cheated on each other; outwardly it was all entirely ordinary.

I cannot write about the time Lucile spent with my father.

This was a given from the start, a formal constraint, an empty chapter, hidden from writing. I knew this even before I began this book and it was among the reasons that prevented me from getting down to it for so long.

For Lucile, these were years of great loneliness (as she often said), which contributed to the destruction of her self (in my view). The meeting between Lucile and Gabriel still seems to me like the meeting of two great sufferings, and contrary to the law of mathematics which states that multiplying two negative numbers produces a positive, this encounter gave rise to aggression and confusion.

I didn't question my father about Lucile. I simply asked him for some documents in his possession (the police report written a few years after their separation at the time of Lucile's first committal and the social services report that followed – I shall come back to these); he sent them by return without demurral. Since I claim to be writing a book about the woman he probably loved – and hated – most, my father is amazed that I have not asked him for his memories, that I don't want to listen to him. But my father knows nothing. He has rewritten his own story, and in doing so rewritten Lucile's as well, for reasons of his own, and here is not the place to comment on them.

To demonstrate the supposed coherence of my strategy, I didn't interview any of the men who shared Lucile's life either close up or from a distance – not Forrest, her first Platonic love, nor Nébo, her great passion, though both of them attended her funeral. That way I could argue and prove to my father that he was not being discriminated against. I'm not sure he will fall for it.

I didn't talk to any of the men who shared Lucile's life, and on reflection it seems to me that that's OK. I don't want to know what sort of wife or lover Lucile was. That's none of my business.

I am writing about Lucile through the eyes of a child who grew up too fast, writing about the mystery she always was to me, simultaneously so present and so distant, and who, after I was ten, never hugged me again.

When Lucile left Gabriel, she was twenty-six. She first found refuge with her parents in Versailles, where we stayed for several weeks and I attended a local school. I have retained a confused memory from that period of a blackboard covered in white chalk marks, which the other children could read but which were impossible for me to decipher. Eventually, my father came to get us; then we were taken off by Lucile again; and then by Gabriel, until an adjudication that reconciliation had failed was eventually signed.

Later, Lucile moved in with Tibère, who lived in an apartment on rue Mathurin-Régnier in the fifteenth *arrondissement*. She had met him a few months earlier through Barthélémy, who had become junior artistic director of an advertising agency. Tibère was a red-haired giant, freelance photographer and committed naturist. Seen from our level, he came from another world and inspired a vague feeling of fear in us. The only memory I have of this in-between period – apart from the squares of chocolate that Lucile melted on bread for our tea and the TV programme I watched on Thursdays in which a boy in a cape called Samson told children's stories – was of the toothache which crushed her for weeks. Lucile wept with the pain. It is one of the very first images I have of my mother, already suffused with a sense of my powerlessness in the face of an overwhelming pain.

★

My parents' divorce was terribly banal, dominated by a ruthless custody battle, conducted around fairly indulgent statements collected by both sides. Lucile was found to be at fault (her infidelity was proved by an affidavit of adultery produced by a bailiff). She obtained custody (or Gabriel conceded it to her, according to some versions). I had just turned six; Manon was two.

Lucile had found work as a secretary in a small advertising agency, which had chosen her from a hundred candidates. None of the others had met Gilberte Pasquier.

At the start of the next school year, Lucile and Tibère looked for somewhere to live. Lisbeth had got married a few years after Lucile and had settled in Essonne. Through Lisbeth's husband, Lucile and Tibère heard about a house that was available nearby. When it came to drawing up the paperwork, legend has it that Tibère, lacking identity papers, presented his naturist's card. The lease was signed. We moved to Yerres, about twenty miles from Paris. The Grands-Godeaux estate was divided in two by the street of the same name. On one side were red-brick apartment blocks, and on the other, ten or so detached houses scattered around narrow paths surfaced in pink tarmac. A little further towards the station there was a baker's, a chemist's and a Co-op.

Julien, Tibère's son, came to live with us. Manon went to nursery and I started at primary school. A few days after school began, Lucile was summoned for a lecture by the head teacher: it was very harmful for children to get ahead of the school curriculum. That was how Lucile discovered that I knew how to read and write. It was decided that I could move up a class.

That day, perhaps, the idea took root in Lucile's mind that whatever happened, I would get by. It lasted a long time.

In the mid-seventies, Yerres represented the start of a new life for us. In my memory it's surrounded by a strange, shining halo. Lucile and Tibère painted the floor in the living room white and mattresses dyed green served as sofas. Little by little, our house was invaded by a joyful, unquantifiable mess, the reflection of our way of life in which rare restrictions were more a response to the weather or mood than good manners. We were allowed to put our elbows on the table and lick our plates, draw on the walls, come and go as we pleased. We spent most of our time outdoors with other children. We were afraid of Mr Z., the neighbour opposite, who was said to be unable to tolerate noise and wouldn't hesitate to get his rifle out. We were scared of the wily yellow dog which seemed to come from nowhere and roamed around outside the apartment blocks with its tail down. We were scared of the flasher who jumped out of a bush one winter evening when we were leaving the community centre. For all that, our territory kept expanding.

In the evening, friends and friends of friends came for dinner, a drink, or to share a joint or two. Thick smoke would fill the living room. We ate mainly pasta shells and spaghetti with or without tomato sauce, and we drove an old Peugeot 403, which was also painted green. Lucile went to Paris every day, Tibère walked about the house naked, stole shrink-wrapped roasts from the Co-op and between photo shoots played at being a house husband.

The rumour started to go round the neighbourhood that our house was a hang-out for hippies and drug addicts, which was repeated to me at school, without it making much sense to me. We were different; we weren't like other families; everything else passed me by, didn't take on any meaning. Every Thursday lunchtime I was invited home by a friend in my class whose mother later boasted of feeding me the only steak I ate all week. When Lucile heard this, I stopped going.

We soon got to know the Ramauds, a single-parent family with seven children who lived next door. Between our house and theirs a sort of free exchange of goods (food, games, pens, dolls) and people was established. It lasted several years. I dreamed of having a bra like Estelle's, the oldest girl, and being attractive to boys like her.

We played together more or less according to age and sometimes we all joined in huge games. With my friends I rehearsed over and over Claude François's dance routines, the star of the free shows we gave on the communal lawn.

Sandra lived in one of the apartment blocks on the estate. In spite of the rumours, her parents allowed her to visit us and even to sleep over. She was my first childhood friend. On Wednesday, Sandra went to catechism with the other local children. You could have cake there and drink as much orange juice as you liked. I asked to go but Lucile said no.

In our own way, we led a regular life; things went on the same way more or less; Lucile went to Paris and Tibère did the shopping and looked after the house.

Every other weekend, Gabriel came for us. He parked his BMW outside and waited for us in the street; we felt as though we ruled the world.

For half-term and other weekends, we sometimes went to Pierremont, where Liane and Georges had settled. My grandparents had left Versailles, Georges's agency had folded and, with the exception of Tom, Lucile's brothers and sisters had left.

The year I turned seven, Lucile took to me to London. I don't know what prompted this trip, perhaps my having reached the age of reason. At Portobello market, Lucile unearthed two Terylene miniskirts (one pink, one green, both trapezium shaped), which she bought for me. I wore them until they came halfway up my bottom and for months they were the centrepieces in my wardrobe (they were succeeded by peach-coloured trousers in smooth velvet, which I got from the daughter of one of her friends and of which I was equally proud).

Nothing was serious, not the crabs that Lucile and Tibère caught in the Brunoy cinema (according to the official version) and which took up residence for a time in our hair (Manon even had them in her eyebrows), nor the mornings we arrived at school late, nor the day I arrived in class with my head still covered in Marie-Rose sauce, whose vinegary smell was recognisable from a hundred yards away (Lucile hadn't had time to rinse my hair), nor the end of the shrink-wrapped chickens and joints of meat (Tibère had been caught in the Co-op), nor Julien's insistence that I stroke his penis until he ejaculated, which

I agreed to do solely on condition that I could wrap my hand in a face cloth.

That period had its darker patches.

In the summer we went to the naturist camp at Montalivet, where Lucile and Tibère rented a bungalow among the pines. We met friends there, a shifting community of people who drifted in and out; some people would move on, others stayed and pitched their tents in the forest. We were naked on the beach, naked in the supermarket, naked at the pool, naked on the paths strewn with pine needles, and my friend Sandra, who came with us, was asked to provide visual proof that she had sunburn before she was allowed to go on the beach with bikini bottoms on.

The photos of those years, taken mainly by Tibère, are the ones I like best. They sum up a whole period. I like their colours, their poetry, the utopia they capture. Lucile had some prints. After her death I had some others printed up from slides I found in a box in her apartment. There is one of my mother amid the crowd at a demonstration in Larzac. Another in which Lucile, wearing multi-coloured suede bell-bottoms, is holding Manon in her arms. Among these photos, one series enchants and overwhelms me: Manon, whose little green and white dress seems straight out of a seventies reconstruction, is playing with a hosepipe; her skin is tanned and her thighs are plump and she makes a succession of improbable faces. There is another in which we are all posing together (a dozen of us), stark naked in front of the bungalow at

Montalivet, the little ones at the front and the grown-ups behind, perfectly aligned, with chins up and summer smiles.

In some shots Lisbeth, Justine and even Violette appear. I think this was a period when Lucile was less alone, when she grew closer to her brothers and sisters. Lucile sometimes posed for Tibère and it seems to me that she was never more beautiful.

In the slanting light of the end of the day, Tibère photographed Manon and Gaëton, the son of one of Lucile's friends, walking off along the beach. They are holding hands, suntanned and naked; the sand sticks to their skin. Tibère made a poster from this shot, which sold thousands of copies in supermarkets all over France.

In my own collection there is also a picture of me and Manon in Yerres, on our way to school with our satchels on our backs. On the rue des Grands-Godeaux, we are turning to look at the lens. I'm wearing an unlikely mini-kilt and after the holidays our hair is almost white.

These pictures and every detail in them (clothes, haircuts, jewellery) are part of my personal mythology. If periods can be summed up by the places that contained them, Yerres remains for me the emblem of *before*. *Before* the worry. *Before* the fear. *Before* Lucile went off the rails.

With time, that's what won. Memory makes its selection.

A few months ago, a journalist who has long been a supporter of mine and whose tact I value, contacted me to ask if I would take part in a series he was making for radio on writers and places. Did

I have a significant place? A seaside resort, family home, writing cabin in the middle of the forest, a cliff battered by the waves? I thought immediately of Yerres, on the face of it less suited to his summer schedule. Yerres was a sort of golden age for me; it belonged to me, belonged only to me. I'm not sure that Lucile or Manon would talk about it in this way.

We lived there for four years: two with Tibère, then two without. I think Lucile left him, or maybe they separated. Tibère represented a fresh start for her, the man of her transition. He left behind his son Julien, who stayed with us until we too moved out.

I have more fragmentary memories of the period after Tibère left. The people around Lucile are no longer exactly the same; some of them have gone, new ones have appeared and some are just passing through.

This was the time when Lucile met Nébo and fell hopelessly in love with him. He remained until the end of her life her great damaged love. Nébo was of Italian origin, his hair was so black it seemed it could never change and his eyes were green, sea-green. He possessed a beauty and magnetism that was impossible to ignore. He was said to be a ladies' man, a man who didn't get attached, at any rate that is the memory I have of him: a sulphurous reputation that surrounded him and made him inaccessible. For a few months, Nébo spent his evenings in our living room with the white floor, appeared intermittently with his friends or on his own, but didn't attempt to make any contact with us. I listened to the adults' conversations, the names they mentioned – Freud, Foucault, Wilhelm Reich – and tried to remember acronyms I didn't understand.

Estelle Ramaud took her holy communion and got a watch and some lacy bras. I was stricken with a spiritual crisis and demanded to take mine immediately, to which I received the response that firstly, I hadn't been to catechism and secondly, I didn't have breasts yet.

We were burgled for the first time and Lucile's jewellery and the turntable were taken.

Lucile decided it was time to bring a bit of order to our home and that henceforth we were going to tidy our rooms.

Lucile began working for a manufacturer who made leather handbags in many colours.

Nébo stayed with Lucile for a few months, then took off. He left behind a painful, enigmatic after-image, and left Lucile entirely to her sadness.

The circle around us was shrinking. The green mattresses were fading, the paint on the floor was beginning to flake off.

Lucile set off early in the morning and got back late. We hung around the machines that dispensed sweets for a franc, we played marbles on the pink tarmac paths, we listened to Dave and Ringo on a slot-fed record-player, we cut our dolls' hair. Between getting out of school and Lucile coming home was a time when childhood reigned supreme, an aimless time that eating a hard-boiled sweet was enough to fill, a time which trickled through our grubby fingers and seemed endless.

Some evenings we formed a welcome committee, watching on the bridge above the tracks in the pale glow of the street-lights for the train that would bring Lucile back from Paris. Beneath our insouciance, we were probably beginning to be aware of something heavy weighing her down, something linked to her loneliness and her tiredness, which we could do nothing about.

The last summer that Julien spent with us, she took us to the Isère, where she had rented a house. On the motorway, the police stopped the apple-green 403. The car was too old, or not in order; there was some problem. Lucile negotiated, argued. It seemed complicated to us. And then suddenly Lucile began to cry, her face buried in her hands. The police let us go.

In a huge house amid farmland in Blandin, Lucile began to paint. She had brought her box of watercolours with her, whose names fascinated me – burnt sienna, vermilion, cobalt blue. We got to know Marcel, a local farmer. Aged around thirty, he lived with his parents and didn't have any children. He adopted us for the summer, showed us how to milk the cows, let us spend whole days riding on the back of his tractor, showed us the dark stables. He was our hero.

★

At the end of the month, we went back to Yerres to start packing up. Lucile had decided to leave the house and Julien had to go back to live with his mother. We left behind dirty walls, peeling paint on the floor, the garden a tangle of weeds.

We said our goodbyes to Mrs Ramaud (our neighbour) and Mrs Gilbault (my friend Sandra's mother), promising to send news, to visit, not to lose touch.

Lucile left the local children the fond and admiring memory that they mentioned to us years later. Lucile was younger than the other mothers, she wore light dresses and high heels, worked in Paris and walked like a dancer.

When Lucile spoke to the other mothers or mentioned them (even when she knew their first names and these women called her by hers), she would say *Mrs* Ramaud or *Mrs* Gilbault. There was in this a sort of respect probably due to the difference in age but mainly, it seems to me, due to the idea that these women were ladies in a way that she would never be, grounded in existence and capable of remaining there.

This morning Barthélémy, who now lives in Marseilles, phoned me in response to an email in which I'd asked him for a few details.

He asked me if I was making progress and I said I was. I would have liked to tell him what a relief it was to have left Lucile's childhood behind, that distant, secret time on which I've never gained the slightest purchase, which continually eluded me just as I thought I was getting closer to it. I didn't want to worry him.

From the point at which Lucile became a mother, that is to say, from the moment I appeared in her life, I abandoned all attempt at an objective third-person narrative. I probably thought that my 'I' could blend into the narrative itself, try to carry it forward. It was a trap, of course. What did I see aged six months, or four years, or ten (or forty for that matter)? Nothing. And yet I continue to unfold my mother's story. I mix my child's eye view with that of the adult I became. I cling on tight to this project or else it clings on to me; I don't know which is more awkward. I would love to be able to tell Manon's story, to include her more in my account, but it seems to me that that is impossible without the risk of betraying her. Writing doesn't give access to anything.

Other people ask me, as Barthélémy did, if I'm writing, where I've reached, or whether it's going well. Those who know venture a timid question, avoid mentioning the project by name, hedge it round with polite circumlocutions or ellipses.

Then I provide lots of detail about the torments I'm wrestling with, the strategies I use each morning to delay getting down to it (filling the washing machine, emptying the dishwasher), my various stress-related ailments (lumbago, muscular contractions, cramp, stiff neck) conspiring to prevent me from sitting down in front of my computer, the hair I tear out in a literal as well as metaphorical sense, the twenty-five cigarettes I dream of chain-smoking without pausing for breath, the mint/raspberry/caramel/pine-flavoured sweets I suck with a passion now that I have given up smoking, the feeling of fighting physically, of really coming unstitched. And on the subject of stitches: the hems, holes and buttons that have needed attention for months, but have suddenly become urgent. I lay it on a bit thick, exaggerate a little, it's better to laugh about it, isn't it, in short, I take the drama out of it. The truth is that I'm not sure I'll stay the course, make it to the end; I have the feeling of being trapped by my own strategy whose overriding necessity no longer seems so obvious.

Yet nothing can stop me.

Sometimes I dream of returning to pure fiction, I revel in it, I invent, fantasise, imagine, opt for the most novelistic, the least probable, I add adventures, permit myself digressions, follow tangents, free myself from the past and its impossible truth.

Sometimes I dream of the book I shall write *after*, when I'm set free from this one.

At the end of the summer of 1976, we moved to Bagneux, which was nearer Paris; Lucile had found a flat for rent in a small apartment block with a white façade. I have no recollection of the reasons which led to this change; I imagine that Lucile wanted to be nearer her job and could no longer pay the rent for the house in Yerres by herself. It is also true that we had been burgled several times and in the end we had nothing left: not an LP, or a bracelet, or a pocket calculator.

In September I began my first year of secondary in a school on the outskirts of town, while Manon started at the local primary. For the first few months, I went to collect her, but quite soon she made her own way home. Manon made friends in our building and it wasn't long before she was taking full advantage of her autonomy (she told me later that she spent hours on some nearby waste ground searching through skips in the hope of unearthing treasure). For my part, thanks to an invitation made over a jar of Nutella, I got to know Tadrina, one of my classmates. Tadrina wore brightly coloured clothes, lived in Fontenay-aux-Roses, *on the other side*, in a huge apartment that was full of antiques, paintings and works of art. To me, she represented an affluent, contented form of middle-class life; I envied the way she lived, the thick carpet in her living room, the attention lavished on her by her parents. We spent hours at her house strutting around in her mother's evening wear or listening to the complete works of Boby Lapointe, most of whose lyrics we knew by heart. We invented role-playing games, collected perfume samples and made candles which we sold in her apartment block so that I could go on her next skiing trip with her (a door-to-door operation which brought in 39 francs 50 centimes). Tad was not at all the spoilt child I had suspected, she was one of my enduring childhood friends.

In the evenings, I waited with Manon for Lucile to come home. I'd decorate the walls of my room with colour pastels, make crocodiles out of beads, perfect the script of my telephone pranks (despite the lock that Lucile had put on the dial, it hadn't taken me long to find the key. This was one of the main pastimes for Tad and me).

Lucile wasn't yet thirty. It seems to me that she was then still part of a group, a gang, belonged to a sort of nebula with multiple arms which included her brothers and sisters, her friends and theirs, and hinged on certain key places. Violette and Milo were in shared apartments in Paris, Lisbeth had stayed in Essonne, Justine was living in a community in a big house in Clamart. They were linked to one another and surrounded by others whose first names – Henri, Rémi, Michel, Isabelle, Clémentine, Alain, Juliette, Christine, Nùria, Pablo, Séverine, Danièle, Marie, Robert, to which were always added a few Chilean and Argentine refugees – are intimately linked to that period for me. Today, when I occasionally hear them mentioned – where they are living now, what they have become – it is hard for me to imagine them at the age they are, and even in the case of those I have seen since, the image of them at the age of fifty or sixty cannot entirely supersede the one I have retained from childhood. They are side by side. Their names, like those of the more or less communal places they lived in (Clamart, Eugène-Carrière, Vicq-d'Azir, la Maison des Chats) are a part of our story, remain linked to it in a confused but profound way.

At that time, threads still connected Lucile to other people, and to those places where people talked, laughed and drank, where nonetheless dreams of a different life were being extinguished. Because around us, the time of disappointments had come. There was a political parting of the ways, activism was running out of steam, the revolution was either becoming diluted or more radical in a France in which comfort and consumption barely masked the shock of two oil crises. As far as I know, Lucile was never an activist, never joined any political movement, didn't belong to any of the women's groups which flourished at that time. But for the people she loved and encountered, these were the years of disillusionment.

Soon after we moved to Bagneux, Lucile got to know Niels, who was younger than her and lived in Clamart with Justine and some others. Niels became Lucile's lover. He came to eat with us and spent the night; he also spent weekends with us. Unlike other men whom Lucile allowed to enter our domain, Niels (perhaps because he was so young) found favour in our eyes. He paid kindly, cautious attention to us; I think from my point of view I was grateful that he kept his distance. We went to see him in Clamart, went walking in the forest, drank hot chocolate in the kitchen. A sense of calm is linked to these memories.

During the few months they spent together, Lucile and Niels saw a film about Edvard Munch, an exhibition of German expressionism, drank wine and talked late into the night. Lucile shared a profound sense of despair with Niels and they had intense conversations on the possibility of suicide. We found that out later. And yet, with this young man who was haunted by the idea of death, Lucile found a sort of peace. Niels and Lucile's relationship brings to mind the Italian adjective *morbido*, which, contrary to what someone (like me) who doesn't speak Italian might think, doesn't mean 'morbid', but 'soft' or 'gentle'. Today, when I try to understand the link which united Lucile and Niels, it seems to me to take on that ambivalence: my mother experienced a sort of peace, or relief, through being close to someone whose torments were at least as painful as her own.

The day before a weekend they were due to spend together, Lucile was waiting to hear from Niels. There was no word. Lucile rang the house in Clamart where, because it was the Easter holidays, Justine was the only other person there with him. Justine hadn't seen Niels but promised to pass on the message. Lucile called back several times, getting more worried, and asked her sister to go and look in his room. Justine, who was five months pregnant, eventually opened his door. She found Niels dead, lying on the floor, his brains splattered all over the room. He had fired a bullet into his mouth. He was twenty-one.

Lucile went to the funeral. Niels left our life as he had come into it.

Every evening when she got back from work, Lucile smoked on her own: grass or hash (I don't know when these words, along with others, entered my vocabulary), which she hid in a little pink metal tin.

She told Manon, who saw her preparing a joint and asked what she was doing, that it was a secret and she mustn't tell anyone.

In school the teachers warned us about the dangers of drugs. The school was in a high-risk area, the subject kept coming up, even in Mrs Lefèvre's dictations, in which a drug-smuggling dog was arrested by the police. These anti-drugs talks left me with a profound unease, conflicting with the hours that Lucile spent far from us, far from everything. For every evening, almost as soon as she got back, Lucile shut herself in her room. No conversation or account of the day was possible until she had smoked alone in her room.

Very quickly I found this ritual unbearable. I was the one who woke her up in the morning, I was the one who worried about whether she got to work and I was the one who got incensed when she couldn't talk to us any more. Until then, Lucile had been my mother. A mother who was different from other mothers; she was more beautiful and more mysterious. But I was now becoming aware of the physical distance separating us, I was looking at her with new eyes, those of the school, of the institution, eyes that compared her to other mothers, searching for the kindness which had disappeared from her eyes.

A vision of an ideal mother soon filled my mind. The ideal mother was middle class and stayed at home, keeping an eye on the well-being of her children and the wallpaper; she had a dishwasher, rustled up meals in subtly flavoured sauces, pursued dust all day long and insisted that you put on your slippers when you came home. The ideal mother didn't get high every evening, prepared breakfast before waking her children up, saw them off to school with a confident smile and a little tear in her eye. My rebellions had nothing in common with my classmates'; mine were all about the purest sort of conformism. I dreamed of an ordered, confined, regular life like the graph paper on which I stumbled through my geometry exercises. I probably had no other way of expressing the confused but growing fear which had begun to take hold of me. I was drifting away from Lucile or she was drifting away from me; I resented her for not being stronger, for not facing up to things.

One Sunday Lucile took us to the theatre to see her brother Milo play a servant in a play by Molière. Afterwards we went to congratulate him and I noticed the tight curls of his hair, like those on a collectable doll, which bounced when he talked.

Another Sunday, I went with Lucile to the flea market at Saint-Ouen, where she bought things for the kitchen.

Every other weekend we took the train to Normandy, where Gabriel lived. At the beginning, Lucile took us in the metro to the Gare Montparnasse. Later, we went by ourselves. On the train we amused ourselves by reading or playing games. Gabriel came to collect us in

Verneuil-sur-Avre and drove us to the village where he lived with his new wife. We entered another world, one in which everything was well ordered, where nothing seemed to be lacking.

Because Lucile and Gabriel were unable to speak to each other on the phone, all information about the school holidays, train times and the practicalities of our trips had to go through me: Mum says this, Dad would prefer that, Mum doesn't agree that . . . The rare times they exchanged a few words, Lucile hung up before the end of the conversation and started crying.

One spring day, a phone call told us that Milo was dead. He had shot himself in the head in a wood or a clearing. I didn't take the information in at first. When I told my father (Milo's death meant we had to rearrange our weekends), he asked to speak to Lucile. For the first time, Lucile and Gabriel had a conversation that seemed normal and ended without shouting. I silently thanked Milo for this miracle. A few days later we left for Pierremont, where the funeral mass took place. This time I could not ignore the sadness which was ravaging my family; the air was thick with it, like gunpowder.

In the weeks that followed, I became more worried about Lucile. Fear never left me, and sometimes it stopped me breathing. I didn't know what it meant. Little by little, my anxiety took shape: I was afraid of finding her dead. Every evening when I turned the key in the door, what I thought was: what if she's done it too? It became an obsession. When I went into the flat, alone or with Tadrina, my eyes fell first on the living-room floor (dead people lie on the floor, I had picked that up from conversations), then I went to check her bedroom. After that, I could breathe again. Shortly after the death of her brother, Lucile had written on the mirror in the bathroom in blood-red lipstick: 'I'm going to crack.' Every morning, we would comb our hair looking in this mirror, this threat tattooed on our faces.

Some evenings when Manon and her friends got back later than us, Tadrina and I had fun scaring them. This was a full-time occupation, just like the telephone pranks, dance competitions, Barbies and their clothes, our collection of perfume samples (we had four hundred between us) and the perfume-shop game we played with them. One evening we hid in the hall cupboard, when Manon and her friend, Sabine from downstairs, came into the apartment. While they were having their tea, thinking they were alone, we started making the most terrible groans and whistles. They approached the cupboard in terror, at which point we emitted a volley of demonic, macabre laughter. They both screamed at once and ran downstairs to tell Sabine's father, who had just come home. He came up and found the two of us, stammering, bright red and tangled up in guilty explanations.

Later, Manon reproached me for these terror sessions, the place I occupied and the way I dominated her as an older sibling. Perhaps I needed her to be afraid too, needed her to leave the state of obliviousness she seemed to be in then and share my distress. Perhaps I was simply jealous of her for the relationship she had with Lucile, which I had lost long ago.

★

When Lucile didn't have the strength to cook, we enjoyed a 'Belgian dinner' (hot chocolate with bread and butter). Later, a friend to whom I described this told me that it was a 'Swiss dinner' in her house.

Then the three of us occupied ourselves. We didn't have a television; Lucile refused to give in to that convenience.

On other evenings we would listen to the records that Lucile loved: 'Bella Ciao' (the song of the Italian partisans), Chick Corea, Archie Shepp, Glenn Gould. Jeannette's song, 'Porque te vas' from the film *Raise Ravens*, which we had seen with Lucile, became our household anthem. Images of Geraldine Chaplin bleeding to death haunted me for a long time. What if my mother was going to die in the same way, of a silent, haemorrhaging sadness?

The summer I turned twelve, my father and his wife had a baby boy. It seemed to me that Gaspard was promised an easy life, that things would be nicer for him than they were for us. We liked taking care of him, changing him and giving him his bottle, making him laugh, and later we admired his first steps.

One weekend I spoke to Gabriel about my worries about Lucile. Probably for the first time I said the words: I'm afraid she'll kill herself. He asked for details. I described her loneliness, her tiredness, the hours she spent smoking in her room.

On the train on the way back I could think of one thing only: I was a tell-tale.

★

My relations with Lucile deteriorated even further the day she accused me of stealing the tin in which she kept her hash and of giving it to my father so that it could be used as evidence against her. A few days later, Lucile found the pink tin, which she had hidden herself, and apologised to me. Later still, she read my diary in which I wrote about her and my fears, and she promised, swore to me that things would be OK.

Lucile knew that I was observing her from the lofty height of my twelve years, with that air of knowing everything without having learned anything, that way of silently showing my disapproval. Lucile knew I was judging her.

One evening when one of my aunts was taking us home after we had had dinner at her house, the car behind us, which was a little too close, bumped into us with a loud noise of crunching metal. Manon and I were both in the back. Lucile leapt up, shouting 'My daughter! My daughter!' and threw herself on Manon. This use of the singular, even in a moment of intense panic, seemed to me proof of her dereliction. I had had no physical contact with her for ages. Manon sat on her knee, Manon hugged her, put her arms around her. Manon wasn't aware of anything: Manon was *her* daughter. I had become her enemy, I was on my father's side, on the side of the bourgeois, the rich and the reactionaries. I didn't count any more.

Of course, writing this now, and no longer in any doubt that Lucile loved me, the episode in the car appears in a different light, making me question the way I behaved for so long, pretending to be so strong when I am so fragile, so that people end up believing me.

One evening Lucile took me to the theatre to see *The Thousand and One Nights*, put on by Jérôme Savary and his Grand Magic Circus. I was wearing a red blouse my mother had given me, my clothes were chic, and as far as I remember, it was the first time I had been to see a show (apart from the puppet show in the Luxembourg Gardens). I was amazed to discover a rich world in which the women were curvaceous and powerful. The production had a sense of humour and excess which made a great impression on me and gave me the confused feeling that they were depicting life at its fullest, freest and most marvellous. The gold of the costumes and jewellery sparkled in the light; I wanted to hold on to those reflections, never let go.

Around the same time, a boy in the technical stream at school developed a passion for me. He must have been fifteen or sixteen; the way he spoke and the things he said suggested that he might have been backward. He watched out for me at the end of the day, and would follow me in the street, waiting for me in underpasses and by the entrance to apartment blocks. He knew my timetable and my routes. Little by little he terrified me. Tad and I worked out all sorts of strategies to avoid him and escape his attention. We would double back on ourselves, or sometimes remain inside the school for several hours to put him off. One evening when we had done some shopping for Lucile in the local minimarket, the boy was there, concealed in the darkness of a doorway. Just as we reached him, he threw himself at me and tried to kiss me on the lips. I pushed him away, Tad grabbed a big tin of peas and stood between us, her arm raised threateningly (we replayed this scene endlessly afterwards).

The boy looked at me and in his clumsy voice uttered this sentence, which we still quote today for comic purposes: 'You got nuthin' to say to me?'

We ran off at full pelt. On the hand which I had quickly wiped my mouth with, I still had the sensation of his wet lips, his sticky saliva. When I got home, I scrubbed it with a nailbrush. I didn't tell Lucile. Lucile couldn't do anything for me. *Nuthin'-to-say-to-me* (which is what Tad and I called him thereafter, since we didn't know his real name) haunted my nights for a long time.

Apart from in French, my school results were in free fall. I wasn't working, I wasn't learning, I was spending my time reading, lying on my stomach on my bedroom floor. Tad and I began stealing from the shops in town – bars of chocolate, packets of biscuits, lip gloss – lots of little challenges we won hands down.

I was regularly struck down with migraines, which forced me to leave school early and stumble home to lie down in the dark, with a pneumatic drill juddering in my skull and a wet flannel over my eyes.

On Wednesdays, Manon and I took the metro and the RER to the dental school on rue Garancière in the sixth *arrondissement*. We spent hours in the hands of trainee dentists of varying degrees of skill, Manon in the morning and me in the afternoon. Bérénice, one of Gabriel's older sisters, would meet us there and take us to a café for lunch and then to her house for tea, where I felt that we were at last in a safe place.

But when we got home, we returned to reality, which became clearer by the week: after the deaths of Niels and Milo, Lucile was losing her grip, and Manon and I were the only spectators of that shipwreck.

When I conducted my interviews, the years we spent in Bagneux produced the fewest memories of Lucile. No one remembered where she worked, how she spent her time, who she saw, or how she got through those years. I think that gradually Lucile cut herself off from her friends and family, she slipped out of sight to conceal the fact that she'd gone off-course, or to try, like everyone else, to live her own life.

At the bottom of a box which I cart around from cellar to cellar, I found the diary I began when I was twelve. It is my most precious source for that time and the next ten years.

At the start, in a hesitant hand, I talk about Lucile, the distance that has grown up between her and me, my mounting fear of finding her on the floor one evening when I get back from school. Lucile is in remission and Manon and I are living with the dread of the event or detail that will push her under.

The so-called 'suicide period' figured in the list of themes for my interviews (for soon Baptiste, Lucile's cousin, who also lived in Clamart and who was the father of Justine's child, also shot himself in the head). Beyond my own memories, I wanted to explore the magnitude of this earthquake: to find out what was said about these deaths, what was murmured and whispered – what theories or what certainties, how it was possible to survive this.

★

It is impossible to ignore any of this if one wants to understand Lucile's trajectory, what drove her in the months that followed to lose her grip on reality for good.

Legend has it that all three of them – Niels, Milo and Baptiste – went to an expensive restaurant one evening when they had a bit of money to burn and swore they would do away with themselves. The legend talks of a pact which Lucile knew about, which in fact she was tacitly associated with. Even recently, in the course of my interviews, several people mentioned this theory or remain convinced of the existence of this pact. As for the restaurant where it is alleged to have taken place, some people mention Lasserre and others Pré Catalan. Justine, whom I asked about this, doesn't believe this pact ever really existed.

Because it had been recommended to me so often, I watched the film *Mourir à trente ans* for the first time. Romain Goupil's film is about political engagement at an early age, combat and disillusion-ment. You have to take into account how things were back then, and consider how that influenced them. That is true for all three of them. At the time when these suicides occurred, this political or philosophical vision of actually doing it sometimes prevailed over everything else. Later, some people wondered about how, for each of them, these disillusionments had resonated with much more personal weaknesses.

Everyone who came into contact with Niels remembers how the idea of suicide was perpetually there in his conversation. His cousin

Alain, who was one of his best friends, told me some of the memories he had of him, the way he spoke about his relationship with Lucile when he was with him, and he gave me a photocopy of a diary that he had kept in a school exercise book in the two weeks that preceded his death. I hoped to find some trace of my mother in it, but there was none. The text proceeded in scraps, disconnected, crossed out, stifled; it struck me that there was no space for anyone left.

I asked each of Lucile's siblings to tell me about Milo, who disappeared at such an early age. In this group of nine children, he was the third brother to die. I don't know if the sadness was adding up or multiplying, but I think that it was beginning to feel like a lot for one family.

Lisbeth told me, with her typically provocative humour: 'Oh, you know, we were starting to get used to it.'

People told me that Milo had been fragile, he had often clashed with his father and had been destroyed by him, he had never found his place, he was the closest to Jean-Marc and so had been particularly affected by his death, that he survived doing odd jobs, he had believed in the revolution, drank too much too young, that he had been badly let down in love, that he was born two weeks after he was due, he was clumsy and always dropping things, he was the first of the siblings to get his *baccalauréat*. And when Georges asked him seriously what he was going to do with it, Milo replied, stubbing out his cigarette with a victorious smile: take a holiday. A long one.

He gave Lucile the lyrics of a song by Mouloudji that he had copied out by hand, which the two of them sang back then and which we sang with her too. I still remember the tune and the last two verses:

> So many paving stones in the world,
> Paving stones large and small,
> How many sorrows lie buried
> In my poor wandering soul.
>
> I'm dying, I'm dying from all this,
> I'm dying, I'm dying from all this,
> And my song ends here.

One Saturday morning Milo left home and bought a pistol in a shop (though he didn't have a firearms licence). He took a suburban train and walked far into a forest 'somewhere to the east', I was told. No one remembered the name of the place (I found it in a text written by Lucile; it was Fort de Chelles), which Milo had probably chosen because it had no family significance and no memories attached to it. A few hours later, a walker saw him from a distance, lying on the ground. The man thought he was a drunk and went on by. The next day the walker found him in the same position. This time he went over. Milo had his papers on him; Liane and Georges got a call from the police. Then they told the children. Apart from Violette, who had just gone on holiday.

As with the others, I listened to the three mp3 files of conversations I had had with Violette, at her home and mine, in order to transcribe them. When she came to Milo's suicide and the fact that they had thought it unnecessary to tell her because she was on holiday in Drôme, Violette stopped and slipped out for a few minutes. While she was gone, you can hear me saying aloud, 'That's crazy.' When Violette comes back into the room, I express my surprise that she wasn't told. But she doesn't seem shocked. I argue the case: telling you would have shared the shock, the terror, so that you could face the sadness at the same time as the others. The fact is she didn't hear the news until her return a week later. In the meantime, Barthélémy had accompanied his father to identify the body at the Medico-Legal Institute and Milo had been buried at L., beside Antonin and Jean-Marc. Violette got back from her holiday just in time for the mass, which was held in Pierremont. This was followed by a meal to which members of my family, friends and neighbours were invited. This moment was dominated by Georges's suffering; he was a compact, bitter bundle of hatred cast in everyone's face.

Listening to my recording, I can hear how painful mention of that day is for Violette, how much it hurts to talk about it. Her voice alters even more when she talks about the mementoes that she and her sisters found in Pierremont when they cleared the house. Liane had collected some fetish objects for each of her sons who had disappeared. For Antonin, there was a tiny cardboard suitcase, an exercise book, a carefully written Mother's Day card. For Jean-Marc, a notebook, a swimming medal and a scout cross carved in wood. For Milo, in a plastic bag which had probably been used to return his things, were his travel card, a lighter and the diary in which he had written those words on the very day he did it . . .

'In which he had written what?'

Now Violette is crying. In a choked voice, I hear myself offer her a handkerchief, which she accepts. There follows a silence lasting a few seconds, during which neither of us can speak, and then I launch in again in a voice that seeks its own resolve: 'In which he had written what?' I'm not crying. I want to know. I'm a sadist, clearly, a vampire eager for details. I'm turning the knife in the wound, delighting in the wet sound of entrails, splashing around with delectation – splash, splash – I'm pushing it all the way in, that's what I'm thinking at that moment, and what I think when I listen to the recording.

Violette blows her nose noisily, then eventually completes her sentence: 'In which he had written: "Forgive me, I never wanted to live."'

There follows another silence of two or three minutes, enormously oppressive, and then suddenly we burst out laughing. Doubled up, in stitches, we're dying laughing. Between two hiccups, I mutter: 'Torture . . .'

Violette starts laughing again and admits that she was reluctant to come (this is our second session), she didn't want to, really didn't, she had even wondered *why am I going*, and then she thought that she had to. It was important.

Violette asks me if I realise the effect my project is having, because now Lucile's brothers and sisters are talking to each other about it, they are talking about things they haven't talked about in years, what each of them knows of the stories about the living and the dead. Then Violette says something which makes me smile: 'You know, you've started something.'

★

Later in the conversation, which I listen to again, to catch the slightest breath, so as not to miss anything of the gift she, like the others, has given me by agreeing to take part, Violette says that she can't wait to read the book. She'll be touched, she says, to read my Lucile. She goes on: 'Because I believe that in spite of everything, she gave you a good start in life. There are photos of Lucile that have a gentleness, you know, that she alone possessed in this family.'

So I try to explain what I would like to write. When I was conducting these interviews, several weeks before starting writing, I had no idea what lay in store for me. For it is exactly that: I would like to take the chaos into account but also the kindness. My voice changes; this time I'm the one who falters.

Suddenly my computer, which has been on standby, announces in a serious female voice (as it does about three times a day): 'YOUR ANTI-VIRUS SOFTWARE HAS BEEN UPDATED.'

Violette looks at me mischievously and asks: 'Happy now?'

In Bagneux, Lucile gave me a copy of *Waiting for Godot*, because Manon had nicknamed me Didi and I called her Gogo. Didi and Gogo are the nicknames of the two characters in Samuel Beckett's play, two tramps who are waiting for a third thief as if for a Messiah who will never come. I discovered this play at the age of twelve, and although I probably didn't understand very much of it, it did prompt this question: what were Manon and I waiting for, what messenger, what saviour, what miraculous protagonist capable of getting us out of there, of breaking the unhealthy spiral in which Lucile had been caught up and taking us back to how it was before, when Lucile's sadness was not so all-consuming, not so visible to the naked eye? What were we waiting for if not for our mother to renew her ties with something resembling life? In my view, the man she was with at that time didn't give her anything, on the contrary, he was shifty and he was dragging her down. Robert had a stupid laugh, walked on tiptoe and made the carpet squeak. Robert was stoned and didn't see anything, especially not how badly things were listing and that nothing was stable any more.

Lucile was smoking more and more and, when she ran out of cigarettes, she would eat her hash in a cake or raw like an ogre.

One evening when Lucile was in the bath, she called me several times. The doors were open and I was sitting on the floor in my room, cutting my nails. Lucile called again, asking me what I was doing. Suddenly I saw her get out of the bath, covered in foam and dripping wet. She burst into my room and looked around. Lucile imagined that 'something was going on between Robert and me'; that's how I wrote about it in my diary, choking with indignation. How could Lucile imagine that I would get within six feet of that revolting man I found utterly disgusting? Not for a second did it come into my mind that Lucile could be afraid for me; her aggression towards me led me to believe the opposite: that I was the object of her suspicion.

Lucile had left the leather-bag manufacturer a few months earlier to become a secretary in a consulting agency specialising in distribution and sales promotion. She got to know one of her colleagues, Marie-Line, who gradually became her friend. Marie-Line must have been the same age as Lucile; she had her hair in a bob and wore round-necked blouses and fine-wool navy-blue cardigans. She was married to a man who worked in a bank and dressed in a suit and tie, which struck me back then as an undeniable proof of his seriousness. Marie-Line and her husband had a little girl who was younger than Manon. From time to time they invited us to lunch in the fifteenth *arrondissement*. Their apartment was modern and perfectly tidy. Or else Marie-Line came to us. Today Marie-Line would be called 'Sloaney', but I don't know if the term existed back then. Very quickly, Marie-Line came to embody the maternal and domestic ideal in my eyes.

One evening when we had just got back from school, Manon and I decided that the white mice that Lucile had given us a few weeks

NOTHING HOLDS BACK THE NIGHT

earlier must be unbearably lonely shut up in separate cages. Very careful observation of these little creatures led us to the conclusion that we had two males and that therefore there was no risk in putting them together. A few weeks later, about ten pink larvae lay squeaking in the cage belonging to Jack (Manon's mouse), who was, in all probability, a female. The baby mice were making a ridiculous amount of noise and Lucile would be back soon. We had to kill them with ether and throw them in the rubbish chute, with death in our hearts and our stomachs churning.

We lived our childish lives. Waiting for Lucile to come home, we invented magic potions and dinosaur food, we swapped our dolls, pens, exercise books, we sat and drew, we examined each other for lice, pulled each other's hair, danced to the music from *Grease*, which we had seen at the cinema. Sometimes we went downstairs to our neighbour Sabine's to watch TV.

Once a week Lucile went to Paris to have her piano lesson with Miss C. When she got back, she would study the sheet music and sometimes practise for hours, playing a passage she stumbled over again and again. Playing the piano had become the only possible activity for Lucile. She found it hard to talk to us, listen to us, she became impatient with our games. She rarely cooked and was sleeping less and less. But at the piano, she sat upright and concentrated. I will always associate Satie's *Gymnopédies* and Chopin's waltzes with her, just as I associate Bach with my father, who played the flute.

★

For a few days, Lucile came home from work looking even paler and more tired. She couldn't sleep any longer. She was writing something, she told me, something very important.

One evening after dinner, Lucile went to lie down in her room. I retreated to mine, where I reread *L'Évasion des Dalton* or *Le Naufragé du A* for the hundredth time. At around ten o'clock Manon came looking for me. Lucile wasn't well, we needed to call Marie-Line, her friend from work; that's what Lucile had said herself – call Marie-Line and get her to come right away. I didn't go near Lucile. I was terrified that she might die in front of our eyes. I dialled Marie-Line's number; she tried to reassure me and said she'd be there as soon as possible. It took several more minutes before I dared enter my mother's bedroom, where Manon had stayed with her.

We waited for Marie-Line, who arrived half an hour later with her husband. Lucile had smoked a lot but hadn't taken sleeping pills, or at any rate not enough to put her in danger. She talked to Marie-Line, who stayed late and coaxed us to go to bed. The next day, when we went off to school, Lucile was still asleep. I came back that evening full of apprehension and found her in the same position. She hadn't gone to work. Lucile mentioned for the first time the text which she had finished the night before, which she would let us read soon, the text whose ending had eluded her for several days, against which she had collided as against a wall, but which she had eventually got down on paper.

Lucile had had *a close brush with madness and suicide*. Those were her words and that's how I wrote them down, word for word, in my diary. Writing had allowed a memory to emerge which she had banished far away, very far, where she thought it could never get at her. Lucile spoke to me about shame, the power of shame. Now she was feeling better. She promised to smoke less.

Lucile got back on her feet, literally and metaphorically, and returned to work.

A few days later she made photocopies of her text, gave it to us to read and sent it to her parents and all her siblings.

Lucile's text is called *Aesthetic Quest*. We found multiple typed copies of it along with other texts after her death. In its pages, she talks about the wish to die, the madness which stalks her, the brightly coloured drawings we do for her, our Mother's Day presents, how touched she is by their attention to detail. She describes the unhappiness which keeps growing and which she allows to overwhelm her until reaching its height:

> *I like feeling this bad, so separate from my body yet so attentive to its pulsing, its pronounced lefthandedness, its weakness.*
>
> *[...]*
>
> *11 o'clock, first joint, first anxiety. How can I control my thoughts, do my ironing, talk to my children, listen to anything apart from the void. Will my hands shake at the keyboard. Will I manage to work, instead of mechanically rehearsing with the aim of achieving improbable perfection.*
>
> *[...]*
>
> *I am so reluctant to go to sleep. The bedroom is calming. I am stiff, I think about it and tell myself I am right. I want to wear out this body*

*and by doing so make it live. Why would I spoil it, have I been spoiled
perhaps?*

[...]

*Shall I make my father atone, knowing that in front of my mother he
cannot refuse me my slightest whim. Like the gold necklace I got him to
give me recently.*

[...]

*I buy a lot of cigarettes, I have loved men, my mouth is bitter. I am
dazzled by Baudelaire's* Petits poèmes en prose, *to think I had never
read them.*

[...]

*I tell Delphine that I have been writing for several days. I feel guilty, she
thinks I'm strange.*

[...]

*My writing, if it lasts, can only be an immense malaise. I renounce life,
I lie down to die.*

My daughters are quiet.

After a few pages of painful fragments added one after the other
without any apparent coherence, Lucile's text ends with these words:

*We are off to our house in the country. I am with my lover, we are with
my father.*

I am not affectionate yet I love my friend.

*That night I can't sleep, I feel hunted. Forrest is sleeping upstairs.
I get up for a pee, my father is watching me, he gives me a sleeping
pill and drags me into his bed.*

He raped me while I was asleep, I was sixteen, I have said it.

Writing about your family is undoubtedly the easiest way to fall out with them. Lucile's brothers and sisters won't want to read what I have just transcribed nor what I am likely to say about it; I can sense this in the tension around my project now, and my feeling that I am bound to hurt them disturbs me more than anything else. They must be wondering what I am going to do with this, how I shall broach it, how far I am prepared to go. Since I am trying to get closer to Lucile, I cannot leave out the relations she had with her father, or rather that he had with her. It's my duty to ask the question at least. But the question is not painless.

I'm firing at point-blank range and I know it.

One day I told my sister over lunch how terrified I was after reading Lionel Duroy's fine book, *Le Chagrin*, which goes back over his childhood and describes the fundamental, irreparable way his siblings became estranged from him after the publication of a novel he wrote fifteen years earlier, in which he had portrayed them and his parents. Even today, none of them speak to him: he's a traitor, a pariah.

Is fear enough to make one silent?

Looking rather distressed in front of her *croque-monsieur*, my sister promised me her unconditional support. 'You have to see it through,' she said; 'don't leave anything in the shadows.'

★

I left convinced that the only route I could take from where I had reached, from where we had all reached, was this one.

The man I love (and who I have come to believe loves me too) is getting worried at seeing me lose more sleep the further I go with this book. I try to explain that it's normal (and nothing to do with the fact that I have got lost in an experiment in a new genre; nothing to do with the material I am dealing with; this has happened to me with other books that were pure fiction and so on). I tough it out, wave aside his concerns.

Is fear enough to make one silent?

At the age of thirty-two, Lucile wrote that her father had raped her. She sent the text to her parents and her siblings, she gave it to us to read. For several weeks, I imagined that something very serious was going to happen, something that would have repercussions, that the family would collapse, inevitably causing terrible damage. I was waiting for a drama.

Yet nothing happened. We continued to go to Pierremont for the weekend occasionally; no one chased my grandfather with a broom; no one punched him in the face on the stairs; my mother herself spoke to her father and didn't spit at him. I was twelve years old and the logic of this escaped me. How could such a revelation not be followed by consequences? In school, grammar was the only subject that interested me. Yet in Pierremont, in the absence of a subordinating conjunction – 'so that', 'as a consequence of which', 'following which' – nothing happened: no tears, no shouting. My mother visited her parents and they fretted about how tired she was, how thin and drawn she looked, the fact she wasn't sleeping, how hard life was for their daughter, who was bringing up her children alone.

A few months later, Lucile retracted. Now she spoke of an 'inappropriate' relationship rather than an incestuous one; she denied her account of the act itself.

Like thousands of families, mine learned to live with doubt or simply sidestepped it. If necessary, they would acknowledge a certain ambivalence, an atmosphere that created confusion, but that was a far cry from imagining the worst . . . Lucile had simply imagined she'd been raped. That enabled everyone to breathe, though there was precious little air.

Proof that something was the matter with her was not long in coming.

Years later, when Manon and I were adults, at a time when Lucile was OK, my sister asked her about it again. Lucile said yes, it did happen. And that no one had reacted to the text that she sent.

The text remained a dead letter and all Lucile received in return was frozen silence.

A few months ago, when I asked my mother's siblings to talk to me about her, they all agreed with genuine enthusiasm. Paying tribute to Lucile, trying to get close to her? Yes, of course.

For all of us, Lucile – her gentleness and her aggression – remains a mystery.

It scarcely need be said that the possibility that my grand-father raped Lucile was high on the list of things I wanted to discuss. Yet, when I began working on the book, I was far from certain.

When I listen again to the conversations I had with each of them, it seems to me that the question is always there from the outset. It hangs in the air even before it is asked. In spite of the silence, years later, Lucile's text has left its mark. They know I shall come round to it; they either delay the moment or else pre-empt it; some acknowledge Georges's '*adoration*' of his daughter; they mention '*fascination*' or '*passion*'. His love, the way he looked at her, could indeed have been oppressive for her, could have put ideas in her head. But aren't all girls in love with their fathers? They tread carefully, weigh each word. Incest? No, definitely not. Not in reality.

Only Justine (who broached the subject right at the outset) acknowledged the possibility that it may actually have happened.

Justine was the last of Lucile's siblings I interviewed. As she lives in the country and doesn't often come to Paris, we had trouble finding a date for me to visit her and in the end she came to me. I was more apprehensive about this interview than the others because Justine and Lucile's relationship was often adversarial, extremely tense, as though a pain that was impossible to share had crystallised between them. After listening to Lisbeth, Barthélémy and Violette, who were instinctively unable to imagine that Lucile could have been telling the truth, I was particularly interested in Justine's account, as she never minced her words (and she had distanced herself from Georges for a few years).

Justine told me about the month she had spent alone with Georges one summer when she was eighteen or nineteen, at the time when her father took his children to Pierremont singly or in groups to help with the building work. Justine told me how Georges endlessly pestered her to take her T-shirt and bra off, to strip off, to relax. He wanted to take pictures of her, to help her to discover her sexuality, to teach her how to masturbate. Justine escaped at the first opportunity to walk by the canal and Georges locked her out. She was afraid the whole time. He took a series of pictures of her that Justine never found. Georges was not a man who took no for an answer.

I asked for details: how far did he go? He '*fiddled*' with her, but didn't rape her. Maybe he was scared she would talk, because Justine, unlike Lucile, was vociferous. Justine experienced Georges's oppression, his looks, the threat he represented.

Today, she claims her own share of hatred for this man who ruined her youth and long damaged her capacity for happiness. *This man who could have been content with being a wonderful father.*

Another day, also as research for this book, I met Camille. She is Gabriel's younger sister and was one of my mother's best friends when they were in their early twenties. I wanted her to tell me about Lucile and her first loves, to find out what sort of young woman Lucile was, to discover how she laughed and danced, what she thought about the future. I was hoping that Camille would help me gain access to the luminous, sparkling Lucile of the television programme. I wanted the carefree, flighty Lucile.

I hadn't imagined for an instant what Camille would tell me, yet it came out very quickly, without being spelled out, when I asked her about Lucile, Georges and the Poirier family: it was an incomplete sentence that hung in the air, but the signal was clear. Camille hesitated: this was off the subject; we had already suffered so much; she wasn't sure she needed to bring *that* up. I pressed her.

Camille didn't talk about Lucile's relations with her father, but about her own. She was sixteen and had met Georges only a few times before. The Poiriers had invited her to Spain. It had been arranged that he would take her to Alicante, where Liane, the children and Gabriel were already on holiday. Her father had died the year before, her mother was old; they had agreed that it would do Camille good to have a change of air, get away with the young people, have some fun. A few days later, Camille found herself in the car with Georges, whom she hardly knew. On the way, they stopped first to pick up one of Lucile's cousins, then to have a rest at the home of some friends of Georges's. The three of them – the cousin, Camille and Georges – found themselves in the same bed, with Georges taking the middle place for himself. During the night, Georges pressed himself against her and started to caress her. A terrified Camille said nothing. In Spain, she kept out of his way, and then she was struck down with appendicitis and immediately rushed home to France.

For months, Georges demanded that Camille call him and meet him in various places. He was crazy about her. He made appointments with her which she got out of, gave her code names so that she could phone him at the agency, addresses where he would be waiting. The more she fled from him, the more threatening he became. If she didn't accede to his demands, he would tell her mother how she had pressed herself against him that night, how she had tried to enflame his desire, to seduce him. Camille knew nothing about sex and the thought of her family hearing such dreadful things terrified her. All the more so since her mother kept insisting that she thank Liane and Georges for having so generously invited her and that she accept Georges's repeated invitations to their home. Time went by, but Georges didn't give up. He never missed an opportunity to remind her what she owed him.

Eventually, he got his way. First, one evening after a dinner he had got her to agree to, then a whole weekend at Pierremont, where he set a trap to get her alone with him. Terrified by his threats, Camille gave in. She had shameful, painful memories, which she didn't talk about for years, of these two days which she spent shut up under Georges's control (on the pretext that the neighbours shouldn't see her), during which she had to submit to his erotic games and *punishments*. The next school year, she went to a college in England to escape Georges's clutches. She felt guilty for years.

When she returned to France, Camille married and had children, in spite of the imprint that Georges had left on her body and the feeling of guilt that has never left her.

After Lucile and Gabriel's divorce, Lucile and Camille lost touch. Camille also got divorced and remarried a few years later.

She was at Lucile's funeral.

I told Camille about Lucile's text and her retraction: the way we rallied around the idea that it was a figment of her imagination; put it down to her illness; my lingering, unanswered doubt. Camille was stunned. She told me she often had the feeling that Lucile was protecting herself from her father, that she was avoiding being alone with him.

They never spoke about it. One weekend when Camille was at Pierremont with Lucile and Gabriel, Georges came into Camille's bedroom, naked, in the middle of the night. But when he heard Gabriel, who must have seen him in the corridor, it scared him off. Later, on the journey home, when the two of them were alone in the car, Lucile asked Camille about her father: what was he doing there in the middle of the night? What had he wanted? Lucile was on edge, aggressive. Camille said nothing.

If she *had* said something, if they had talked about it, would their lives have been different?

After her visit, Camille wrote to say how relieved our conversation had made her feel. After all these years, she felt less guilty.

During my research, Manon reminded me about something she had mentioned in the past but which I had blocked out. One day when she was on holiday at La Grande-Motte, Georges, for a reason she doesn't recall, decided to buy her a bathing costume. At the time going topless was *de rigueur*, but Manon chose a sporty white one-piece with lining. As she was thanking him for the gift, Georges came close to her and stroked her shoulder, saying: 'If you're really good, you can have other gifts.'

Manon was sixteen; the implication of what Georges said was not lost on her. She confided in Lisbeth's children and one of them couldn't stop himself passing the confidence on to Liane. Liane, in an icy tone that Manon hadn't heard before, reprimanded her: 'It's not nice to say things like that about your grandfather.'

Lucile kept all her correspondence. When she died, we found most of her father's letters in her cardboard boxes. Manon stored them at her house along with the rest of her papers and writings. When I began working on this book, I asked her for them. Manon had read them and told me there was nothing in them, nothing specific. Georges wrote to Lucile from time to time with news, that was all. When I began sorting them by date, I was struck by a strange fact: during the summer of '78 (a few months before Lucile wrote her text), Georges had sent her eight letters in less than three weeks. Liane was making her 'July Tour' at the time (visiting family and friends) and Georges was in the south of France by himself, where my grandmother would join him in August. Eight letters in three weeks, sometimes two on the same day. I shuddered at the thought of finding some clue or detail that my sister had missed and read them very carefully. But the letters gave nothing away. Judging by what Georges wrote, Lucile was having problems at work and was worrying about her health. Georges advised her to go and see a haematologist and get some rest; he insisted that she should come and join him, hoped at one point that she would get away for the weekend of 14 July, reminded her that if necessary he would buy her ticket; then, after 14 July had come and gone, insisted that she come down in August.

Two months after Milo's death – which he never mentions – Georges was worrying about Lucile. He probably feared for her, that's all.

★

When I mentioned to Violette that I would like to take Georges's recordings home with me that day we were in her cellar looking for the cassettes, she got into a terrible rage. She became shrill and agitated, trembling with anger; she refused, she didn't want to, it was out of the question that she would give me them if they were going to be used against her father. Helplessly, I told her that all I was after were some of Georges's memories about his career and anecdotes about the rue de Maubeuge, which I wanted to describe but hadn't yet captured the atmosphere. This was true, in that I did not for a second think that I would find the slightest trace on the cassettes of the ambiguity in Georges's relationship with Lucile.

At the time when Georges was recording his memories, he told Violette that he had devoted one cassette to his sex life. She made clear to him that she didn't want to hear about it. A fortnight later, he claimed he had destroyed it. She told me this herself.

Violette let me take the cassettes.

Lucile and Georges are both dead; it's too late to find out the truth. Lucile was bipolar and it seems that incest is one of the factors which may trigger the condition. I haven't found data on this. The text Lucile left among her papers says that Georges gave her a sleeping pill, then raped her.

Among the writings we found in her flat (which she didn't judge necessary to throw away, and therefore left for us to see), I discovered a draft of her text written in pencil in a school exercise book. It shows how she redrafted this point:

'Final tableau = We are off to our house in the country with my lover, we are with my father. I am not affectionate ~~I am too afraid in case my father sees us. My Friend~~ Forrest is sleeping upstairs. I get up for a pee, my father is watching me, he gives me a sleeping pill and drags me into his bed ~~to relax me, I am so nervous. I don't know if he raped me,~~ He raped me while I was asleep, sixteen years ago, and I am saying it.'

When Manon returned to this subject years later, Lucile told her that Georges made her sit on the edge of his bed, then started to caress her. She fainted in terror. There was no mention of sleeping pills. That is more or less the version she wrote in 1984, when the psychoanalyst whose patient she had been for months, and who kept coming up against her silence, asked her to keep a diary:

'Saturday 29.12.1984. Today my father gave me a round watch to cover up the tattoo on my wrist, which he doesn't like. I like the tattoo, it's part of me. My father doesn't know that he is the origin of this tattoo. Ten past ten is the time I woke up in their bedroom after having spent a night with him when he may have raped me. I don't know. All I know is that I was very afraid and fainted. It's the most afraid I have ever been in my life.'

Until the end of her life, Lucile kept that round watch tattooed on her wrist. Ten past ten, the time she woke up, the time that watches in jewellers' windows are set at.

What if nothing happened that night? And fear was all there was, that huge fear, and the unconsciousness that followed?

★

Sometimes I am haunted by a different idea:

What if Lucile, unable to talk about it or write it down, came up against an even greater taboo, that of her own state of consciousness? What if Lucile didn't faint, though frozen in fear, and Georges abused his power, his control, to make her submit to his desire, to convince her to give in? What if Lucile, like Camille, was unable to say no; didn't know how to?

Then shame would have distilled its poison and made any words impossible without distortion. Then shame would have carved out its own channel of despair and disgust.

I reread these words from *L'Inceste*, in which Christine Angot reveals how her father abused his power over her: 'I'm sorry to talk to you about all this, I'd much prefer to be able to tell you about something else. But this is what made me mad. I am sure of it; it is because of this that I went mad.'

We shall never know. We all either have our own convictions or have suspended judgement.

Maybe that is the hardest part: not being able to hate Georges, but never able to absolve him either. Lucile bequeathed this doubt to us, and doubt is a poison.

A few months after she wrote this text and the silence which surrounded its distribution, Lucile was committed for the first time. Juxtaposition is to writing what collage is to images. The way I write these sentences, the way I place them, reveals my truth. It is mine alone.

Lucile could no longer bear the cooped-up atmosphere of our house in Bagneux, the carpet grimy with age, the double-glazing cracked from top to bottom, her long journey to work on public transport. At 1 p.m. one day in late July, she visited an apartment in the ninth *arrondissement*, very near the district where she had lived as a child. It was much bigger than others on offer for the price and seemed clean and light. The kitchen and bathroom were huge and well-appointed. The estate agent pressed her and she signed there and then. Lucile arranged the move, repainted our rooms, then joined us in the South, where we were on holiday with Liane and Georges. Everything passed off as though the text had never existed, as though none of this (the dark hours, the accusations) had ever happened. All three of us went home at the end of August. It was not long before Lucile realised what a mistake she had made.

Our new apartment at number 13, rue du Faubourg-Montmartre was directly opposite the Palace nightclub and the offices of the sports newspaper *L'Équipe*. Beneath our windows two lanes of buses and countless tourist coaches threaded their way down this narrow artery to Pigalle or the Folies-Bergère at all hours of the day and night. It was one of the noisiest streets in Paris; there were people everywhere all the time. To get to the stairs in the hall of our building, we had to walk round the queue for Studio 43, a local cinema the nature of whose programme (B-movies, Z- or X-rated films, two for the price of one) has remained obscure to me to this day. From the kitchen window, we watched monstrous rats feeding calmly from the bins of the local fast-food joint, neon signs flashed on and off all night, and it wasn't uncommon for us to be woken up by the sound of shouting and sirens when the Palace closed. Hiding behind the curtains, I'd get up to watch the quarrels, the police raids, the fights being broken up.

Lucile was still working as a secretary for the same promotion company. She frequently mocked her boss, dreamed of long holidays in faraway places, and sometimes told us anecdotes about the office.

Manon's bedroom opened on to the living room, where Lucile had put her bed. Lucile's mattress rested on wooden palettes, which served as a bed-base. Almost every night, Manon heard Lucile crying.

I had started in the fourth year at a school on rue Milton, which I went to by bus. My childish closeness to Tadrina was long gone and I was finding adolescence a real torture: I wore braces on my teeth, which my cousins called 'the nuclear power station', I had curly hair that was impossible to tame, tiny breasts and puny thighs. I blushed whenever anyone spoke to me and didn't sleep the night before I had to recite a poem or give a presentation in front of the class. In order to appear more at ease in this Parisian environment, which I found so intimidating, I created a character for myself: a sad, lonely girl, eaten away by a secret drama, and turned down any invitation likely to distract me from my misery. Manon, who was at a local primary school where most of her friends were Jewish, pretended to be Jewish too, and invented religious festivals and fervent prayers for herself. To explain the shape of her face (broad and smooth, like Faye Dunaway), Manon told anyone who would listen about the day she had hit a tree when galloping at high speed on a runaway horse.

Manon was a happy, confident, smiling child. I was a serious, solemn, cerebral adolescent. We spent most of our time stealing from shops; the local area offered rich pickings. Pains d'Épices, a model and toy shop on passage Jouffroy, where we plied our trade several times a week and left with our pockets full, and Monoprix, in an era before anti-theft systems, became our places of choice. In order to explain this sudden affluence to Lucile, I piled lie upon lie: I had swapped some of my junk, miraculously found money in the street, had friends who had grown out of their clothes and given them to me, kind-hearted mothers who gave me gifts – the rest we hid in our drawers.

One day Manon got caught and received a lecture from a sales assistant; we only just avoided disaster.

Lucile couldn't bear the incessant noise from the street, the mice that invaded the kitchen the moment our backs were turned or the rats the size of rabbits, rummaging through the bins all night.

Lucile was isolating herself in an ever darker world in which curls of smoke were sometimes followed by powder.

★

Virginia was in my class and lived directly opposite us on the sixth floor of the *L'Équipe* building. She couldn't have cared less about my problems, or her own, or any problems in fact. Virginia lived in a tiny apartment with her mother, who was a cleaner. She prided herself on dragging me along to parties and on cinema trips, and gave a loud whistle from the window every morning to signal it was time to go. It didn't take long for her energy to breach my self-created barriers. Thanks to her, I joined the most prestigious group in the school. I discovered The Specials, Madness, Police and The Selecter. I skipped classes I thought were boring in favour of heated discussions in cafés or trips to Galeries Lafayette. I was unambiguously entering a new world, a world which pulsed and throbbed and was alive.

On 4 January 1980, my grandmother's sister Barbara and her husband Claude Yelnick, then communications director on *France-Soir*, were invited on to the TV programme *Apostrophes* to talk about the book they had written together entitled *Deux et la folie*. The book described from both their viewpoints Barbara's illness, which was characterised by alternating periods of hyperactivity, indeed delirium, and deep depression.

Probably the broadcast coincided with the end of the Christmas holidays, because I remember the whole family gathered in reverent silence in the 'television room' in Pierremont, which was dedicated to the cult of the small screen (which was in fact huge and took pride of place in a cabinet designed specially for it). Some people were sitting in large armchairs covered in soft sheepskin; the rest of us sat on the blue carpet. We waited with bated breath. The programme had hardly begun when the first whispered comments began: Why's she dressed like that? Who's he going to start with? No, really, his suit's perfect. The first exasperated shushes flew across the room. And then: Come on, pay attention; Barbara and Claude are going first; isn't that chic/great/amazing? Can you be quiet? And who is it who keeps coughing like that?

When we got back to Paris, Lucile began painting on the wall of the living room a tormented fresco, consisting of arabesques and spirals, dark green on a white background. That's how I remember it: tortured and threatening.

One evening, Justine's boyfriend Pablo rang the bell; he was holding a basket of oysters he had just stolen from outside a brasserie on the boulevard Montmartre. He'd been in the area. A few minutes later he went back to ask for a lemon and sympathised with the waiter, who was lamenting how he had been tricked the moment his back was turned. Pablo opened the oysters and we tucked in to the feast.

In the next few days, I thought Lucile seemed increasingly agitated.

Another evening for dinner she served us frozen raspberries straight from the packet, which we found impossible to eat.

For a few days, Lucile had only been buying sweet foods (I added in my diary: '*which are dead expensive*').

★

On 29 January Lucile invited Manon and me to a special meeting whose agenda soon became apparent. Lucile wanted to announce that she was telepathic. Consequently she knew what was going on even far away and could control most things. Just as she said this, we heard mice squeaking in the kitchen. Lucile added that she could also make mice disappear, but then said immediately: 'Ah no, what an idiot I am. They're not things' (a sentence which I reproduced verbatim in my diary). Wherever we went, she could see us in mirrors and could protect us from afar. And we had powers too. Manon was a witch who could hear everything and could decipher, thanks to her power of hearing, the hostile world around her. Lucile added that she'd have to take her to an ear, nose and throat specialist so as to make the most of this power. As for me, I was the Delphic oracle: I could predict the future and my predictions would come true. But I had to be careful not to predict bad things. Lucile held a pair of scissors close to my neck and I felt the point brush my skin. I held my breath and watched her trembling hand. She sat down again and explained that she had written a letter to a famous psychoanalyst, which, because she had no stamps, she was going to send him that very evening telepathically.

The next day was a Wednesday, our day for the dental school. Manon received treatment from the dental students in the morning and I had an orthodontics session in the afternoon. As we were about to set off, Lucile announced that it was out of the question that we should take the metro: the Parisian transport network was not entirely under her control. She gave me money so we could take a taxi, because she did control of all of the taxis in Paris. No vehicle escaped her vigilance. Lucile asked me with the greatest seriousness if I would prefer our driver to be a man or a woman. After several seconds of reflection, I said I'd prefer a woman. Manon and I no longer dared look at each other. We went down the stairs in appalled silence.

My mother was an adult. My mother had read a lot and knew lots of things. My mother was clever. How could I imagine that my mother was talking nonsense? I was thirteen years old. I went hesitantly towards the line of taxis, torn between respect for what she had said and the stirring of my own awareness, between the desire for the driver to be a man and the desire for her to be a woman. Something was happening which couldn't be expressed, which was beyond my ken. The idea of secretly taking the metro and giving her the money back later briefly occurred to me (taking taxis wasn't part of our lifestyle and struck me as a shocking waste of money). But I was scared that she would discover my betrayal through her powers. Manon was silent. With a knot in our stomachs, we went towards the front of the taxi rank.

At the head of the queue, there was a man behind the wheel. We got in the car and I told him our destination – rue Garancière – with the note that Lucile had given me burning a hole in my hand. I felt bad.

That same evening, Lucile came home with a black eye. She told us that Jacques Lacan, the great psychoanalyst, had hit her.

Lisbeth came from Brunoy for dinner. Lucile's brothers and sisters were starting to get worried about her; she was saying odd things on the phone. Lisbeth had been sent to find out what was going on. Lucile, with her black eye and in a state of great agitation, took us to Chartier's. As was usual there, we shared our table with other diners. During the meal, Lucile talked a lot, laughed, sobbed, stole chips from the plate of the man beside her, waved her arms and summoned the waiter for the slightest thing. She was convinced that he was making us wait deliberately; he had a grudge against us: she'd already noticed he had something against her personally.

I watched Lisbeth. I was waiting for her to say something: don't worry about it, what's happening is entirely normal, there's no reason to panic or even be afraid; your mum will go back to normal, a good night's sleep and there'll be no trace of it; but Lisbeth looked just as much at a loss as we did. After dinner, we went back to the apartment and Lisbeth went home. As I was about to put the light out, Lucile said that tomorrow she would buy me the pink velvet trousers with fine ribbed stripes that I had previously asked her for without success.

For several days Lucile had been spending money she didn't have; it wouldn't be long before we found this out. Lucile was spending without counting the cost.

Later that night Manon heard her crying in bed again.

The next morning Lucile decided she wasn't going to work (she hadn't gone the day before either). She also reckoned that we deserved a lie-in. We had gone to bed late, and so she excused us from having to go to school for an unspecified period, but from the way she said it, we imagined that it could last for some time. Moreover, for some days Lucile had sensed from a distance that Mr Rigon, the headteacher at my school, was very irritated. It would be best to avoid all contact with him. I had no desire to stay with her; I was beginning to think she wasn't right in the head. I insisted on going to school and tried to persuade Manon to do the same. Manon refused. She wanted to stay with Lucile, whose distress was apparent to her.

In the bus on the way to school, I tried to analyse the situation. Should I be worried? Even having gone back over the events of the past few days, I found it impossible to acknowledge that Lucile was really going off the rails, still less that she could become a danger to herself and to us. Lucile was going through a bad patch, that was all. When I got to school, I met Virginia and Jean-Michel, another friend from my class, who were planning to bunk off PE to go to Galeries Lafayette. I debated for a moment with them; I had just got off the bus and was reluctant to turn around again, but in the end I agreed. For some reason I can't recall, we went back to Virginia's. Almost as soon as we got there, I went over to the window. From the sixth floor, I was able to look down and see what was going on in our apartment. I saw Lucile standing in the living room: she was naked and her body was painted white. This sight took my breath away. Paralysed, I couldn't take my eyes off her, though I could hardly believe it entirely. I looked for Manon, but she wasn't to be seen. It was nearly two hours since I had left the apartment: something was wrong, seriously wrong. I didn't want to go to Galeries Lafayette any more; I wanted to stay there and for all this to stop and return to normal. I watched Lucile for a moment longer. I was finding it harder and harder to breathe. She was still standing there and from her gestures of impatience, I understood that she wanted Manon to come over to her. Lucile stamped her foot. Manon didn't appear; she was clearly refusing to obey. Suddenly Lucile seized the plank of wood that we used as a backrest on the old barber's chair and raised it above her head with both hands. The plank remained suspended in the air, ready to be brought down on Manon. I raced down the stairs, rushed across the street without looking, and in a few seconds was in the hall of our building. I climbed the stairs two at a time and arrived breathless at our door. Violette had just arrived. She had rung the bell two or three times and got no reply. I screamed: 'She's hitting her, she's hitting her!' I pressed the bell as hard as I could, shouted again. Violette took me in her arms and my body pitched backwards. Violette supported me for a few seconds; I felt unable to breathe. In my panic, I finally realised that I had a key. I opened the door and we rushed into the living room. Lucile was holding Manon by the hair to stop her getting away. Violette ordered her to let her go. Manon flew into my arms. Now that I held her against me, she began to cry. Lucile had wanted to put acupuncture needles in her eyes and had managed to insert one below her right eye. Suddenly, uniformed men appeared behind us. Someone had called the police. Everything got unbearably jumbled up in all the confusion. Lucile was naked and painted white, looking crazed, her body shaking. Manon was terrified. Virginia and Jean-Michel had arrived. Someone suggested taking my sister to the doctor along the street at number 7. I let go her hand and Jean-Michel hugged her.

We had to leave the apartment. We had to leave Lucile, naked and white, to face half a dozen cops.

At the doctor's, a police sergeant came to get us.

The doctor removed the paint flecks that Manon had in both eyes and cleaned the small trace that the needle had left under her right eye. Then we left his office and, while Lucile was being taken care of by the police in our apartment, we were kept apart from her in the police van parked across the street. A crowd gathered at once. On the other side of the windows, people were pushing and shoving, craning on tiptoe. Their eyes were trained on us, eager to see bruises and bleeding wounds. I wanted to spit in their faces.

When Lucile was dressed – Violette had made her have a bath to calm her down and try to get the paint off – we swapped places with her in the van. So that we didn't have to see her, they took us away before she was brought down.

It was eleven o'clock in the morning; life in the street went on as though nothing had happened; nothing had stopped, not the deliveries or the noise of car horns, not the smell of frying from the shops or the flashing neon signs. Nothing apart from our lives.

Violette picked us up that winter Thursday like two damaged packages. She was twenty-five.

That afternoon we went back to the apartment to collect some things for the night. That evening Violette made up beds for us in her little studio apartment. We eventually got to sleep, curled up in quilts she'd brought back from her travels in South America.

Next morning I woke up dazed and stiff. I insisted on going to school. I knew that I wouldn't be going back. Every hour felt like it was the last: last French lesson, last history class, last notes exchanged across the classroom, last secrets whispered in the playground, where a few weeks earlier I had bashed my head against a wall to get out of a German test. (The tactic had worked so well that I was taken to hospital. Thereafter I couldn't sleep, feeling guilty for costing Lucile a pointless X-ray.)

None of that mattered any more. My mother had gone mad; she had suffered a delirious episode; my mother had something the matter with her. The word 'episode' made me think of TV comedies, but I couldn't see the funny side. I didn't understand what they were trying to explain to us: Lucile was very tired, she needed rest, she hadn't meant to hurt Manon, she wasn't in her right mind, she loved us with all her heart but her nerves had cracked, things would work out, things always work out in the end.

★

That evening as arranged we caught the train to Normandy, where our father was still living with his wife and our little brother. With my forehead pressed to the window, I watched the countryside that we almost knew by heart go by. I shut my eyes, trying to find a time out of time where none of this had happened.

When we arrived, we had to describe things we didn't understand ourselves, things which obeyed no logic, made no sense, which could only be expressed a little bit at a time, and yet they *had* happened.

The following Monday I was unceremoniously sent to L'Aigle school in Orne, and Manon went to the primary school in the same town. Exiled and dazed. The shape of my so-called cowboy jeans (wide at the top and narrow at the bottom) hadn't yet reached those parts, so there was astonishment at such a garment and sniggers behind my back.

A few days later, our stepmother bought us new clothes. A few weeks went by before we were able to return to Lucile's apartment to collect our things and several months before we could see her again.

This was where we were to live for several years. We didn't yet realise how our lives had been turned upside down.

In Gabriel's nice house, at the end of a little dirt track, we were going to discover a different sort of brutality, which we would be unable to put into words for years.

To me 31 January 1980 represents a sort of initial point of severance, one of those which seem to remain intact in the memory, anchored in the body, one of those which you know will never be completely erased any more than the pain which is attached to them.

Later, the body will assimilate the fear; it will enter the bloodstream, be diluted and become a constituent part of how it functions.

For Lucile, I am sure of one thing: there would be a before and an after.

I have written about Lucile's first committal in a few pages. I know how inadequate they are, how partial and reductive all this is. Even today, I am looking at the scene from afar, unable to decipher it, I am – literally and metaphorically – in the building across the street.

For questionable authenticity, I could have copied out word for word the police report my father sent me, which was written on the same day by the police officer Jean-Michel R., the subject of which is given as follows: 'Transfer to the Lariboisière Hospital of a person suffering a nervous breakdown, who committed abuse of a minor under the age of thirteen (her daughter). CID boss in attendance.'

I'm not sure that would have enabled me to get closer.

★

During the series of interviews I conducted for this book, I asked Manon and Violette to describe that day. I wanted to compare my recollection with theirs, to reconstruct how things happened. On some points of detail, our memories differ (was my cousin Frank there the day Lucile claimed she could control the taxis? Did we both sleep at Violette's the night she was taken away?), but the essentials are brutally the same.

That January morning, Lisbeth had called Lucile after I left. She found her more and more confused and became worried about Manon being alone with her. Lisbeth rang Violette, who didn't live far from us, and asked her to go round.

During her crisis, Lucile stood naked and white at the window and demanded that Manon describe the passers-by. Gradually, a small crowd, attracted by the shouting, gathered on the pavement opposite. Someone must have called the police.

I would like to be able to write what happened to Lucile minute by minute, to capture the exact moment when things got out of control, examine the phenomenon under the microscope, grasp its mystery, its chemistry.

Before I began writing this book, in that singular, precious time when the text is being thought about, being fantasised, before a single word or any music has come from the keyboard, I envisaged writing about Lucile going off-course in the third person, as I did about some scenes from her childhood, through a new, reinvented 'she', which might have opened up the unknown for me. For example, I would like to have written about her visit to Jacques

Lacan ('she burst into the waiting room despite his receptionist forbidding it, and asked to sit down'), to describe her wandering around the city, fill in the blanks, reconstruct the impossible: the time of pure madness which even Lucile herself did not fully know about.

But I didn't know how.

A few years after it happened, my mother wrote about her first breakdown, and the immense void that followed. We found these pages at Lucile's home jumbled up with others: rambling, morbid thoughts, thoughts about love, more or less legible fragments scribbled in pencil, poems in verse and prose, undated loose-leaf sheets. It was all stored in a tin filing cabinet that I had given her ages before.

This text has no title, but it has been typed up and, like the others, copied several times. I began by recopying it into my own text in its entirety: twenty closely typed pages, a raw account, steeped in guilt. I thought that nothing could translate Lucile's suffering better than her own words. But once the text was there, stuck in the middle of my pages, it seemed as though it didn't belong, couldn't be integrated with my own material, at least not like this, as a single block. Then I decided to keep just a series of extracts, separated by ellipses, a selection worthy of *Reader's Digest*, but this didn't blend in any better. In fact it resisted: it revealed its own bitter and uneven timeframe and its fluctuating register.

Later it became clear to me that I had to take responsibility for my words, my silences, my hesitations, my breaths, my convolutions – in short, my own language. And try to make the fairest use of Lucile's words, to keep the most intense, distinctive themes.

The text begins with these words:

'This year, in November, I will be thirty-three. A rather uncertain age, I think, if one were superstitious. I am a beautiful woman except that I have rotten teeth, which in a certain way I'm very pleased about, sometimes it even makes me laugh. I wanted it to be known that death lies beneath the surface.'

Lucile then describes the days leading up to her crisis. She cries alone in the street, in a Chinese shop, then in Galeries Lafayette; she buys a piano on rue Vivienne, then all sorts of objects and clothes that don't suit her. Later, she finds herself at Lacan's office – to whom she sent a letter a few days earlier – demanding to see him. When his secretary tells her that he won't see her, Lucile asks to rest in his waiting room. When the psychoanalyst comes out of his office and asks what she's doing there, she flings herself on him and grabs his glasses, shouting: 'I've got him! I've got him!' Lacan slaps her face, the secretary manages to pin her to the floor before both of them throw her out, without any form of help. This scene, as Lucile describes it, explains the black eye that she came home with the day before her committal. Years later, at a time when I became interested in Lacan's seminars, I asked Lucile if this story was true. Did it really happen as she described? She assured me it did. At the end of his life, Lacan saw patients every ten minutes for astronomical sums and, by then suffering from cancer which he refused to have treated, didn't greatly trouble himself about them. No more than he did about a woman suffering a full-blown crisis who burst into his office. That's what Lucile told me. I never tried to verify this version. I believed it.

Lucile had a precise recollection of 31 January: my refusal to stay at home, my setting off for school, the almond croissants that Manon bought for breakfast, the titles of the chapters of *The Master and Margarita* that she read aloud to her, the threat the cover of the paperback suddenly represented, the fresco that she had been painting on the living-room wall for several weeks, which she suddenly judged malevolent (it seemed to her as though the interlinked lines formed a swastika) and which she had to get rid of at once. She asked Manon to help her cover it over with white paint, but became impatient with how slow she was. She shook her and hit her to make her go faster. And then the worst happened: the mad idea, which struck her as a certainty, that she had to treat Manon with acupuncture needles in her eyes (having stuck several needles in her own head as my sister looked on in terror).

In the police van, Lucile took off her clothes again. Under the brown blanket they put round her, she had hallucinations which she remembered: her brother Jean-Marc getting out of his coffin in the blue overalls he liked wearing. In the Lariboisière Hospital, they assessed her as too aggressive to admit. She was then transferred to the psychiatric services of the thirteenth *arrondissement* and ended up in the Maison Blanche Hospital, which she left two weeks later, still in a highly delirious state.

I wrote earlier of how much Gérard Garouste's book affected me. I wish Lucile had lived long enough to read it. First, because she loved painting, and second, because I'm sure that if she had read his book she would have felt less alone. Lucile drew a lot and sometimes painted, and left behind a certain number of texts and an impressive collection of reproductions of self-portraits from all periods and countries, including one by Garouste. She was born the same year as him and lived opposite the Palace nightclub where he painted the sets and also spent some of his nights. In *L'Intranquille*, Garouste describes his first delirious episode in detail. He too remembers it all: the way in which he fled the house where he was on holiday with his wife, the journey he made hitch-hiking and by train, giving his wedding ring to a stranger, throwing his identity card out of a taxi window, stealing money from his parents, the 500F notes he gave to children in the street, slapping a woman for no reason, the priest in Bourg-la-Reine whom he wanted to see at all costs, his outbursts of violence.

'Some delirious episodes are unforgettable,' he confesses, 'others are not.'

Lucile didn't forget anything about that day in January 1980 either. She wrote:

'That day my life crumbled irreversibly. I mistook hawks for handsaws, fish for fowl. I could no longer distinguish the real from the imaginary. I was about to spend 48 hours of hell before I got to the psychiatric hospital, ceaselessly wandering about, talking, acting, going too far.

'It was time with reverberations that would go very far and cost me very dear. It was irreversible time.'

The memory records everything, and sorting happens afterwards when the crisis has passed.

I have never before put 31 January into words, not in the diary that I kept then (I lacked the time, or the courage), nor in the letters I wrote to my friends in the days that followed, nor later in my first novel. The end of January still represents a sort of danger period for me (I discovered Lucile's body on 30 January). It's something which is rooted in the body's memory.

I found the account that my sister gave of what she experienced that morning when she was alone with Lucile overwhelming. I had forgotten it in part, probably because of the unbearable details it contained. Manon was nine and a half. She didn't receive any psychological help; she remained with the loneliness of what could not be spoken. It belongs to her; that too is probably part of her character.

One day a few months ago when I was taking a taxi to Roissy airport, the driver began asking me where I was going, the reason for my trip, my job . . . I rarely take taxis (my editor, who knows my phobia, links this to Lucile); the truth is that I always end up feeling sick in the back of cars. This morning however I made an effort to answer the driver, a little evasively at first, and then as he persisted, I ended up telling him that I was a writer.

'What caused that?' he asked me, exactly as though it were an illness, or even a punishment or a curse.

In the rear-view mirror he looked at me sympathetically.

What caused that?

When I meet readers in libraries, bookshops or schools, I'm often asked why I write.

I write because of 31 January 1980.

Confusedly, I know that the origin of my writing is there, in those few hours which caused our lives to fall apart, in the days which preceded it and the time of isolation which followed.

I remember hearing that my mother had the same illness as Barbara, Liane's sister, who for several years, in a desperate repeating cycle, veered between bouts of delirium and periods of profound apathy. The illness had been passed on from one to the other, that was all. As if it were as simple as that: hereditary madness passed from generation to generation by a complex route, a calamity which affected the women in the family and about which nothing could be done. Liane would sigh in the kitchen, with that sad look, her hands cradling her warm teacup. It was in the blood, it had to be coped with, it took patience; and after several years, Barbara had stabilised, had stopped going in and out of hospital, and came through it. And Liane would conclude by saying: 'Close the door, my princess. It's freezing.'

★

There were only a few weeks between the *Apostrophes* programme and Lucile's first crisis. I had never taken stock of this timing; in my memory these two events were not so close. That's not significant. Thanks to the INA archives, I was able to watch the programme again. I had forgotten what it was like. My memory was of the television room at Pierremont, imbued with the solemn tension of the moment. I think Lucile was there with us but I'm not sure. I felt emotional watching Barbara and Claude's performance, though I only vaguely knew them, the way you know people you meet at funerals and family get-togethers (which is to say, they were two complete strangers). They are both dead now. On *Apostrophes*, they are sitting side by side, as though they are joined; his attention is entirely on her, and vice versa; everything else seems of secondary importance. Both of them talk about the hollow years from which they have emerged, the series of committals, the pain he experienced when he had to sign the papers, the letters she sent from hospital asking for a divorce. She is beautiful and has incredible presence and much more charisma than him. He takes her hand several times, she smiles when he mentions his somewhat fickle past, 'Let him who has never done the same cast the first stone at me,' he adds with conviction. With great dignity, she laughs.

I had never read their book. I ordered it on the Internet, where you can still find it second-hand. There have always been very close ties between Barbara's family and my grandmother's. It was thanks to Barbara, I remembered, that Liane and Georges met. And then thanks to Georges that Barbara met Claude, her second husband. There was just three years' difference in age between the two sisters and they both raised large families, like their own mother. Though they were very different, it seems to me that they shared (except during Barbara's periods of illness) the same elemental force drawn from the earth, an inextinguishable energy, a gift for life. Both of them had faith in love and both laid claim to the limitless devotion which, they thought, a wife ought to show towards her husband. Both of them married men with strong personalities who needed to be the centre of attention. They were pious without being sanctimonious (their conception of religion, it seems to me, in no way excluded physical pleasures) and strongly marked by the education they had received.

In *Deux et la folie*, Barbara mentions the death of their two brothers one year apart, both scarcely out their teens: one following a war injury in Indochina which was mistreated, and the other from pneumonia after a swim in an icy river. By one of those detours that delirium takes, these deaths also came back during her first crisis, as though she bore some responsibility.

In the course of my research for this book, I learned that some of my grandmother's sisters were very probably sexually abused by their father when they were girls. Barbara makes no mention of that.

I have never really been interested in psychogenealogy nor in phenomena transmitted from one generation to another, which fascinate some of my friends. I don't know how these things (incest, child mortality, suicide, madness) might be passed on.

The fact is that they run all the way through families like pitiless curses, leaving imprints which resist time and denial.

L ucile stayed at Maison Blanche for twelve days. She received several visitors, including Forrest, some of her brothers and sisters, and friends from the Maison des Chats. A few days after her arrival, she was told of the death of Baptiste, Barbara and Claude's son. He had shot himself in the head. If the pact was genuine, Baptiste was part of it. He was the third and last of the so-called 'suicide wave'.

Lucile left Maison Blanche before the delirium subsided. She had only seen the psychiatrist twice, once on admission and once on discharge, and as a result of the many injections she had had, she hadn't suffered. Lisbeth enabled her to avoid a hospitalisation order by taking her home with her along with medication Lucile refused to swallow. The situation rapidly became impossible. To the great delight of Lisbeth's children, Lucile didn't do as she was told, she messed around, and kept coming up with new tricks and schemes to escape. Crawling across the carpet on all fours, she tried to make it to the door while her sister had her back turned and invented unlikely appointments in order to get out. When she was locked in, she said anything that went through her head in a continuous stream after her years of silence.

Gabriel had begun the process to regain custody of us.

Lucile, who had just got out of hospital and was still in a delirious state, made a first appearance before the judge. Accompanied by a friend and scarcely able to stand, she cried, laughed uproariously, made puns and noisily demanded a cigarette (though she had been recommended not to smoke). Eventually the judge gave her a Camel.

A background report was ordered.

One Saturday in the days that followed, Lucile rang us in Normandy. She asked to speak to each of us in turn, asked the same questions several times, kept changing her mind about which one of us she wanted to speak to, enquired about the weather. She asked Manon to describe her toys and made me repeat the same words, still convinced that I was the Delphic oracle. The conversation lasted over an hour. It was the only contact we had with her for several months.

Lucile eventually escaped from Lisbeth and fled to Barcelona, where she moved in with Milo's best friend. Henri and Nùria received her with great kindness, despite the agitated state she was in. They showed her the city, accompanied her on her adventures. In a few days she amassed a vast number of objects: fountain pens, painted plaster Jesuses, a collection of little cactuses.

At this time, Barthélémy, who worked for a supplement of *Libération*, had them publish the text which Baptiste had written a few days before his death.

Lucile returned to Paris, resumed her wandering, and gave money away in the street. Those close to her began to think that she was going to have to be hospitalised again. Lisbeth and Michel B., one of Violette's friends, spent a day with her in the hope of taking her gently to the emergency services at Saint-Antoine Hospital. Lucile demanded they stop at cafés, danced on tables, sang old songs by the sixties singer Sheila, delaying the moment of her imprisonment. Once she got there, she commented on the body of the doctor who admitted her and expressed concern about his mental health when she discovered that he was left-handed (as she was). In the ambulance which took her back to Maison Blanche, Lucile again sang at the top of her voice and ordered the driver to go faster (though she was usually terrified in cars).

A few days went by before Lucile was transferred to Belle-Allée clinic near Orléans, where she spent three or four months. A treatment plan was put in place, Lucile saw doctors several times a day but remained in a delirious state despite her medication.

In the texts which she wrote later, Lucile recalled the subjects of her fantasies: painting, the Philokalia, mythology (Aphrodite and Apollo), the architecture of Viollet-le-Duc, *Les Très Riches Heures du duc de Berry*.

(Another sentence I read in Gérard Garouste's book, said by his doctor: 'You have deliriums that stem from your cultural background.')

Lucile sent us some letters from Belle-Allée in which she tried to describe her life in the clinic, how she spent her time, the doctors who were treating her. We wrote back reassuringly, telling her about our schools, our activities, our new friends (Lucile kept all

our letters from when we were children; we found them in her flat
after her death).

After a few weeks, the delirium eventually subsided. It was followed
by shame; a grubby, guilty sense of shame that would never leave
her.

Lucile opened her eyes and saw her life in ruins. She was about
to lose custody of her children, she had spent money she didn't
have, she had said and done foolish things.

It had happened. It couldn't be fixed.

Several months later, when her condition seemed to have stabilised, Lucile eventually came out of the clinic. She returned to the
apartment on the rue du Faubourg-Montmartre and went back to
her job while her dismissal procedure was going through.

Shortly before the summer, the time came for us to see her again.
The weekend had been organised far in advance; it had been
arranged that she wouldn't come to get us alone. Gabriel drove us
to the station at Verneuil-sur-Avre. All three of us cried in the car.

In the train which we now took in the opposite direction, we tried
to prepare ourselves for the reunion ahead. Our apprehension grew
ever greater. We were unable to play any of our usual guessing games.

When we got to the Gare Montparnasse, we walked side by side
towards the exit, feeling more fear than joy.

★

Lucile was at the end of the platform, amid the bustling crowd, a tiny blonde figure wrapped in a navy blue coat. Lucile was there, with Violette and a friend, near us now, and suddenly there was no other face but hers, pale and thin. Lucile kissed us undemonstratively, none of us knew what to do with our arms, and our legs weren't holding up too well either.

We set off towards the metro. Lucile took Manon's hand. She was walking ahead of me. I looked at her back, how frail and fragile and broken she looked. She turned round and smiled at me.

Lucile had become a tiny little thing – breakable, glued together, patched up – irreparable, in truth.

Of all the images I have retained of my mother, this one is probably the most painful.

The custody assessment took place in the months following her discharge from the clinic. On several occasions we were asked to meet psychologists and psychiatrists, to take tests, answer questions, draw families and houses on blank sheets of paper and colour them in with felt-tips.

Lucile, Gabriel, his wife Marie-Anne, and some other family members were interviewed too.

At the end of the assessment, the medico-psychological report recommended that custody of the children be granted to Gabriel, with substantial visiting rights and overnight stays for Lucile.

At the same time, Lucile was dismissed from her job and had her bank account closed. She was thirty-three and had lost almost everything in life that kept her going.

For a few months she continued to pay for the apartment on the rue du Faubourg-Montmartre, which had become too big for her, in the hope that we would be coming back. She signed on, took an intensive English course, and let herself be lulled by a distant echo, which reached her only in snatches.

For several years, Lucile lived on antipsychotics.

Her expression was fixed, clouded over, as though a grimy film covered her eyes. Behind those eyes, you could guess at the pills taken to a set timetable, the drops diluted in glasses of water – and time stretching ahead of her, unchanging. You couldn't catch her eye; she stared at the ground or just above it, a little below the horizon.

Sometimes Lucile's mouth remained open without her realising and she would yawn wide enough to dislocate her jaw. Her hands trembled because of the medication, as did her leg when she was sitting down; it would jerk even more noticeably, in a way that she couldn't control. When Lucile was walking, with her arms folded at waist height, her hands looked like two corpses. Lucile was like everyone who takes high doses of antipsychotics: their eyes are the same, they stand in the same way, their movements look mechanical. They are far away, as though cocooned from the world; nothing seems able to reach them; their emotions are contained, regulated, controlled.

It was unbearable seeing Lucile like that. There were no words that could translate the feelings of revolt or pain, just sometimes the desire to shake her to get some reaction from her: a laugh, a sob, a tiny cry.

She didn't emerge from this state of lethargy until she returned to one of delirium a few years later. In the meantime, she was trying to survive, to fill the time, which was now so empty.

Violette would call her and encourage her to go out. She'd take her to the cinema, where Lucile nearly always fell asleep.

On the Sundays when we weren't there, Lucile would meet friends at the swimming pool. There, as elsewhere, it was a case of keeping her head above water.

★

Every other weekend, we took the train to see her. She would be waiting at the Gare Montparnasse. We'd catch the metro to Rue Montmartre, a station that's since been renamed and whose endless stairs would turn our legs to jelly, as if that were needed. Yet as the months passed, a tentative, fragile bond developed.

Lucile wanted to hear about our new life: we told her about our little brother, school, friends, neighbours, the horse, tap dancing, the dogs, the canteen – but we weren't really saying anything in our letters or face to face. There wasn't anything that could be said.

Lucile would invite our childhood friends round on those weekends, would be attentive to us, try in her way to make things nicer.

I rediscovered memories of a time long gone. I wandered with my friends on the boulevards, went to the cinema.

I think this was the period when, with some of my friends, I invented the game of 'Maître Capello', a parody of a TV programme, which we recorded on a tape recorder and was the source of much hilarity.

Lucile didn't read any more. She didn't go to the art exhibitions she used to love. When we weren't there, she lay on her bed for hours, staring into space. Lucile was being treated by a psychiatrist, who prescribed her drugs, and a psychotherapist, whom she saw twice a week and who was working with her long-term, though their sessions faced the obstacle of her silence. Lucile had nothing to say.

She was struggling to give us her least damaged, least exhausted side; she was struggling to remain in life. It was for us that Lucile got up and dressed, put make-up on. For us she went out and bought cakes for Sunday lunch.

Each act cost her dear; that was impossible for us to miss.

For a few months, Lucile had been looking for a secretarial job and had responded to three or four ads in her trembling handwriting. But the fact was she was incapable of getting through a job interview.

When she ran out of money to keep on the apartment on the rue du Faubourg-Montmartre, she moved in to a little two-room courtyard flat, on the rue des Entrepreneurs in the fifteenth *arrondissement*, with the support of some friends and relatives.

The following spring, the excitement about the 1981 presidential election seemed to draw Lucile out of her silence. For the first time in ages, she appeared concerned about something external to herself and us. She hesitantly expressed a wish – which was very rare – and tried to explain why to me. From these conversations I concluded that François Mitterrand was clearly the man of the future: our saviour. François Mitterrand personified renewal, *a fresh start* – words which were very precious to Lucile – all her hopes combined, tangible proof that she was still one of us. Mitterand's 'peaceful force' – that was what we needed – and for the walls of silence and loneliness to gently tumble down.

I had just turned fifteen. I rebelled against Gabriel the only way I could. I wanted to talk about the death penalty, I wanted to talk about social determinism, I wanted to talk about underdeveloped countries, denounce the limited life of provincial worthies. I turned up the volume on my record player to listen to my records, among which the singer Renaud figured prominently. Over and over he sang: 'Society, society, you won't get me.' I'd had enough of dreams of comfort and conformity, of peaceful middle-class life, of plush carpet and immaculate interiors: I had become a rebel.

At just after 8 p.m. on 10 May 1981, in the train taking us back from a febrile weekend with Lucile (we had gone right into the polling booth with her), a triumphant ticket inspector went through the carriages announcing that the left had won. Half the passengers cheered, while the rest greeted the news with appalled silence. Mobile phones didn't exist; we absorbed the messenger's words: yes, he was sure, he'd heard it on the driver's radio, which was linked to the control room; it was definite, absolutely certain, around 52 per cent of the vote. Between Versailles and Dreux stations, as the train travelled through the countryside, it struck me that we were saved. François Mitterrand was President of the Republic.

When we got off the train, our feet trod new ground. As darkness fell, a shining path had opened up before us, a path whose victories, twists and setbacks were still unknown. Gabriel had come to fetch us from the station. He was tense, as he always was when we came back from Paris, and he was tense because François Mitterrand had just won.

That evening, I fell asleep thinking of my mother. I imagined her in the Place de la Bastille, though I knew she was incapable of going there. I imagined her amid a jubilant, ever-growing crowd: Lucile dancing, twirling her floral skirt, Lucile happy.

A few months later, I listened over and over to the song by Barbara about that day in 1981 and the hopes it still embodied:

Look! Something has changed, the air seems lighter — it's indefinable.

Look! Under a sky that's clearing, everything's sunny — it's indefinable.

A man with a rose in his hand has opened the way to a different

future . . .

People want to talk, to love, to touch.

And start everything afresh.

Ultimately, I don't know what the point of all this research is, nor what will remain of the hours spent rummaging through cardboard boxes; listening to cassettes distorted with age; rereading administrative documents, police and medico-psychological reports, texts infused with pain; comparing sources, statements, photographs.

I don't know what *the cause of it is*.

But the further I go, the deeper my conviction that it was something I had to do, not as an act of rehabilitation, nor to honour, prove, re-establish, reveal or repair something, solely to get closer. Both for myself and for my children – who, despite my efforts, feel the weight of distant fears and regrets – I wanted to go back to the source of things.

And I wanted some trace of this quest, however futile, to remain.

I am writing this book because I now have the strength to examine what troubles and sometimes assails me, because I want to know what I am passing on. I want to stop being afraid that something will happen to us, as though we were living under a curse, and to be able to make the most of my good fortune, my energy, my happiness, without thinking that something terrible is going to destroy us and that sadness is forever waiting in the wings.

★

My children are growing up and even if it is very banal to say how amazing and overwhelming I find that, I will say it: my children are their own beings; their personalities make me feel awe and delight; I love a man whose path unexpectedly crossed mine (or the other way round), who is both very similar to and very different from me, whose unexpected love simultaneously fulfils, amazes and fortifies me. It is now 10.44 a.m. and I am sitting at my old PC, whose slowness I curse but whose memory I love. Today I know how fragile all this is and that now, with the strength I have regained, I must write to the end.

Tears can wait.

Approaching Lucile, whether very cautiously or with my sleeves rolled up, also means approaching other people, living people, with the risk of ending up more distant from them. My sister was one of the people I asked to talk to me about Lucile, to share their memories with me.

Manon told me about that January morning, and how impossible she found it for months afterwards to go to sleep in Lucile's presence, her childhood nights haunted by the fear that her mother would burst into her room to finish what she had begun. That affected me deeply.

Manon told me about the subsequent years from her point of view, the silent onlookers that we became, unable to stop Lucile's suffering.

Manon told me many other things which have nourished this book and which I hope I have not misrepresented.

Manon made me promise to destroy the recording of the long

conversation we had (which I did). Soon after, she sent me two texts that she had written, one following our meeting and the other just after Lucile's death.

Coming from Manon, who is so private, this was a splendid gift.

Of the period which followed Lucile's committal, few traces remain. The police report is wretched and relatively vague. The custody assessment that Gabriel gave me, addressed to the family court in Paris a year after Lucile was hospitalised, refers to the various interviews which led to a recommendation in Gabriel's favour. It describes in broad terms the personalities as they appeared to the psychiatrists, and compares the different viewpoints of my parents, both of whom were seeking custody. Lucile's concerns about her ex-husband's violence or the secluded environment in which she fears we would live are mentioned, as are Gabriel's doubts about his ex-wife's ability to look after us and the way we had previously been left to fend for ourselves. Both of us were careful not to reply to the question of whether we would prefer to live with our mother or our father. The psychiatrists emphasised our wish to stay out of parental conflict. And as for me, the personality test revealed a strong desire for independence.

What Lucile had to say about the months that followed her hospitalisation bear the mark of guilt and great sadness.

Of the weekends when we began to visit her again, she writes:

'Organising these two days worries me the whole fortnight: meeting at the Gare Montparnasse, the train, which is often late, what we're going to eat, and especially what we're going to do and talk about. With them too I have no voice. I don't know how to talk to them any more. I have fallen from my pedestal as a mother. Even face to face with them I no longer exist, yet seeing them is my only profound pleasure/pain in this life. Despair of these days flowing by one after the other, with no vital thread or chopped in pieces.

[...]

'I still have feelings for my children, but I can't express them. I can't express anything. I have become ugly, I don't give a damn, nothing interests me apart from finally reaching the time for sleep with my medication. Waking up is horrible. The moment when I go from unconsciousness to consciousness is a wrench. Forcing myself to have a shower, and find some acceptable old clothes to put on.'

Of Dr D., the analyst she saw twice a week for years, she writes:

'He's the first person in the world I trust. This is huge. I owe him great gratitude. I cry my distress to him in hushed tones. I don't hide my thoughts of suicide from him and as the months go by things emerge which will be sorted out for ever. My situation with my father, my mother and each of my brothers and sisters. Who benefits from it, who takes advantage of it. My self fragmented in that terrible group of siblings. New relationships to build, especially with my daughters.'

★

Among Lucile's things, we also found some papers about the custody assessment and the charges for it. On 2 December 1981, Lucile received a letter from the office of the lawyer who was looking after her case. I reproduce it here for its postscript, an incongruity within the judicial system, which perhaps sums Lucile up better than a whole book:

Dear Madam,

Following the hearing concerning your objection to costs, and so that you may avoid having to pay the assessment charges, I must ask you to seek legal aid, which will of course bring about the postponement of the hearing concerning the merits of your case.

PS – Maître J. thanks you for your kind thoughts and the drawing, whose choice of colours he greatly appreciated.

Photos from this time show what we had in common with other people: short hair, tight trousers, Benetton pullovers and cotton scarves, and what we couldn't have in common: Lucile's vacant expression, her hunched shoulders, her mouth, which was never entirely closed.

I cannot ignore how much the book I am currently writing disturbs me. My troubled sleep is concrete proof of it.

After a night of waking myself up with loud crying (which hadn't happened to me for years), I try to convince the man I love not to worry. I dreamed I was being locked up.

Yet I continue to fire off emails, both urgent and impromptu, to all and sundry, asking for names, dates, details. In other words, I'm getting on everyone's nerves.

Lucile had withdrawn, far from us and far from everything. She was no more than an extra in a film whose script seemed to elude her more each day, standing in the middle of the set, not hearing when she was asked to come back to the centre or move to the side. She no longer captured the light; she ignored it and sought a place where she would be completely unnoticed and could slumber with her eyes open, but without people thinking she was absent or had given up.

There was nothing François Mitterrand could do.

In the course of 1982, Lucile, who had still not found a job, opened a strange junk shop with a friend of Justine's on the rue Francis-de-Pressensé near the L'Entrepôt cinema. The premises were small and rather characterless. There they assembled trinkets, lamps, boxes, carafes, other miscellaneous objects and a few cosmetic products, arranged side by side with no connection between them. Everyone donated what they could; cupboards, cellars and attics were emptied to provide a minimum level of stock. The almost empty shop was open every day except Sunday. Lucile and Noémie took it in turns to be there and were rarely disturbed by a customer. Sometimes a passer-by, prompted by adventurous curiosity, pushed open the door of 'Lucky Dip'. A few months earlier, Justine had opened the Pleasure Boat nearby, a bar and restaurant, where the dish of the day, made by Justine herself, soon became a great hit. Lucile was bored stiff at the back of her shop; she was visited by the local winos, and, in slow motion, continued to lead her uncertain existence, which intersected with ours twice a month.

For the weekend, Lucile would fill the fridge with things we liked, and give us money to go to the cinema or buy a waffle. Lucile looked on as we lived our lives, chatted or laughed with our friends. Lucile listened distractedly to our inconsequential stories, Lucile listened to us on the phone, arranging to meet up, organising outings. Lucile watched us finishing our maths exercises, our French home-work. She never asked us anything; she demanded nothing of us. Lucile didn't judge us; she refrained from commenting on our child-ish or adolescent whims, observing us from a distance.

We were living beings, she could feel that; life in us had endured.

For the weekend, the whole of her self was mobilised in order to cope.

Sometimes a fleeting glance, a brief frown, a smile would remind us of the woman she had once been.

At Christmas and for the long weekends at Ascension, Pentecost and All Saints' Day, we continued to go to Pierremont, where our family would gather en masse: uncles, aunts, brothers, sisters, cous-ins, always supplemented by some friend who was a little bit pale, depressed, or lacking in red blood cells.

Liane and Georges never lost their appetite for entertaining on a large scale. If there was enough for fifteen, there was enough for twenty.

We took the train with Lucile as far as Laroche-Migennes, where Liane would come to pick us up in one of the old Renault 4s that she drove until they fell apart. I sat in the front; Lucile was scared in cars. It was best to keep your legs up: the floor was open and the road flashed by under your feet.

In the blue bathroom at Pierremont, I would watch Liane and her set ritual on emerging from the shower: she'd rub herself with an exfoliating glove, smear her body with a thick layer of Nivea, then put on her first bra, followed by a second, the first pair of pants, then a second, her girdle, bodystocking, a short slip and a long one (I'm not exaggerating). It's like an icebox in this house, my princess. In pride of place in a plastic mug on the shelf were her seven toothbrushes. Liane had one for each day of the week: Monday's was blue, Tuesday's red, Wednesday's yellow and so on, according to a precise rota she had completely mastered. Liane reckoned that toothbrushes had a right to a rest: six days between two appearances allowed the bristles to recover properly and guaranteed all of them the longevity they deserved. (I'll take this opportunity to mention in a different, but to me equally fascinating, context, the system of tension clips that Liane devised and used under the mattress on her bed so that the fitted sheet was pulled extremely tight. The elasticated corners of the sheet intended to do this were not enough. Liane couldn't bear wrinkles.)

In the bathroom at Pierremont, in the interplay of reflections between the bathroom cabinet and the huge mirror on the wall, you could see yourself from behind. I spent a certain amount of time, depending on my age, studying my hair or else the shape of my bottom.

In the blue bathroom at Pierremont, after an interminable game of Trivial Pursuit, we proceeded in small groups to our evening ablutions. Lucile had gone to bed long ago; I shared these moments of intimacy with Violette, Justine or Lisbeth. We swapped toiletries, discussed brands, nabbed each other's cotton wool, shampoo, soap, cotton buds, almond oil, moisturiser, rose water, oh my, that smells nice!

In the bathroom at Pierremont, and also in the yellow kitchen, we talked about lost loves, suitors, aspirants, the passage of time (and of sorrows), the walk we might take along the canal, the new design of woollen pyjamas perfected and knitted by Liane, forthcoming birthdays and holidays, the fresh eggs we needed to get from the farm, the joint of lamb that had to be taken from the freezer first thing.

In the blue bathroom at Pierremont one winter evening, Violette explained to me with utmost seriousness her own vision for the preservation of toothbrushes. Unlike her mother, Violette neither advocated nor practised toothbrush diversification. She opted by contrast for a single specimen of superior quality. According to her, conserving the bristles depended on careful and meticulous drying, preferably with a hand towel washed with fabric softener.

In the blue bathroom at Pierremont, given how many of us there were, you put your toilet bag down wherever you could, on the end of a shelf or on the floor. Whatever happened, you knew you wouldn't find it again in the same place and it wasn't out of the question that it would be removed entirely. Because the blue bathroom at Pierremont was first and foremost Tom's domain; Lucile's youngest brother's rituals were impossible to ignore. Tom took several baths and showers each day at set times, which he pinned up on the outside of the bathroom door. Tom had succumbed to a real passion for the toiletries, after-shave lotion, soaps and shower gels, which were always coming on to the market, offering a multiplicity of fragrances and the promise of manliness. Tom organised his territory as he saw fit. And you could be sure there was no question of getting in his way.

Tom had learned to read and write. He could count and add up. He knew the theme tunes of every American TV series and *Au théâtre ce soir* by heart. Tom loved *Columbo*, Michel Sardou and *Ric Hochet*, and was beside himself with delight when his brothers and sisters visited. He kept his room meticulously tidy, closely followed premier league football, was a passionate supporter of Auxerre, and on championship days, noted down each team's score on blank pieces of paper. In the same way, Tom recorded a variety of information on slips of paper, which he then put into folders. Tom, in spite of his disability, was viewed by his family as a sort of intellectual, whose humour, talent for imitation and ability to connect ideas never ceased to amaze us.

Georges had spent hours with him, accompanying every stage of his development, and had fought to get him into school. Georges had made Tom a humorous boy, not one of whose neurones went to waste. Tom was, I think, his father's greatest achievement.

★

Meals in Pierremont were both our main activity and our main topic of conversation: what we had eaten the day before, what we would eat the next day, what we would eat on a future visit and which recipe would be used. In addition, we spent the day in the kitchen, planning, preparing, clearing up, loading and unloading the dishwasher, making cakes, tarts, sauces, ice cream, desserts; we went into raptures at the thirteen or fourteen flavours of Liane's home-made ice cream; we stopped to have tea, coffee, an aperitif, a herbal infusion; we kneaded, stirred, simmered; talked about other people, our studies, illnesses, weddings, births, divorces, redundancies; we proclaimed truths in a lofty tone, corrected and contradicted one another, nudged each other, and we rebelled against the standard method of making seafood vol-au-vents.

Voices in Pierremont always ended up being raised, doors slammed, and just as it was about to come to blows, the apple-shaped kitchen timer would go off, reminding us that it was time to get the gratin out of the oven.

Beside us, sitting on a stool in silence, Lucile asserted her right to abstain from the rule of the kitchen. She didn't have a view on anything. She sometimes agreed to peel a few potatoes.

I wish I could describe this house, which I loved so much, the dozens of photos of us all, at every age and from every period, jumbled up and stuck on the stair wall; the poster of Tom beside Patrice Martin, holding the Handisport waterskiing trophy he had just won; the poster of Liane on a mono-ski at the age of seventy-five, a jet of water accompanying her slalom; her Barbara Cartland collection reserved for her (frequent) sleepless nights; Georges's collection of bells stored in the hall; my grandmother's over-abundance of kitchen equipment – she owned and hung onto every kitchen utensil and gadget invented in the past fifty years.

I wish I could describe this house which was open to the four winds and where the building work never ended; it was like a tired, irascible old lady whom nothing – no repainting, repair, renovation, though often carried out over many years and at the cost of great human effort – could ever satisfy. As I knew it, the house at Pierremont, with its flaking paint and spiders' webs, remained a sort of magnificent ruin, racked with rheumatism, full of draughts, and where lorries frequently came to grief. For the most singular characteristic of this old building was its location, at the end of a drive which was a direct continuation of the line of a major highway. And so several times in the middle of the night, a tired or inattentive driver was surprised by the tight bend and came thundering through the main gate with a sharp squeal of brakes. Later the council had concrete crash-barriers built in front of the entrance.

In Pierremont when we were children we slept with our cousins in the so-called 'four-bed room', which contained a minimum of six beds and could fit in as many as eight on especially busy days. When heavy lorries went by, the windows shook and rattled noisily, while through the slats of the shutters, we watched the dazzling beams of the headlights dance on the ceiling.

In summer, Liane and Georges went to a small village in Gard about fifteen miles from La Grande-Motte. Georges and his nephew Patrick had bought a barn a few years earlier, which they had done up in order to be able to accommodate as many people as possible. For lack of funds, the original plan for a hotel-restaurant had been shelved and Georges, at a difficult time, had to sell his shares to his nephew, who then became sole owner. The Poirier family nonetheless enjoyed a group invitation for the month of August, as a result of which we spent several summers with Patrick's family. In the course of those weeks, uncles, aunts, brothers, sisters, cousins, nephews and nieces passed through Gallargues, in addition to which there was always some friend who was broke, run down, getting themselves together, who hadn't had a holiday for one, two or even four years, who was passing through and in the end prolonged his or her stay. The total headcount could reach thirty-five, including those sleeping in tents.

The set-up was precise and known to everyone: every day a couple of adults – if possible comprising one of either sex but not necessarily linked by marriage or in a known sexual relationship – with the help of two children and/or adolescents, took charge of the domestic duties for the day: shopping, cleaning, cooking dinner, tidying up for the next day. The rota of couples on duty was arranged at the start of the stay. Apart from those exhausting days, idleness was guaranteed.

★

During the summers following Lucile's first committal, we joined Liane and Georges for two or three weeks in the big house in Gallargues. Lucile didn't have enough money to take us anywhere else and she would probably have found it impossible to spend the holidays alone with us. She knew how much we loved this communal interlude, seeing our cousins again, those huge meals where it was hard to count the ever-changing number of guests.

Every morning, armed with cool-boxes and towels, the family would gather first on the banks of the Ponant (a lake which is linked to the Mediterranean and belongs to the commune of La Grande-Motte), then a few hours later half of us would decamp to the real beach at Grand Travers. The women wore bikinis and spread monoi-scented suncream on their tanned skin; they chatted and smoked while the children played at the water's edge or quarrelled about who would get in the boat. Georges now had a mid-range speedboat with a 60-horsepower engine.

At around eleven o'clock, a radiant Liane would come down in her Renault 4, take off her bizarre orange plastic sunglasses, don a life-jacket and slalom on her mono-ski while astonished holiday-makers looked on. Every day she wore a differently coloured one-piece, chosen each year from the Trois Suisses catalogue, which showed off her generous bust and her narrow waist. Liane had a whole collection of them.

Tom, after months of mental conditioning and intensive training, had finally managed to rise out of the water on his skis with his family's wildly enthusiastic encouragement. In time, he had learned to cut through the waves and mono-ski and Georges was now training him for the French disabled championships.

Wearing a bandana, which earned him the nickname 'Pirate', a sunburned Georges spent most of the day at the wheel of his speedboat, calling out to some, teasing others, demanding that the women around him went about topless. In the course of these summers, Georges had become the star of Ponant. Thanks to this aura and despite having no qualification, he had decided to teach waterskiing. This increased his notoriety, enabled him to meet people and to pay for the petrol for the skiers in the family. Georges was funny and patient; he was a good teacher and his waiting list kept growing. The lake was his domain; here as elsewhere, Georges was impossible to ignore.

He devised all sorts of practical jokes for his grandchildren, the most memorable of which was probably 'the laughing cassette'. In the garden at Gallargues, Georges recruited about ten volunteers from whoever happened to be available. Around a microphone, in a carefully planned crescendo, we chuckled, tittered and clucked, the hilarity growing until genuine, collective, uncontrollable laughter made us all double up. Once the cassette had been recorded, the fun could begin. Around La Grande-Motte, Georges would pull up at a red light in his Renault 21, with its windows down. Inside, two, three or four of us, looking gloomy, adopted the same stubborn expression at Georges's command. Then Georges would turn the cassette on and set the volume as high as it would go. We meanwhile had to remain stony-faced, raising not as much as an eyebrow. Lugubrious. With blank expressions, we watched for the reactions in the cars beside us, which we eventually turned and looked at, with mournful expressions, while inside our car the cacophony of laughter redoubled. Given how hot it was, most people drove around with their windows down. Once they had identified the source of the hilarity, they stared at us, craning their necks, looked at each other in puzzlement, and usually ended up laughing themselves. Sometimes someone would jump out at the last minute amid a chorus of horns (the lights would have changed to green in the meantime) and ask us what radio station we were tuned to.

In the evening, back at the house in Gallargues, Georges rang a bell to announce it was time for aperitifs and for getting together. With sparkling Listel we toasted the day's feats on the water, commented on imminent arrivals and departures, reorganised room allocations and chatted. I loved this house, too: the people, the noise, the hours in the scorching sun, evening walks through Gallargues's narrow alleys, the festivals and dances in neighbouring villages.

Yet despite all the laughter, the arguments, the yelling and memories of explosive events (the time that Georges in front of thirty people forcibly ejected a representative from Lepetit, the cheese company – whose guest he was I don't know – who had had the misfortune to defend pasteurised Camembert), these noisy, communal summers never made us entirely forget Lucile, there yet not there, her way of being right in the middle of the commotion without ever joining in.

★

Lucile countered the surrounding hubbub with her exhausted silence.

When I think about those times, a memory comes back to me which even today remains bitter:

In Paris, alone in her little apartment, Lucile had eventually bought a television set. Every Wednesday, she would watch *Dallas*, then in its heyday. She never missed an episode and made no secret of it.

When the family got together, mentioning *Dallas* in front of Lucile became a running joke, a routine gag. For in order to make Lucile smile – exactly like triggering a conditioned response in an animal through some Pavlovian reflex – all you had to do was sing her the theme tune. And everyone, my cousins, aunts, even Georges, would join in.

Then Lucile, who had read Maurice Blanchot and Georges Bataille, and whose smiles were so rare, would smile broadly, even laugh. It broke my heart.

In a blind rage, I dreamed of lashing out at them, trampling on them. I hated them all, because it struck me then that they were all responsible for what she had become, and they were laughing themselves silly about it.

The fog Lucile found herself in lasted nearly ten years.

During this time, she gave up her shop on rue Francis-de-Pressensé (where no one, apart from a few friends and two or three brave souls ever ventured) and found a job as a secretary with an educational publisher. I think – though I'm not sure – that she was introduced to the firm of Armand Colin by a young woman she had met in this neighbourhood. Her work consisted mainly of typing out manuscripts and various administrative tasks. Lucile didn't do too badly and was confirmed after her probation period. Working, there or elsewhere, became a trial for her, as was the rest of her life, and at the end of every weekend, the prospect of the new week paralysed her with anxiety and she felt as though she would never get through it.

I think that afterwards, when Lucile had emerged from this period, these ten years constituted a single block to her, blank and featureless, whose different phases she couldn't distinguish, a single block of which she had a painful, stiff memory, uniformly dark, though she experienced two manic phases during it.

The first occurred after my *baccalauréat*. I had just come back to live in Paris and had moved in with her in her little two-room apartment on the rue des Entrepreneurs. Lucile had put her palettes and mattress in the living room and I slept in one of the single beds in

Manon's room. Manon was still living in Normandy and came down every other weekend. I had just begun a foundation course, was discovering student life and getting reacquainted with the rhythm of Paris. Lucile's regular, monotonous life ill-concealed her inner turmoil; she sometimes emerged from her torpor with a jolt, brutally, in the middle of a sentence or some passing fancy. Little by little the all-too-familiar signs of a relapse appeared. Lucile began to fuss about, buying new kitchen equipment (including a new SEB pressure cooker), talked about pay rises she was going to get which seemed exceptionally high, as well as a one-off bonus that would enable us to go to Djerba for the Christmas holidays. Lucile came and went with increasing frequency on various pretexts, devised plans and projects, and then one night, she didn't come home. I waited up late for her. At last she burst in with that distant look in her eye, and told me about the crazy evening she'd spent at Immanuel Kant's place, and her first meeting with Claude Monet, which wouldn't be her last, she was sure, because he was charming and they had got on so well together. I rang Lucile's sisters. Justine took the initiative and did all she could to inform Lucile's work, where people were starting to be surprised by her sudden agitation and the money she was handing out in the corridors to 'poor people' who were no poorer than she was.

Quite quickly arrangements were made and Lucile was taken to a ward in Sainte-Anne Hospital, where she spent several weeks.

During the visits I was soon allowed to make to the hospital on the edge of the city and yet within it (for Sainte-Anne is a city within a city), I discovered a type of misery and abandonment I didn't know existed. One day while I was reading, I wondered what the exact meaning of the word 'dereliction' was and looked it up in the dictionary. I realised I had already seen it in the flesh. Here men and women dragged themselves around the overheated corridors, spent whole days in front of a badly tuned television, rocked on chairs or hid under blankets little better than prison ones. Some of them had been there for years and had no prospect of going elsewhere, because they represented a danger to themselves or others, because there was nowhere else to put them or because their families had long since given up. When I came back from these visits, haunted by this atmosphere, I would write about the doors locked behind me, the bunches of jangling keys, the patients roaming the corridors, the sound of transistor radios, the woman who kept repeating 'My God, why have you forsaken me?', the man who asked anyone who came within sight for a cigarette up to ten times, the mechanical, loose-jointed bodies, flesh gone flabby through inactivity and boredom, the fixed stares, dragging feet, these beings whom nothing seemed able to free from this, whose medication stopped them screaming.

Within a few days, Lucile had got to know everyone on the ward and was keen to introduce me to them every time I visited. Mrs R., Mr V., Nadine, Hélène, Mrs G., a whole tour which generally concluded with a tall woman dressed in black, who would look at me in the same wild-eyed way and repeat to Lucile, 'Your daughter is beautiful', as though she were pronouncing a curse. Lucile shared her room with a Hungarian woman with transparent skin, whose face seemed to have escaped the effects of time.

I was seventeen. I knew nothing about mental illness. The distressed looks which caught my eye in this ward sometimes haunted me for days.

Within a few weeks, Lucile obtained permission to go on outings. One Saturday afternoon I went to collect her from Sainte-Anne, where she was waiting for me, sitting on a chair with her hands clasped on her little handbag. We spent a few hours out, after taking the bus back to the area where we lived. In Monoprix, a smooth, singsong voice offered us crazy prices, 50 per cent reductions on all household linens – sheets, towels, quilt covers – crazy prices which we had only a few minutes left to take advantage of. As far as craziness was concerned, I was terrified by the idea of Lucile running off, escaping my vigilance, or not wanting to return to the hospital. But when evening came, Lucile started looking at her watch. She was afraid of being late; she had to get back in time for dinner and her medicine. Lucile didn't have to be asked to go back. She felt all right there, sheltered from herself. She was so tired.

There would be other outings, other afternoons stolen from the heavy air of the ward, other moments of freedom, far from the empty hours spent in the common room where no breeze ever stirred the air.

In the train that took us to Pierremont for the weekend, Lucile, whose delirium had not entirely gone, talked to everyone in broken English to the delight of the whole carriage. I had no idea how to stop her, and mouthed lame excuses behind her back. Lucile wanted to sit here and not there, then there and not here. She asked other passengers to change seats, others to move their bags – 'Would you mind please to move your bag somewhere else because you know it is difficult for me to stay here, I mean in a train. I'm sorry I'm desease you know, but let me introduce you my daughter she is very gentle but a bit susceptible.'

The following Christmas, there was no more talk of Djerba or the beach; Manon joined me in Paris and we took Lucile to Pierremont, where magnificent festivities had been in preparation for weeks. This year the theme for Christmas Eve was based on three colours: red, white and silver. We obeyed the dress code, exchanged all sorts of symbolic gifts and splendid 'vouchers', written with love, as everyone was broke. Lucile had resumed her role as extra and didn't say a word.

When Lucile got out of the hospital a few weeks later, I left her apartment. I didn't want to live with her any more. I embarked on a series of more or less happy cohabitations, as opportunities arose, which lasted almost two years.

Lucile went back to work. They had been compassionate enough to keep her on.

Manon started coming for weekends again.

I dreamed of a calm time for her, a chance to catch her breath, but I had nothing I could offer her apart from my presence at Lucile's when she went there, the length of a lunch, a walk, a dinner, and my simple and probably blind desire to get us out of there.

★

This was also the time when Lucile met Edgar, a watercolour painter ravaged by alcohol, whose talent hadn't saved him at all. Edgar became her lover. They drank together – litres and litres of beer. Lucile swelled up before our eyes and grew even further away from us.

I woke up in the middle of the night and sat up on the side of my bed. I was searching for an image in the darkness, a voice in the silence. Gradually the memory which had disturbed my sleep came back to me: a super-8 film that Gabriel made before we lived with him, one of those films he shot during the school holidays with a plot and incidents we loved inventing. To be more precise, it was about me in one of those films, my unbearable, shrill voice. Little by little, the memory became sharper; I wasn't entirely sure of my recollection, it was something about writing and madness. Maybe I was making it up, maybe I had reconstructed this sequence, invented it. I needed to see the film to be sure. I had a copy of it somewhere on DVD, buried in the mess in my living room. I forced myself not to leap up at 3 a.m., lay down again in the dark, tossed and turned, waited till the next day to undertake the search which would free me from doubt.

This morning I found the film. I must have been thirteen and Manon nine when my father made it. I can't pinpoint it with certainty, but it dates from *before*; before Lucile's illness and our sudden move to Normandy. With humorous direction from our stepmother and a classical music backing-track added in the edit by my father, we parodied a television talk show, a cross between *Apostrophes* and *Le Grand Échiquier*. Before she herself fell into the abyss which cost her her life, our stepmother Marie-Anne was a very beautiful woman of considerable imagination. The sequence is entirely improvised; none of it was rehearsed. Marie-Anne first interviews Manon, who plays Cunégonde Gertrude, a singer with an international reputation, just before she opens at Olympia for a four-week run. With a boa wound around her neck and pencilled eyebrows, Manon's Edith Piaf manner is hilarious. The adorable little girl she was, hesitant in her role as star, moves me to tears. When Marie-Anne mentions the rumours of a romance involving her (there is talk of the TV presenter Yves Mourousi and Prince Charles), Manon replies that she could win a hundred other hearts. A bit later, Marie-Anne begins the next interview. This evening, she says, she has the pleasure of welcoming Jeanne Champion, a writer whose books have been translated internationally and whose thirteenth novel, *The Montaurian Brothers*, is a bestseller. I appear on the screen, all made up, my lips painted and my eyes darkened, while Marie-Anne describes my cruel childhood, marked by my mother's repeated committals and my father's alcoholism, in short, the years of sorrow from which it seems I freed myself through writing. 'Some passages are very tough,' she adds by way of warning. I answer a few questions, add that the novel has just been translated in the United States by Orson Welles (probably the first American name that came to mind; we just about manage not to giggle). A little later, Manon improvises a song (with hilarious lyrics) while I pretend to read out an extract from my novel, which I make up as I go along, despite finding it increasingly hard not to laugh. It was this voice which came back to me in my sleep, this put-on voice mimicking melodrama, this terrible voice which talks about a 'maaahd-house'. There is something pathetic about my appearance which I cannot define, beyond the strange premonition contained in my stepmother's questions. I am between two states – childhood and adolescence, combat and renunciation – I am wearing a horrible brace on my teeth and can't stop fidgeting. I hate this film, my voice, my mannerisms, my bare shoulders, the amount of jewellery I'm wearing.

(In a state of doubt, I have just checked on the Internet that Jeanne Champion exists. The real Jeanne Champion paints, has written six novels and did indeed publish a book called *The Montaurian Brothers* in 1979.)

Another memory came back to me in the course of the day. A long time ago, along with the father of my children, who is a director, I devised a short film project for which I wrote the screenplay. It described the first day trip made by a woman who was hospitalised at Sainte-Anne, whose daughter, terrified by the thought that her mother might escape, came to get her and took her to Paris. The sounds, the voices, the scraps of dialogue from the television, the announcements in shops, conversations overheard on the bus, played a central role. We sent it to the National Cinematography Centre for a grant and by some miracle the screenplay cleared the first hurdle. We went crazy. It was rejected subsequently and returned to us with this comment: 'The description of the psychiatric environment is not realistic.'

Manon told me the other day that several people (notably our father and brother) had asked her if she had a problem with me writing about Lucile, if it didn't worry her, disturb or unsettle her or whatever. Manon said that the book would be my vision of things, that was my business, it belonged to me, just as Violette had said to me that she would be happy to read about my Lucile. Manon today possesses that form of wisdom, beyond her wounds.

I haven't written about how, after my return to Paris and Lucile's stay at Sainte-Anne, I stopped feeding myself for an academic year, to the point of feeling death within my body. That was in fact exactly what I wanted: to feel death within my body. At the age of nineteen, weighing 5 stone 9lbs and measuring 5 ft 8½ inches, I was admitted to hospital in a state of malnutrition and almost in a coma.

In 2001, I published a novel which tells the story of a young woman who is hospitalised for anorexia: the cold which takes her over, being fed through a nasogastric tube, the encounters with other patients, the progressive return of sensations and feelings, being cured. *Days without Hunger* is a partly autobiographical novel in which I wanted to maintain – apart from some flashbacks – a unity of time, place and action. The construction took precedence and none of the secondary characters really existed. The novel has an element of fiction and, I hope, poetry.

My current strategy strikes me as both more risky and more futile. These days there always comes a point when the tools fall from my hands, when the act of reconstruction escapes me, because I am seeking a truth which is located outside me, which is beyond my reach.

★

Anorexia is not simply a matter of some girls' desire to look like the – admittedly increasingly thin – models who populate women's magazines. It is often overlooked that fasting is a powerful and inexpensive drug. The state of malnutrition numbs the pain, the emotions and feelings, and functions initially as a protection. Restrictive anorexia is an addiction which makes the sufferer believe she has control when in fact it is leading her to her own destruction. I was lucky to meet a doctor who was aware of that at a time when most anorexics were shut up between the four walls of an empty room with a weight contract as the only thing on the horizon.

I'm not going to revisit this period of my life here; all that interests me is the effect it may have had on Lucile, its impact.

Lucile, more powerless than ever, was the distant spectator of my collapse. Without a gesture, with no word of anger or sorrow, without being able to express anything at all, all the time that I was falling, Lucile faced me, without words, yet without turning away. Lucile, whose tardy words, 'But you're going to die!' and the tone of powerlessness with which she said them, revealed to me the impasse I was in.

A few years later, when I was a mother myself, I often thought of the pain I had inflicted on my own mother.

A few weeks before I was taken in to hospital, Lucile's psychiatrist, to whom she must at the very least have mentioned the situation, asked her to bring me along with her. Lucile rang me. She insisted. Dr A. thought it could help us; I ought to do it for her if not for myself.

I followed Lucile into his office. I had no desire to be there. I couldn't bear any of it; all of it made me beside myself, I had nothing to do with these psychiatrists, psychoanalysts and other psychotherapists who had not been able to get Lucile out of her distress, each one was as bad as the next, all losers, who had turned my mother into a robot. Dr A. asked me some questions which I have forgotten. I was tense, on the defensive. I didn't want to talk to this man, to enter into any kind of pact with him; I wanted to show him how much I disapproved of him, how I wasn't taken in by him at all. What could he do, apart from prescribe some additional drops to dissolve in a glass of water? Suddenly Dr A. asked me to sit on Lucile's knee. Playing for time, I asked him to repeat what he'd said. I was thinking, who does he think he is, the idiot? I was wearing jeans made for a twelve-year-old. I can no longer recall the colour. The question had taken my breath away. He repeated gently: I would like you to sit on your mother's knee. So I got up and sat down on Lucile's knee and in less than ten seconds I went to pieces. It had been months since I had cried, protected as I was by the cold, my low blood temperature, hardened by loneliness. I was starting to go deaf from malnutrition and in the course of a day, a very limited amount of information reached my brain.

But this was a wave, a breaker, high tide.

While I was sobbing on my mother's knee, Dr A. suggested she give me a Kleenex. Lucile rummaged in her bag and handed me a tissue. Dr A. said: 'You see, Mrs Poirier, your daughter does still need you.'

★

Both equally stunned, we left his office and walked side by side down a boulevard in the eighteenth *arrondissement* whose name I have forgotten. I didn't put this scene in my first novel for a reason I have also forgotten; perhaps at that time I felt it was still too raw. In that book written in the third person, in which the character Laure is my double, I described however how *her* mother came to see her in hospital several times a week, tried to find words and gradually recovered the power of speech. And how Laure's mother, brutally thrust back into her role, had dragged herself back from the depths to regain a semblance of life.

Another day when we were having lunch together, Manon came back to the conversation we had had about Lionel Duroy and how he had been rejected by his siblings after his novel came out. Manon still supported my project, reiterated her support, but she'd been thinking about it and she was afraid. Afraid that I would paint too harsh, too negative a portrait of Lucile. For her part, it wasn't a case of denial but propriety. For example, she confessed that the scene in *Days without Hunger* in which the mother, having drunk too much beer and unable to get out of her chair, wets herself, seemed very brutal to her.

I reminded Manon that that actually happened (as if she could have forgotten).

That argument was absurd of course and didn't justify anything. My memory contains other scenes involving Lucile, more brutal still, which I shall probably never write down.

Before Lucile returned to a state of delirium again, all three of us experienced a period of calm, a strange interlude: a fore-taste of peace.

A few months after I got out of hospital, Manon – whose life at Gabriel's had reached crisis point, making staying there impossible – landed up at Lucile's in the middle of the school year. Lucile seemed to be doing better; she was applying herself at work, had stopped drinking and was beginning to communicate a little again.

The following year, to avoid having to go all the way across Paris every day (Gabriel had moved to Neuilly and Manon had contin-ued to attend a school there), my sister started at a high school in the fifteenth *arrondissement*.

With Manon, Lucile danced to Les Rita Mitsouko, took English classes provided by the city council and shared her thoughts on stupid soap operas on television.

With Manon, Lucile rediscovered a sort of lightness.

At this time, I was sharing an apartment with a friend a stone's throw from Lucile's, and after a few months of indecision, I had gone back to my studies. I was gradually learning to slow down, to control my dizziness, to accept my own vulnerability, to tame the appetite for life that had consumed me.

Lucile was trying to show us both a new side of herself; she was considerate and attentive; she had started cooking and devising new recipes again; and every week she left me a bag of the sweet things I loved hanging from her window.

After my classes, I would go to the rue des Entrepreneurs for tea or an impromptu dinner, or to see something at the film-club; there I'd find my mother and sister, whose relationship was gradually assuming a new shape and regaining visible form. We told each other what was happening in our lives; Lucile always offered less than us, was more circumspect. On Sundays we went to the cinema at Beaugrenelle or Kino-panorama; in spring we made the most of the first sunshine, lying on the grass on Saint-Lambert Square or sitting on the benches in Georges Brassens park. In both summer and winter, we walked for hours.

Lucile always loved walking in Paris, exploring new districts, stopping for a fruit juice or hot chocolate, setting off again, going on, allowing herself to be carried along and intoxicated by physical tiredness. Walking is probably the activity which Manon and I, together and separately, most often shared with her.

This was a calmer period, yet all at once the light could still go out of Lucile's eyes and she could shut herself off; gloom could over-whelm her on a rainy day; Lucile could suddenly abandon her reserve and vent her anger because she felt rejected or overlooked. We knew how much of Lucile's life came down to a matter of dosage, how fragile it all was. But Lucile was there, in her own way: a precious presence that never intruded. This was a time of calm which allowed us to recover our strength.

But once again, Lucile was caught in the backwash of her pain and guilt. She shattered the beginnings of an *after*, the signs that things could be rebuilt.

When Manon got back from holiday, she realised that Lucile had started drinking again. She tried to talk to her about it, but Lucile replied that she was forty years old, had no friends, no lover, and a job that bored her to tears, so it was understandable and even desirable for her to take refuge in the realm of the imagination. Lucile didn't hide anything from us. Quite the reverse: we couldn't miss the provocative way she opened bottle after bottle of beer in front of us, or pinned up an article in the bathroom about the risks associated with the regular consumption of Rohypnol, a sleeping pill she had been on for years, and the dangers of mixing it with alcohol. I saw her behaviour above all as a sort of cry for help, a refusal to see us grow up and away from her, a confused desire to reverse our roles, to attract our attention. For several weeks, Manon kept me informed about Lucile's demeanour, which became more mysterious and evasive. As far as her fantasies were concerned, Lucile went on about the malevolent intentions she ascribed to the few people around her, claimed she was being spied on and was the victim of various attempts to swindle her, not to mention the gas, which she had discovered left on in her apartment several times.

Then Lucile got it into her head that Manon was smoking crack and threw her out. She sent her back to live with her father.

★

Lucile, along with seventeen other employees, had just been made redundant as part of a down-sizing by the publisher for whom she had worked for several years. Anxiety overwhelmed her.

In a state of distress which boded ill, Lucile, aggressive and touchy, came up with more and more mysteries concerning her private life; she invented lovers' trysts and mysterious plans that were only hinted at in our presence; she decided to give notice on her apartment, which she wanted to leave though she couldn't reveal why, although it was due to a piece of good news which meant she would be able to shower us both with gifts. A few days later, Lucile decided to give all her possessions (furniture, clothes, electrical goods) to a homeless charity and arranged for them to call on the day she had decided she was moving out. Something big was afoot. We heard from a friend that Lucile was planning on breaking in to the Museum of Romantic Life to steal George Sand's jewellery. She refused entry to Liane, who used to call regularly to help her, and hung up on people who expressed concern about how she was doing.

In the space of a few days, Lucile had become impossible to reach. One evening, when I had got her to agree to meet at the Café du Commerce, Lucile explained to me that Armand Colin's IT system was now under her control, thanks to the course that she had taken a few months before. Moreover, her whole life was now governed by computer logic, so all she had to do was push a few buttons in order to trigger certain events; it happened nonetheless that she might make a mistake, in which case, she told me, lights would come on and start flashing. Even so, there was no cause for panic.

She admitted she had stopped taking her medicine. She couldn't bear to live like a vegetable any longer; she had had enough of that life ruled by antipsychotics; she wanted to experience things, feel them, *be alive*.

A few days later, Lucile told me on the phone that she was thinking of moving into an attic room, but refused to give me the address. Justine and Violette were planning to intercept her when she left work to persuade her to go in to hospital, but Lucile hadn't been to work for several days. She had disappeared from circulation.

By some coincidence, which probably wasn't one, I was struck down at the same time with a dreadful infection which, within a few weeks, meant I ended up in an ambulance one October morning being rushed to Boucicaut Hospital. The infection had reached my liver, I was jaundiced, and, literally and metaphorically, incapable of lifting a finger. Paralysed with pain, I hadn't told Lucile – who, according to the latest news, was roaming the fourteenth *arrondissement* in pursuit of a tramp she had fallen in love with – but Bérénice, Gabriel's sister, who used to look after us when we went to the dental school and whose presence had done me good several times in the past. The hospital admitted me immediately.

That evening or the day after, Lucile, in a state of manic excitement, burst in to the room, which I luckily had to myself. Violette, who was visiting, allowed herself to be bundled out amid a stream of reproaches and abuse. She seemed worried to be leaving me alone with Lucile, who a moment before looked as though she were about to slap me (her hand was frozen in mid-air), and was now reproaching me for being ill and asking me to reflect on who benefited from this.

'Enough of your play-acting!' she shouted as soon as the door closed. 'Look at you with your emergencies and your drips!'

I refused to discuss it. I had given up. I could scarcely lift a finger. At least things were clear: I wanted to be left the hell alone, to be forgotten; I wanted to be sheltered from the vast battlefield that Lucile was in the process of setting out. The hospital gave me a sort of neutral, protected space: a place of retreat.

Pinned to my bed, hooked up to an impressive antibiotic drip, facing my enraged mother, who was pacing the room like a caged beast, the situation suddenly appeared to me in its most pathetic and – at the point we had come to – its most comic light.

A frenzied Lucile, her eyes staring from lack of sleep, left as she had come, with a carton of cigarettes tucked under her arm, after dubbing me a 'stupid murdering bitch'.

Violette came back into the room after Lucile had gone. Lucile had passed her at the foot of the stairs and called her 'pitifully obese', which was untrue.

Lucile returned several times, increasingly agitated. She gave me a resin reproduction of a dancer by Degas from the shop at the Louvre, which she insisted I put on top of the television (she bought Manon a statuette of an Egyptian cat from 300 BC). Lucile talked about the many presents she would soon be able to give us thanks to her redundancy money and other mysterious income. She told me about Graham Hardy, her alcoholic tramp violinist, who lived in one of the last remaining squats in the fourteenth *arrondissement* between the rue de l'Ouest and the rue de Gergovie. Graham was the fallen scion of an old Scottish family, who survived by playing his fine music in the metro. A rumour was going round locally that he had fled Scotland after killing a man. In the course of a few visits, Lucile brought me piles of useless things from home: she was emptying her apartment. I let her cover my bed with paper, boxes and Tupperware.

One evening, at a loss as to what I should do, I rang Justine and then Violette. But they had their own lives, their own problems and sorrows and no desire to sign their sister's committal papers. Faced with their reluctance, I shouted that I couldn't take any more of this, I was twenty-one, I was overwhelmed with exhaustion and refused to carry all this on my shoulders. Calmly, we came to the conclusion that the only place where it would be possible to get hold of Lucile was my hospital room. This didn't promise the most restful conditions before my imminent operation, but there was no alternative. Lucile was bound to be back.

The next day, Lucile turned up in my room at ten o'clock in the morning, looking more sallow than ever. Her body was shaking. I reminded her that visits weren't allowed before 1 p.m. and asked her to come back in the afternoon. Lucile agreed, but before she went, she deposited the things she had brought me: a plant mister,

Manon's bonsai, a series of old, unidentified soft toys, a very special pack of cards for telling the future, a whole series of useless knick-knacks. Her pockets were full of them. Lucile announced that she had just won the jackpot, a cool 30,000 francs, because she had managed to blow up Apple's nerve centre. Given that her case was entirely exceptional and clearly unprecedented, the Macintosh management had offered her a very lucrative post which wouldn't take much of her time. She promised she would be back later and I immediately told Justine.

It was terrible waiting for Lucile that afternoon. Justine had arrived soon after I called her. The hours went by in dread of the moment when the door would open and reveal to Lucile the trap we had set for her. Once again I was guilty of high treason.

At the end of the day, during which our state of tension had kept increasing, two of my classmates turned up unexpectedly, and then Barnabé, a boy I had met a few weeks earlier and of whom I had high hopes. While I was trying to explain to them that it might be better to come back another day, Lucile burst in like a fury, laden with posters and plants.

'Out, the lot of you, and get a move on!'

A few minutes later, I found myself in the corridor attached to my drip, while in my room Lucile had jumped on Justine and was trying to bite and scratch her, calling her every name under the sun as she did so. Justine shouted to me to call the emergency psychiatric services. One of my friends ran to reception. The door closed again. I remained in the corridor, doubled up with pain and anxiety, my heart pounding, beside Barnabé, who seemed to have realised that I was not the girl from a good family he had been hoping for. Alerted by the noise, nurses came running to help. The door opened on Lucile, who was on the floor and seemingly quite at home there.

For a few seconds, I no longer took in any of the panic around me: lying on the floor, suddenly remote from the commotion she had created, Lucile smiled at me, a strange smile, infinitely sweet and disarming. Time stood still.

Justine asked the nurses not to leave Lucile alone. In the corridor, I saw how pale Justine's face was, distraught with sadness. I realised how hard it was for her to be there, to take on this role, this responsibility, and how brutally this moment was being added to past sorrows. Violette joined us in the corridor. The nurse had stayed with Lucile. We waited for the ambulance to arrive.

When Lucile emerged from the room and began spraying everyone with the plant mister, a conscientious junior doctor took me by the shoulders and steered me into a side room, where he made me sit down and told me not to move.

Lucile eventually agreed to go down to A&E, where the ambulance was waiting to take her to Sainte-Anne. Barnabé fled. It had all been too much. One of my friends stayed with me for a moment, while Justine and Violette followed the ambulance so as to be there when Lucile arrived. And then my friend had to go home.

This transition to solitude was the hardest point, though I needed it to be able to cry.

★

That evening an understanding nurse gave me a sleeping pill, which I didn't take. Early next morning a woman with a reedy voice knocked on my door.

'Good morning! I'm the duty psychologist. I hear you had a bit of a problem with your mother last night. Would you like to talk about it?'

With a sigh, I said no, no thank you, everything was fine. I played it like Lisbeth: force of habit.

In order to write these pages, I read through some of the diaries I kept for a long time, amazed by how precisely I noted, almost daily for several years, the most significant events, but also the anecdotes, the parties, films, dinners, conversations, reflections, the tiniest details, as though I had to keep track of it all, as though I refused to let things escape me.

The truth is I have forgotten a good deal of what is contained in those pages; my memory has retained only the most striking details and a few reasonably intact scenes, while the rest was long ago swallowed up by forgetting. Reading my accounts, what strikes me above all is the way our bodies carry out this natural purgation, this ability we have to cover over, efface, synthesise, this tendency to pick and choose, which doubtless allows us to free up space like on a hard drive, to start over, move forward. Reading these pages, I rediscovered – in addition to Lucile – my student life, my worries as a girl, my feelings in love, my friends, those who are still around and those I didn't manage to keep, the bright flashes of their conversation, their celebratory exuberance, the boundless admiration I felt for them, my joy and gratitude at having them around.

Slipped between the pages of these notebooks, I found a few letters that Manon sent me when Lucile made her leave her apartment and in the weeks that followed. Manon was seventeen. Reading about her despair, I cried in a way I haven't cried for a long time.

I think Manon's connection to Lucile was stronger than mine ever was, and she absorbed more of her suffering than I ever allowed myself to.

Whatever I say and pride myself on, it is painful plunging back into these memories, in bringing back to the surface things that were diluted, erased, things that were covered over. The further I go, the more I perceive the impact of writing (and of the research it requires); I cannot ignore just how disturbing it is for me. Writing strips me bare, destroys my protective barriers one by one, silently dismantles my perimeter fence. Did I need to feel happy and strong and assured to throw myself into such an adventure, did I need to feel as though I *had some leeway* in order to put to the test my capacity to resist, as if that were necessary?

The further I go, the more I long to return to the present, to distance myself from this, to put things back in their places, in their files, their boxes, to take back to the cellar what belongs down there.

Meanwhile, I qualify each word, go back endlessly. I correct, refine, gradate, discard. I think of this process as a street-cleaning machine; it has served me for all my books and is a valuable ally. But this time I wonder if it has lost its bearings. I watch it turn vainly in concentric circles. At night doubts assail me, I wake with a start at 4 a.m., I decide to give up, to slam on the brakes, or else I wonder if I shouldn't go faster, drink lots of wine and smoke tons of cigarettes, if this book shouldn't be written at speed, unselfconsciously and in a state of denial.

★

Even if I have recorded the main themes of Lucile's fictions (the will to dominate and control, supernatural abilities, the endless flow of money, the possibility of showering us with gifts), they remain impenetrable to me.

This too is a form of mental disturbance, as Barbara described it: 'this explosion like a geyser of a timid inner protest which has long been buried, the sudden brutal expression of refusal to let yourself be manipulated or destroyed any longer, which translates into a shift in tone, a rise in volume that normal ears find unbearable'.

I hoped that writing would allow me to understand what had eluded me: these ultrasounds unintelligible to normal ears, as if the hours spent rummaging in crates or sitting in front of a computer could eventually endow me with a special, more sensitive kind of hearing, like that of some animals and dogs, I believe. I am not sure that writing enables me to go beyond a recognition of failure. The difficulty I have in describing Lucile is not so far removed from the distress we felt as children and teenagers when she disappeared.

I am in the same state of waiting: I don't know where she is, what she's up to; this time too these hours are missing from the story and all I can do is gauge the extent of the mystery.

PART THREE

During her final stay in Sainte-Anne, amid her ruined dreams and remnants of the delirium that eventually passed, Lucile told Dr G. about her exhaustion. She didn't want to return to silence and the emptiness of a body cut off from sensations, or to see her ageless, expressionless face in the mirror again. It was time to end the cycle, the repetition. If she had to choose, she would rather die.

Dr G. listened to Lucile's lifeless voice and radically altered her treatment. Lucile long admired this woman and praised her intelligence and cultivation; she was able to get the exact measure of Lucile's inner disaster and reappraise everything.

Dr G. treated her for several years. She was able to talk to Lucile as an equal, in tune with her anxieties and her fantasies. She accompanied each step of her return to life.

And so, after ten years in the wilderness, Lucile returned from far away, returned from all of it, left her time in the shadows behind.

Lucile, who had never been able to climb a rope, pulled herself up from the depths, without anyone ever really knowing how she did it, through what impulse, what energy, what ultimate survival instinct.

It was a struggle, a long, gradual climb towards the light. It was an incredible tour de force, a spectacular life lesson. It was a rebirth.

When she got out of hospital, she went back to her little apartment on the rue des Entrepreneurs (Justine had managed to convince the landlord to ignore the fact that she had given notice). Manon, now no longer a minor, came back to live with her for a few months.

I don't know the circumstances in which Lucile found a job as an assistant in an advertising and PR agency. She was convalescent, she was starting to concentrate on essentials – talking, everyday actions, the metro journey, her PC, the colleagues with whom she had to establish a basic level of contact. She saw Dr G. once a week, and could call her whenever she felt herself begin to falter.

Then gradually, tentatively, Lucile expanded her range, her sphere of operations.

Lucile developed a passion for plants: she took cuttings, pruned, tended the buds, adorned her windows with lush foliage and cascades of flowers.

Lucile wore new clothes and went back to the hairdresser.

Lucile began seeing her friends again and went out with them.

Lucile bought lipstick, applied it several times a day and from then on always carried it in her handbag.

Lucile started wearing heels again.

Lucile walked around Paris with us or on her own.

Lucile began to read and write again.

Lucile sunbathed at her window.

Lucile had her teeth fixed.

Lucile dabbed on Miss Dior.

Lucile told stories, anecdotes, jokes, offered off-the-cuff opinions.

Lucile burst out laughing.

Lucile went to visit friends in Dorset with Manon.

Lucile watched, with the rest of us, the spectacular splits which Liane performed on her seventieth birthday in a figure-hugging green leotard.

Lucile went to India with a friend (a journey which disturbed her almost to the point of having a relapse).

Lucile took an interest in newspapers again and fell for the charms of Joshka Schidlow (a critic on *Télérama*), to whom she probably wrote a couple of letters.

Lucile traded in her old washing machine for a new one thanks to her bonus.

Lucile went off to stay with a family in St Petersburg for a few days (a trip from which she returned in a state of rapture).

Lucile made new friends (Lucile always had a knack for picking out people who shared, in different ways and to various degrees, the little grain of madness which could cause things to come judderingly to a halt).

Lucile fell in love with a chemist in her neighbourhood, whom she unsuccessfully tried to seduce.

Lucile again spent a few months of her life with Edgar the

watercolourist, whom she tried to get off alcohol, but without success, though she retained a deep affection for him to the last.

Lucile had a few lovers in the course of her peregrinations.

This time Lucile's treatment had not erected the impregnable fortress around her in which she had been immured for so long. Maybe it was all down to lithium and molecules. But beyond the chemistry, I like to believe that something in her had come back to life, was fighting back.

One Christmas at Pierremont, when we had all assembled for an orgy of delicious foods, each finer and more festive than the last, probably all dressed in the colour specified for the occasion, a scene took place which was to mark our family history.

The Christmas Eve meal was tense, but there was nothing strange in that. Whenever the family got together, the air initially became charged with joyful electricity, which soon turned into a high-voltage current. Year by year, it seemed to me increasingly difficult for our family to be together for more than a few hours. On this occasion, the issue centred on the presence of Barthélémy's first wife, whom Georges had always loathed, and who had insisted on coming to Pierremont for Christmas with one of our cousins, though Barthélémy was also staying with his new partner.

We had encountered more dangerous minefields and some of us could have adapted to the situation without difficulty – all of us still felt deep affection for the first wife, which didn't mean we felt any the less for the second – if Georges had not trained his hatred and rancour on the interloper.

The tension built up gradually until Georges eventually left the table, after having lashed out at everyone present with a nasty jibe, a particular talent of his.

Then Liane, whom I had never in my life seen cry, burst into tears. She covered her eyes with her hands and, by some effect of contagion, with astonishing speed, like toppling dominoes, almost all the guests at the table began to cry.

And then Liane took her hands from her face, which was incredibly bright and smooth, and gave us her most beautiful smile, saying: 'It's nothing. It's over.'

When I look back on them today, the nineties seem to me the decade when Lucile's new self burst forth, the Lucile of *after*, the only Lucile known to some of her friends who were unaware of what she had been through, the Lucile who marked our adult lives and whom our children knew.

I don't know what the exact link is between that person and the Lucile from *before*. I don't know how to connect these images to those I have preserved from childhood, in the faded halo in which I see them. They are resolutely separate from them.

But it doesn't really matter. Lucile was over forty, she had become a beautiful woman again, shapely, a woman who looked impressive, whom one guessed had once been more beautiful still, but it wasn't a matter of age but of a fault line: anyone meeting Lucile for the first time simultaneously perceived her beauty and the indelible mark of her fall. Lucile was walking a tightrope, gracefully, with just a hint of provocation, and no safety net.

Lucile had whims, phobias, fits of temper, moments of feeling down; she liked to say strange things – which she half-believed herself – she jumped from subject to subject and then back again; she got worked up, made cutting remarks, sailed close to the wind, played with fire. Lucile liked to swim against the tide, put her foot in it; she knew she was being watched, sometimes looked at us challengingly, enjoyed alarming us and demanded we acknowledge her uniqueness.

Lucile didn't like crowds, big groups, lots of people, crowded tables; she fled from chit-chat, but let herself be tamed in one to ones, or small groups, or during a walk, in the movement of striding along. Lucile's feelings remained secret; she never gave away the most intimate part of herself, she kept what she was really thinking for a select few. She was a strange mixture of acute shyness and self-assertiveness.

We had to learn how to trust her, stop fearing a relapse. We had to learn how to smile at her acts of defiance, her crushes, her fantasies, to listen to her mistrust, to respect her rants, without immediately suspecting that she was on a slippery slope or had succumbed again. Lucile was learning to flirt with her own limits, to know them better, to recognise for herself when she was letting herself be overcome with sadness or an excess of exuberance, and go back to see Dr G. whenever she felt she was at risk.

During this time, Manon left Lucile's to live in various places, seeking her own path with its own digressions.

I started work, met the father of my children and moved in with him. I fashioned myself by his side; I loved him passionately and was intensely happy.

Manon and I had become adults, stronger for Lucile's love, but fragile as a result of having learned too young that life could collapse without warning and that nothing around us was completely stable.

In her way, Lucile followed our trajectories. She had us round for dinner, dropped by at weekends in the course of her wandering. Lucile was never one of those intrusive mothers who ring every two days, whom you need to tell every little detail. With both Manon and me, she liked to have a few drinks and wander the streets with no particular aim.

When we went to Pierremont with her for a weekend, a family celebration or a few days' holiday, it was as though Lucile were entering enemy territory. In Pierremont, Lucile withdrew, showed her most defensive and at the same time most aggressive side. Within the family, she became watchful, prickly.

Lucile preferred to see her siblings one to one, at their homes or hers; she had a particular relationship with each of them, nourished with love, gratitude and resentments. Lucile wasn't easy; she imposed her own rhythm and her many sensitivities.

For some weeks, Lucile had been worrying about Lisbeth, who, according to some of her friends, was preparing to take her own life. Lucile's older sister had been living in the South for several years; Lisbeth's children had left home, followed by her second husband's. On the eve of her fiftieth birthday, Lisbeth had said that she wouldn't go much further. She had no desire to grow old. In the weeks before her birthday, she had left her job and attended to various formalities. The family knew Lisbeth was depressed; her intentions had eventually leaked out and the telephone calls became more frequent. The day before her birthday, two of Lisbeth's friends turned up at her house and announced they were staying. The day she turned fifty, a surprise party organised by her children brought her to floods of tears. Her friends stayed on for a few days and Lisbeth abandoned her plan.

The following summer Lucile spent a few days at her sister's, a trip which she made nearly every summer thereafter.

(In the course of the conversations I had with her about this book, Lisbeth, who isn't averse to being provocative, said with the highly sophisticated sense of humour which she judges to perfection, with reference to Lucile's suicide: 'She stole my thunder. She always stole my thunder.')

In her little apartment, Lucile busied herself with various tidying and reorganising projects, began painting and planting, in short, she *faffed about*. 'Faffing about' is a commonly used expression in my family, I don't know where it originated, but it means: starting several activities without focusing on any of them, or else flapping about for no particular reason. So Lucile was *faffing* and this was excellent news: she had enough energy to be able to waste some.

You should have seen Lucile getting on the metro at rush hour, her way of targeting the only available seat or strap as though it was unquestionably meant for her by virtue of her survivor status, known only to her.

You should have seen Lucile walking in the street, simultaneously so energetic and so ill assured, her body leaning forward, her bag against her hip, her way of cutting through a crowd, of going straight to her goal, *ploughing on*.

You should have seen Lucile use her elbows in a crowded cinema queue or in the supermarket to dissuade anyone thinking of jumping ahead of her or who had the misfortune, lost in a daydream, of encroaching by as much as an inch on what she considered her space.

You should have seen Lucile with her face turned to the sun, lying on the lawn in a square or sitting on a bench, the pleasure and sense of peace she found there.

One Saturday lunchtime I received a call from my mother: she had just met a friend at République metro and had realised that she had left a pan of water on the gas. Could I rush round to her kitchen immediately? Drained by an exhausting week, I flew into a rage: 'You really piss me off! I'm telling you, you really get on my nerves. For fuck's sake, as if I had nothing better to do!' (related verbatim in my diary). Feeling a certain relief, I picked up the key Lucile had given me and went to turn off the gas.

Because Lucile bore the shock, could arm herself and put up resistance, we were able to argue with her, show our disagreement, raise our voices. Not that we had spared her while she was still silent, but our rebellions had been more muted, muffled (and probably more aggressive).

Another day, it was Lucile who got into a great rage because I was five minutes late. She complained that I was five or ten minutes late every time we met. This was true. It was a mother's role to wait, to phone, to worry (I long strove, consciously or otherwise, to put Lucile in the place where I thought she belonged).

A few weeks later, on a bench in place Saint-Lambert, I told Lucile I was pregnant. She gave a brief sob and covered her face with her hands to conceal her emotion. Then she turned to me and said: 'You will let me look after the baby, won't you?'

When my daughter was born and her little body was held out to me so that I could hold her against mine, I spoke two words aloud which horrified me: 'My poppet'.

'My poppet' was what Lucile used to call me when I was a child and much later in moments of intimacy or calm. I didn't know if my baby would be a boy or a girl before she was born. Whatever sex she was, I hadn't for one moment thought about what sort of silly pet name I would give her: my kitten, my little bunny, sweetie-pie, pumpkin, schnookums, treasure, angel.

My baby was a girl and my first words were: 'My poppet'.

From the age of fourteen, not being like my mother was a major preoccupation, my main objective. I didn't want to be like Lucile in any way, physically or psychologically, and took any casual comparison between us as an insult. In fact, the resemblance between me and Lucile that my father would sometimes remark on (which no one but him saw, because I look much more like him) was not a compliment.

For years I felt ashamed of my mother in front of other people, and I felt ashamed of my shame. For years I had tried to create my own mannerisms, my own way of walking, to distance myself from the spectre she represented. Even now that she was better, I was no keener to be like her, I wanted to be her opposite, refused to follow her path, in fact I avoided any similarity and took pains to go in completely the opposite direction.

So for several months, picking myself up constantly, I made myself call my daughter all sorts of ridiculous pet names. Then eventually I gave in: I called my daughter 'my poppet' and, probably by extension, called her father the same thing.

When my daughter was a few months old, I let my mother look after her. I don't remember any longer how or in what terms I asked myself if I could let her, nor indeed if I did ask it. Lucile loved holding my daughter in her arms, looking after her, assuming her role as grandmother. Over time, she came to look after her in our home when we went out in the evening, then later, she had her in hers.

At that point Manon expressed her disapproval to me. If she had a child one day, she could never entrust it to Lucile. I was taken aback. I understood Manon's suffering, her unresolved fear, and I pondered my decision: it was instinctive. (Some years later, Manon had two daughters and Lucile often looked after them both.)

Lucile was an odd grandmother. I shall come back to that.

Gradually, Lucile got involved in the trade show run by the advertising agency she worked for. She looked after their PR. She liked telling us about her successes and failures, the disagreements with her boss, the little incidents that spiced up office life. Lucile had never thought of work as a source of self-fulfilment, but it was a form of alienation that now had the merit of distracting her.

A few years later, she felt the wind change. There were rumours of a major staff reduction and indeed imminent redundancies. Lucile was forty-nine, she spoke an approximation of English, and her grasp of IT was much more limited than in her wilder fantasies. Apart from an obsolete typing diploma, she had no qualifications; she had left school after fifth form, and the rare professional courses she had been able to take were long out of date. This time, she took the bull by the horns. She sat an equivalent of the *baccalauréat*, which she passed without difficulty, then put her name down for the competitive entrance exam for several social work schools. She took the written paper and did well. Then she asked for our help in preparing for the interviews. Lucile's shyness under oral exam conditions constituted a major handicap. Manon and I spent several afternoons trying to play this down and role-playing her forthcoming interviews. The first two interviews were a disaster, but she was successful in the third and gained a place at a college in the eighteenth *arrondissement*. Next, Lucile thought about the various ways of funding her three-year course. As she had been turned down for training leave, she negotiated her imminent redundancy in advance, which guaranteed her two years' unemployment pay, though not a day more.

Lucile wanted to change career. She decided in spite of everything to start the course she had chosen and leave the rest to luck: time would tell.

At the start of the next academic year, Lucile slipped notebooks and pens into a student's bag and started at the training college for social workers in Torcy.

We were flabbergasted.

Most of the students in her class had done a year at university or completed a degree, or in some cases had just got their *baccalauréat*. But it didn't take Lucile long to make friends and create around her a disparate little group of people whom we sometimes met.

She had no money – only enough to get by and have a drink now and again. Lucile was an anxious, hard-working student, convinced that she was unable to marshal or connect her thoughts. Her results in the end refuted her initial conviction; Lucile did very well.

One Saturday in July 1997, Lucile set off for a bike ride. On a street in the fifteenth *arrondissement*, she came face to face with Nébo. Her much-missed lover was pedalling in the opposite direction. His black hair had turned grey, but his eyes were the same: green and piercing.

They hadn't seen each other for over twenty years, but they recognised each other at once.

For a few months, Lucile and Nébo tried to gauge the significance of finding each other again. In Lucile's case it was love; in Nébo's,

I can't say. Lucile highlighted her new-found femininity, wore short skirts and perfume, put on more lipstick, wore rubber gloves to do the washing-up for the first time in her life (her reconquered lover thought her hands looked tired). They went to art exhibitions and on cycling trips, they went to Chamonix for a few days during the holidays, they talked for hours.

Later Lucile confided to Manon that Nébo had been the man she could talk to, the one she had told about her deepest torments.

In the third year of her course, Lucile came to the end of her unemployment benefit and applied for income support. Despite having tried to put some money aside, she could no longer cover the rent on the rue des Entrepreneurs and soon had to move. Not far from her training college she found an attic room that lacked light and even the most rudimentary level of comfort. At the end of the academic year, she wrote the dissertation which would complete her course and enable her to get her diploma. She spent days on it and in the end managed to write about fifty pages (*The income support contract: Towards a pedagogy of negotiation*), which she asked us to read, comment on and correct. Things got more complicated when it came to preparing for her viva. Lucile was paralysed with nerves. She rehearsed over and over with Manon and me, her hands trembling as she clutched her paper. Lucile read out what she was supposed to say, convinced she was doomed to fail, unable to let go of her crib sheet. On the day of her viva, she got into a complete panic, clammed up, dug her heels in and was failed. We feared the worst.

But Lucile postponed getting her diploma for a year, found a job in a social rehabilitation centre, where she was in charge of admissions, and took on some administrative tasks.

After a few months, thanks to the help of a social worker she met at the centre who became one of her closest friends, Lucile got a two-room apartment in a housing estate in the nineteenth *arrondissement*. This came as a huge relief to her. Lucile had always been filled with anxiety at the thought of no longer being able to provide for her own needs. Getting this flat reassured her on this score for the first time and was a precious guarantee for the future.

Manon, who had just completed her training in decorative painting, took Lucile's apartment as a place to experiment. She transformed the soulless space into a haven of colour and light, where murals, textures and *trompe-l'œil* vied for attention. Lucile settled in to her lair with its magnificent walls, whose pale green background, which she had chosen, brought to mind the colour of Nébo's eyes. For the second time he had declared, after a few idyllic months, that he no longer loved her.

But Lucile had found her refuge. Lucile was no stranger to sorrow. She watched the garden that hung from her windows flourish: geraniums, white ivy, petunias, busy Lizzies, trailing verbena, abelias, gerbera, dwarf conifers . . .

Lucile's pansies in blue, purple, yellow and white prospered as they turned to the sky.

At the end of the year, she had another go at her viva and got her social worker's diploma. It was her greatest victory.

A part from *Aesthetic Quest*, which dates from 1978 and ends with the claim of incest, and the diary of her empty period written at the request of Dr D., which describes her years of torpor, most of the texts that Lucile wrote date from the nineties. I mean the typewritten ones she worked on. They occur therefore between the end of her last spell in Sainte-Anne and the beginning of her social work studies, at the point that marks in a sense the start of her renaissance.

It was during this period that Lucile wrote an account of her first committal (I found a copy with a handwritten date on it and transcribed some extracts), as well as a text entitled *No romantica*, about Graham, her violinist tramp, written after she heard he had been found murdered in his squat.

There is another text, which I had no memory of and which I don't think I had ever read before I began my research. There is only one copy of it and it is about her childhood. She talks about Antonin's death in the accident, her total absence of memories from before his loss, and the pain which followed: 'Childhood was never harmony again.' In its pages, Lucile writes about how her mother became inaccessible, about the photo shoots that Liane no longer went to with her, the taxis she took to get there. Her few memories of her years as a child star are introduced with these words: 'I was a very beautiful child and I paid a high price for it.'

★

Lucile's texts are confused; they don't obey any chronology or logic; they are built of fragments and end as they begin, brutally.

But in rummaging through the box that Manon gave me, I found a jumble of notes and papers, some dated and others not, as well as a number of diaries, which always broke off or had just a few pages filled.

In these notes, in different ways, the idea of death is everywhere:

'Ennui is never fleeting. There is of course a remedy for that ennui, but it is drastic and unpleasant for others (some people will grow old, others will die).

'I'd love to have an incurable disease and die young. Last year I didn't even catch a cold.'

Yet in other fragments, Lucile shows herself in a more whimsical light. For example, when she regains her desire to be attractive and starts to fantasise about the local chemist, Lucile begins writing a work which she calls, pragmatically, *Diary of an attempt to seduce a chemist in the fifteenth* arrondissement. In it she relates precisely and in detail the different purchases she made in his dispensary (tooth-paste, paracetamol, a toothbrush, sugar-free sweets) and the pretexts of varying degrees of plausibility which enabled her to come into contact with the aforementioned chemist.

A liquid corn-remover gets her a long explanation on how it should be used and refrigerated. Lucile sums up: 'Five minutes of happiness for 11.30 francs.'

But in the course of her visits, Lucile discovers that the young woman in the shop, whom she had thought was just an assistant, is in all probability the owner's wife. A discovery which prompts this reflection: 'Deflecting a Jewish chemist from the straight path under the nose of his wife – I mustn't kid myself that this won't be difficult.'

Lucile has a bit more fun, relates a few inconclusive incidents, then gives up.

Among the fragments left by Lucile which I fell upon are: a text about my son, born three years after my daughter, when he was still a baby, whose fresh skin and babbling moved her; a humorous story written for my daughter; a shocked paragraph on the politician Pierre Bérégovoy's suicide; a piece inspired by the hands of Edgar the watercolourist; some very beautiful poems.

And then on a loose sheet of paper, this sentence, which made me smile: 'To Pierremont, I say no.'

I had never realised the extent to which writing was part of Lucile's life, still less how much the desire to be published had occupied her.

I understood this when I discovered some pages torn from an exercise book dating from 1993, in which Lucile clearly expresses this plan and refers to previous failures.

Autobiographical fragments. I think the title has already been used, but it would suit my texts well. I'm going to send them again to some publishers as yet undecided and add Aesthetic Quest. I haven't managed to immerse myself in a new literary project, no subject tempts me.

[…]

Manon is going to bring me the little electronic machine, I'm going to

revise my texts one by one, immerse myself in them and then type them out
as a single document.

In the pages of an exercise book, I found a rejection letter from
Éditions de Minuit.

A few years later, when Lucile had written a text about Nébo, she
gave it to me to read before she sent it off under the pseudonym
Lucile Poirier (so in a way my mother chose the name for her
character in this book herself) to a select number of editors. I
hoped for her sake that her text might be published. Like the
others, it proceeds by fragments and memories, to which she added
poems, letters, thoughts. Of all the texts she left, *Nébo* strikes me as
the most accomplished. I didn't know it wasn't her first attempt to
get into print. In the weeks that followed, Lucile received rejection
letters equal in number to her submissions.

When I found out that *Days without Hunger* was going to be published,
I gave her the manuscript to read. One Saturday evening when she
was due to look after the children, Lucile turned up drunk, her eyes
watery. She had spent the afternoon reading my novel, and thought
it was beautiful but unfair. She repeated: it's not fair. I took her into
another room and tried to tell her that I understood that it could be
painful for her, that I was sorry, but it seemed to me that the book
also showed − if it were necessary − how much I loved her. With a
sob, she protested: it wasn't true, even at the worst of her torpor, she
hadn't been like that. I looked at her and said: yes, you were.

I didn't say she had been worse, worse than that.

That evening we didn't go out. I didn't want to leave her drunk and alone with my children. Lucile stayed for dinner.

Subsequently I was grateful to her for accepting the existence of this book and following its reception with interest. A few years later, she told me that she had reread it and had been impressed by its skill.

Lucile never wanted to come to any of my readings or book-shop events, even when they were just a stone's throw from her flat, out of reserve or shyness. Even later, with my other books. I think she was afraid of being judged, as though the whole world had read my first novel and couldn't fail to recognise her and point at her.

Lucile was circumspect and kind about each of my books as she was about everything which in her eyes had to do with my private life. Lucile was not the sort who imposed her views. But with a word or a single sentence, she often approved my riskiest choices.

Did I take on Lucile's desire to be published without realising it? I don't know. When my first book came out, I didn't feel as though I had fulfilled something she had dreamed of or accomplished an unfinished or unsuccessful plan. In the conversations we had, Lucile never made any connection or contrast between my desire to write and hers, and kept most of her attempts to get into print a secret. It seems to me, for each of us, it was a matter of something else.

Lucile's writing is infinitely darker, more blurry and subversive than mine. I admire her courage and her brilliant flashes of poetry.

★

I have sometimes thought that if Lucile had not become ill, she would have written more and might have published her writing.

I remember an interview with Gérard Garouste broadcast on France Inter which made a big impression on me. The painter subscribed to the opposite of the received opinion that a good artist was obliged to be mad. By way of example he mentioned Van Gogh, whose genius is generally reckoned to be inseparable from his madness. According to Garouste, if he had been able to benefit from the medication that psychiatry has today, Van Gogh would have left an even richer body of work. Psychosis is a serious handicap, for an artist just as it is for anyone else.

Today only my sister and I have access to Lucile's writing, to its pain and confusion.

These texts call me back to order and perpetually force me to examine the image of her I am giving in my writing, sometimes in spite of myself.

When I write about her renaissance, it is my childhood dream which surges back, my Mother Courage erected as heroine: 'Lucile left her time in the shadows behind. Lucile, who had never been able to climb a rope, pulled herself up from the depths, without anyone ever really knowing how she did it, through what impulse, what energy, what ultimate survival instinct.' Reading that again, I can't ignore the ideal mother who hovers over those lines in spite of myself. Not content with making her presence felt without being summoned, the ideal mother paints herself in tawdry lyricism.

★

Yes, Lucile eventually left behind her ten years of numbness, of feeling anaesthetised. Yes, Lucile went back to her studies, passed her exams, found her refuge. Lucile became an exceptional social worker, involved in her work and highly effective. That is not a lie, but it's only one aspect of the truth. For deep down I know that Lucile always remained suspended above the void and never took her eyes off it. Even later, even when she was herself in a position to absorb other people's distress and try to make them feel better.

Much more than my own, Lucile's writing (its disorder and dead-ends) shows the complexity of her personality, her ambivalence, the secret pleasure she experienced throughout her life in brushing up against limits, in damaging her own body and her beauty.

At the age of thirteen, Lucile smoked her first cigarettes alone in her room, her legs wobbly and her head spinning. When I read her writing today, it seems to me that Lucile liked nothing better than drinking, smoking and doing herself harm.

When his last advertising agency closed, Georges worked in professional training for several years. He left Liane at home and criss-crossed the roads of France. In Chambers of Commerce he found an audience of adult students whom he taught marketing and advertising, and always left them enthusiastic and appreciative at the end of the course. After he retired, Georges – on the strength of Tom's success in the Handisport championships – established a thriving waterski club for the mentally disabled a few dozen miles from Pierremont. Then, as he got older, he became melancholy and gradually abandoned his various activities.

Recording the cassettes for Violette occupied him for several months, as did the 'mood diary' thereafter, which absorbed him for two or three years. Then all Georges could find to write were angry, outraged letters to various institutions and the media. He spent hours alone in his office dozing in his chair or listening to the old songs he used to love on an antiquated tape recorder.

As the years went by, Georges had lost his taste for words and paradoxes, the desire to spar, to debate. Georges had been a captivating, destructive father, and an odd, irresistible grandfather; he became an embittered old man. Bitterness engulfed him.

It seems to me that at the end of his life, Georges cut himself off from his family, with the exception of Liane, whose compassion he was jealous of; Tom, to whom he had devoted so much hope and attention; and possibly Violette, who had always shown him more indulgence than the family average.

Georges could no longer bear most people, the thought of them being around, or the fact that they deprived him of Liane's attention. A few years earlier, when I went to tell my grandmother I was expecting their first great-grandchild, Georges, put out by Liane's outburst of joy, left the kitchen in a theatrical gesture of disapproval, saying icily: 'We haven't heard the last of this.' The births of my son and daughter left him completely unmoved. Georges had had his fill of children (which is understandable) and the thought of the unspecified number of descendants he might soon have gave him no pleasure. Georges now had other preoccupations, in particular when he could have his first drink of the day, which as the years went by got earlier and earlier. Wine had made him happy, then aggressive; now wine made him disagreeable and meant he went to bed early, much to everyone's relief. Georges would clump up the stairs, long since upstaged by Liane.

As time went by, Liane had become a sort of enduring sporting icon for her grandchildren, to whom each of us paid tribute in our own way. Her gaiety, her faith and her humour were irresistible. We loved the musicality of her voice and her laugh, the poetry of her speech, her formal yet affectionate way of talking to us, straight out of the Countess of Ségur. Her vocabulary ('smashing', 'splendid', 'tremendous', 'a hoot!') matched her personality and her boundless enthusiasm. Up to the age of seventy-five at least, Liane stuck with her satin leotards and gave a gymnastics class twice a week that was famous throughout Pierremont. She had long taught the catechism as well as doing a regular day in the local library.

Liane's exploits gave the family something to talk about. One day, when she was over eighty and alone in the house, she fell head-first into the narrow tank of the water-softener at the back of the cellar in Pierremont. Only her calves poked out. By dint of a superhuman effort, she managed to extricate herself.

Another time, my grandmother swallowed a pint of petrol as I looked on in horror. With the aid of a hose, she had set about transferring some cut-price fuel that she had stored in jerry-cans to the petrol tank of her car. And the best method she had come up with to get the siphon started was to use her mouth, which proved very effective. Liane coughed, spat, vomited, turned all the colours of the rainbow, doubled up, stumbled and almost fainted. Looking on helplessly, I saw she was on the point of passing out, when she straightened up and announced, her eyes ringed with purple and a disgusted smile on her lips: 'Filthy stuff.'

And on another occasion Liane remained suspended above the void for several minutes, loosely attached to a ski-lift which she hadn't managed to clamber aboard, while Manon and her husband Antoine, both terrified, tried to haul her up.

Liane, whose generous proportions in the end melted away, became a little old lady in perpetual motion – apart from the siesta she allowed herself every day in front of some soap opera – a tireless imp who went up and down the stairs ten times a day, her back increasingly stooped. Right to the end Liane fought against immobility.

★

At the end of his life, Georges rarely spoke: just a few drops of bile, delivered with a sigh. Exasperation and ennui had deformed his face, and his mouth was no longer able to shed its sneer. You thought twice before catching the train to Pierremont; over time, Georges's bitterness had put visitors off. He was ill and refused to look after himself. Sometimes Georges suddenly fell to the floor from a chair or a stool. His body was huge and stiff. Tom had to be called to lift him. Tom would come into the kitchen, sigh in turn, slip his arms under his father's armpits and heave. But for some years Tom had been living in a hostel for the disabled near the centre where he worked and only came back to Pierremont at weekends.

One winter evening at bedtime, Georges collapsed at the foot of his bed. He remained on the floor; Liane couldn't lift him. As Tom wasn't there, Liane covered her husband up, thinking that she would have more strength in the morning. But the next day she still couldn't manage it. Georges seemed paralysed. When the ambulance arrived, he suffered an unprecedented attack of dementia, which led to him being taken to the psychiatric hospital in Auxerre.

Georges had Korsakov's dementia; his liver and entire system had been eaten away by alcohol. From that day on, he stopped feeding himself. He was transferred to a hospice, where he died a few weeks later.

He and Liane had promised each other they would stay together to the end and would die in the house in Pierremont. Liane had allowed Georges to go off to hospital, which greatly saddened her.

★

Lucile shot a whole roll of photos of Georges on his deathbed.

The mass took place in the church at Pierremont. Tom was sitting in front of me, squeezed into his suit, overcome with a sadness he couldn't contain. Soon Tom's sobs and moans were all I could hear, a hoarse lament, which drowned out the priest's voice and seemed as though it would never stop, a lament that honoured the dead and all the buried grief.

Lucile began her career as a social worker in an AIDS unit at Avicenne hospital in Bobigny. She knew she hadn't picked the easiest option, but she wanted to engage with her new career and, going beyond her good intentions, get the true measure of it.

She stayed there for four years, befriended some of her colleagues, did unpaid overtime, and showed herself to be both capable and combative. Lucile sometimes talked about her work: she spoke of her hopes and disappointments, the administrative process required to get a residence permit or free medical cover, the infinite number of calls needed to find a hostel or a follow-up care centre, the misery she came up against head-on, the deaths, whether sudden or expected, of men and women she had looked after for months. Gradually she learned to leave all this behind her when she came home at night, to enjoy the smallest victories, to accept failure. Lucile learned to keep the necessary distance, not to lose sleep over it.

As far as I know, only once did she break the rules she tried to follow. Lucile asked me to allow a couple of Haitians to use my address so that they could remain in France to continue their treatment. I acted as their letterbox for several years, while Lucile made efforts on their behalf, got their residence cards and medical follow-up, and often invited them for dinner. In spite of the illness they both had, they managed to have a child. I met them sometimes.

When the V.s heard about her death, they wrote Manon and me a wonderful letter about Lucile and what she had done for them.

Between her flower-filled apartment and the demands of her job, it seemed to us that Lucile had found a sort of stability.

Manon went to Mexico with Antoine and gave birth to their first little girl a few months later.

At the start of the summer of 2003, a thirty-three-year-old woman arrived in Lucile's unit. She was a drug addict with AIDS who had suffered abuse and in all probability been forced into prostitution. She had been found unconscious, wedged behind a fridge and covered in cigarette burns. The young woman's condition and her story made a big impact on Lucile. She often mentioned the shock she got the first time she saw this woman, the terror in her eyes. A few weeks later she decided it was time she changed unit and found a less onerous, less exposed position. She applied to the Lariboisière hospital and was taken on.

The image of this young woman continued to haunt her, though, and the summer heatwave did the rest. Because of the heat, Lucile had to reduce her medication and within a few weeks paranoid thoughts had caught up with her. She imagined a plot with numerous dangerous ramifications involving the young woman and a businessman. She became convinced that I was letting myself in to her apartment to steal photos and documents from her, and that the caretaker was turning on her gas when she wasn't there.

★

In spite of my concerns, I went on holiday with friends and family to Gers. I rang Lucile regularly for news; she seemed increasingly distressed and told me one morning that she had 'metal plates in her brain'. Manon had just arrived from Mexico for a few weeks in Paris. She lost contact at the same time as me with Lucile, who simultaneously stopped answering her phone and disappeared from her workplace (she had just started at Lariboisière). Manon and I had several worried conversations. Early one morning, Manon decided to go round to Lucile's to see what was going on. Lucile consented to open the door to her but slammed it in her husband's face. Manon, who was carrying her daughter in a baby chair, found herself facing Lucile alone. In a moment of panic, she gave her a violent shove and managed to get Antoine in. Lucile was having a full-scale crisis and hadn't slept for several nights. When the fire brigade arrived, she escaped down the staircase, refused to go with them, and hid in the lift, from where the firemen eventually retrieved her.

I caught a train back to Paris that same morning. When I discovered that, because of where she lived, Lucile had initially gone to the A&E department at Lariboisière before being transferred elsewhere, I was devastated. She had only recently been taken on there and hadn't yet completed her probation period.

Lucile had slammed the door behind her, leaving the key on the inside, so we had to get a locksmith to open it. Everything was in a state of confusion in the apartment: there were about twenty empty bottles strewn about the floor, Lucile had cut off the telephone – literally, with a pair of scissors – and attached Post-Its and little bits of paper to various objects, books and reproductions of

paintings, on which you could read, in her trembling hand, delirious ravings of varying degrees of comprehensibility.

After nearly fifteen stable years, Lucile had relapsed.

She was transferred to a little room without natural light in a ward
of the Maison Blanche Hospital near Buttes-Chaumont.

She missed Violette's memorable wedding, which all the rest of
the family attended in brightly coloured outfits. Violette, looking
radiant and magnificent, threw the last big party at the Pierremont
house.

Lucile's stay in hospital wasn't very long. The relapse was quickly
checked; she left after a few weeks with new medication.

After a rapid convalescence, Lucile went back to the job she had
only just begun with Lariboisière's coordination and intervention
team for drug addicts.

During her brief spell in A&E, she had been seen by a female
psychiatrist whom she had met at her job interviews and with
whom she had gone on to work. On her return from sick leave,
Lucile was confirmed in her post. She told us how deeply grateful
she felt to this woman; I don't know if she got the chance to tell
her.

These were her best years as a social worker.

A few months later, when she seemed to have settled in and got
into her stride, Lucile's fears, her moments of confusion,

sometimes caught up with her again; she expressed suspicions about various people, and between two interpretations always chose the pessimistic one. Feeling concerned, I decided to call the doctor who had been responsible for her in the hospital. He spelled it out to me very clearly: either he put Lucile back on sedatives, in which case she would be unable to work, or he gave her a chance to lead a normal life and we would have to accept that she might sometimes express irrational or suspicious thoughts.

'Like many people who aren't considered ill,' he added.

This conversation confirmed me in the belief that we had to tame Lucile as she was, the Lucile who had experienced this fresh start, with the *increased volume* that sometimes hurt our ears, because that didn't stop her living her life, or working or loving us. We had to trust her, give her time to control her fears and moods herself.

Lucile made friends everywhere she went in the last fifteen or twenty years of her life, including during this short stay in hospital. She exerted an odd and eccentric form of attraction around her, mixed with a great spirit of seriousness. This brought her strange encounters and lasting friendships.

I think the meaning she found in her work, the feeling of being useful, of being able to measure the results of her efforts, her desire to emerge from her own suffering and try to assuage that of others, was a source of stability for her, and, for the first time in her life, of achievement.

★

Lucile used her holidays to go and see Manon in Mexico. She loved these interludes far from her everyday world, meeting up with Manon and her family, their nice house, the Coyoacàn district, the paintings of Frida Kahlo and Diego Rivera.

After three years in Mexico, shortly after the birth of her second daughter, Manon and her husband returned to Paris.

My children, and later Manon's daughters, called Lucile 'Grandma Lucile' at her request. Things had the merit of being clear. Lucile claimed her status as a battle honour, and it did indeed represent a victory: she had made it this far.

My children's visits to their grandmother followed an unchanging ritual, which − beyond the pancakes and inevitable walks in the Parc de la Villette − they remember clearly. Every time Lucile had them at her house, she let them devise a 'ratatouille' of their own invention; they were allowed to use any ingredient in her kitchen in their concoction and she agreed to taste it no matter what.

So Lucile swallowed the most disgusting mixtures of spices, chocolate, flour, jam, soy sauce, Coca-Cola, Provençal herbs, evaporated milk, olive oil and I don't know what else, under the quietly ironic gaze of my son and daughter.

Lucile was an anxious and ultra-protective grandmother. She had a thousand worries about our children that she never had about us. She didn't take her eyes off them, insisted they took her hand to cross the road (even at an advanced age), never left a window open when they were there, and spent her time imagining or fending off catastrophic scenarios which could do them harm (such as an object, under the influence of a sudden, violent gust of wind, falling and bringing another down, which in turn would inevitably strike – and so on …)

I thought of all the times we had been left to our own devices, so far from her sight.

One day when I was with Lucile in a café, she told me about her terrible worries about my children. For some time, Lucile had been spotting paedophiles everywhere, and she considered every man over fifteen in our immediate or extended circle suspect. Inevitably I felt her anxiety as oppressive, and I was afraid it would oppress my children too. The conversation quickly became heated. Lucile was tense and aggressive. I lost my temper. I forget what I said exactly, but it related to the fact that she had anxieties about our children which she would have been better off having about us. Lucile suddenly got up and, with a terrible clatter, tipped up our table on my knees. In the trendy café on the rue Oberkampf, I contemplated the chicken and chips and *croque-monsieur* scattered in my lap while thirty astonished pairs of eyes looked on. Lucile had disappeared. Mustering all my dignity, I righted the table, collected the chips one by one, left some money and walked out without looking back.

We never spoke of this incident again. Time had taught that to us both: to yell at each other and move on.

★

Lucile loved avenue Jean-Jaurès with its Fabio Lucci and Sympa shops, which sold a jumble of clothes and accessories of questionable quality and taste. She spent hours there, searching the cluttered departments, looking for *the* lipstick, *the* pair of tights, *the* T-shirt, bra, bag or shoes which struck her as just right. Lucile worked her way through all the discount shops, where she had the knack of unearthing all sorts of bits and pieces of varying degrees of usefulness and decorative appeal. Lucile had developed over the years a taste for the cut-price, the bargain basement and the trashy.

Lucile loved junk shops, flea markets and car boot sales, where she discovered unlikely presents for her grandchildren (trinkets, boxes, bracelets, hair slides, Opinel knives, pencil cases, figurines for Nativity scenes), as peculiar as they were useless, which she triumphantly presented to them on each of her visits.

When I think back on those years just after Manon's return from Mexico, it seems to me that they were a peaceful interlude for Lucile, one of those periods of calm in which things seemed finally in place, a time of respite that preceded the tumult. The handful of photos taken by my sister on Lucile's last few birthdays bear witness to this: her smile, a hint of pride, Lucile blowing out her candles with us all around her.

Shortly before she turned sixty, Lucile applied to postpone her retirement and continue working at the hospital. She didn't have the necessary contributions that would have enabled her to retire on a full pension, and she enjoyed her work and was afraid of inactivity.

Shortly after getting permission to keep working, Lucile went to her GP, complaining of shoulder pain. She sent her for a lung X-ray.

The X-ray revealed a mark on her right lung. Follow-up tests were called for.

Lucile called me one evening and announced in the adamant, febrile tone that she had made her own that she had lung cancer. She hadn't had any test results yet. I tried to reassure her. She ought to wait till she knew more, maybe it wasn't that serious, she shouldn't over-dramatise. When was her test date?

I have a clear memory of ending this conversation on a light note, of hanging up and saying to myself: she has cancer and she knows it.

The previous summer Lucile had complained on several occasions of feeling unusually tired. During a weekend in Pierremont when Lucile, Manon and I, and all our children were there (Liane vacated her house in summer), we had put her exhaustion down to work, travel, lack of sleep, the inadequate soundproofing in her apartment, the pace of Parisian life, even her reluctance with regard to household chores. Then Lucile went on holiday with Manon for a week and had a good rest.

Following her subsequent tests, Lucile's presentiment was confirmed.

Initially she asked us not to talk about it. She went to all the meetings necessary to work out a cancer care plan. As a first step, she had to have an operation to remove the tumour (which seemed to be in a relatively good position), then chemotherapy, then radiotherapy.

Lucile waited till the last moment to tell the family.

She complained about Liane's reaction: according to Lucile, she didn't make much fuss about it. Liane couldn't care less, never could.

The day Lucile went in to the Montsouris Institute, I had lunch with her in a café in the fourteenth *arrondissement* which was very near the apartment on the rue Auguste-Lançon (where we had lived with her and Gabriel), and Montsouris Park, where she used to take us for a walk when we were children, and Bérénice's apartment, and the Saint-Anne Hospital.

Those years appeared to me in a sort of blur, scattered across the paper tablecloth, without it being possible for me to link one to the other, while Lucile sat opposite me, tense, trying to put on a brave face. Lucile had stopped smoking. Her future would be expressed in terms of treatments, cycles, radiotherapy and catheters, but she tried to talk about other things, asked me questions about the publication of my book and how things were going at work, where I had been having a hard time.

Lucile had her operation on the Monday morning. We weren't able to see her in recovery; we were told we would have to wait till the next day. However, we were able to get news of how she was doing by phone when she came out of theatre. The operation had gone well, although it had been necessary to remove two of her ribs, where the cancer had metastasised.

The next day I left work early to go and see Lucile. Now prisoner to drains and tubes, she had just got back to her room, and was trying to come round in spite of the dose of morphine which was holding her pain at bay. She managed to say a few words.

For several days, Manon and I took it in turns to be at her bedside.

Four or five days after her operation, I found Lucile sitting on her bed, very disturbed and agitated. I had only just gone into her room when she seized my arm and asked me to get her out of there. In a state of great confusion, she explained that she was being subjected to punishment by the nursing staff. By way of proof, she said her television had been tampered with, so that she could receive only Channel Six, which as I knew she hated, and which broadcast an endless succession of stupid programmes round the clock, programmes moreover which were intended to harm her. She made me swear I believed her and arrange with Manon, whom she'd spoken to on the phone that morning, to get her out of there as soon as possible.

In her weakened state, her panic greatly distressed me. I knew at once what was happening.

I went to find a nurse, who gave a loud sigh even before I was able to ask the question that was worrying me and told me that Lucile was a difficult patient. Understandably so: the instructions to resume her medication, which had been stopped in advance of the operation because it could cause shortness of breath, had been lost along the way. Lucile was on a high dose of morphine without any medication to counterbalance it.

I had a rather curt exchange with the nurse, who agreed to speak to the doctor. Things returned to normal as soon as Lucile came off the morphine and started back on her medicine.

Lucile got out of the institute two weeks later. I went to collect her in a taxi and took her straight to Manon's.

Manon had arranged things so she could have Lucile at her house while she convalesced. I hadn't offered to have her at mine, not just because of lack of space, but mainly because I couldn't. Ill or not, I didn't think I could bear Lucile for more than a few days. I admired my sister for being up to it.

I know how grateful Lucile was to her.

When she had regained her strength and could get about, Lucile went back to her little apartment and the plants which, thanks to my regular watering, had survived her absence.

One Sunday afternoon, Lucile arrived at my apartment for tea as arranged and announced without preliminaries – as she confessed she had told Manon the day before – that she was not going to go any further. She had thought it through: the operation was necessary, the tumour had been removed, but she refused to undergo chemotherapy.

I cannot say what happened at that moment in my head, what sudden, unusually violent short-circuit took precedence over my sense of propriety and my reserve: I burst into tears and shouted at Lucile that she had no right to do that. My panic and my strength of feeling seemed to shock her. In the face of my distress, she dropped her guard. I succeeded in getting her to agree to another appointment with the oncologist (whom she had already seen, though she confessed she had made no mention of her decision), so that he could explain the consequences of that decision in my presence. I wanted her to be fully aware of its implications and then, if she stuck to her decision, I would respect it.

Lucile agreed.

A few days later I went with her to Saint-Louis where the doctor, who had come across others like her, managed to convince her.

I shall not dwell on the months Lucile spent in chemo. Nowadays we all know someone who is enduring or has endured the extreme aggression of cancer and the treatments which go with it.

Lucile didn't lose her hair. She gained weight and spent hours lying down at home, overcome with exhaustion. She swelled up from the effects of the cortisone.

Then Lucile moved on to radiotherapy, which burned her skin.

Throughout this time, I think Manon and I were as present as we could be, each of us in our own way. For my part, I became closer to Lucile, rang her more often, visited her more.

Throughout this time, I was unable to hug Lucile – not even once – nor to rub her shoulder, nor even put my hand in hers. Lucile was stiff and ungraspable; she kept herself at a distance, cloaked in her pain. Apart from quick kisses to say hello and goodbye, Lucile's attitude had long discouraged any physical contact.

I don't recall exactly when we heard that Liane had pancreatic cancer and had only a few months left to live.

Lucile finished this year of treatment drained and exhausted. For administrative reasons, because she had suffered a long illness, she was unable to extend her exemption and was obliged to retire. This came as a shock to her. She was hoping in time to go back to work.

Knowing how far her cancer had progressed, Lucile searched on the Internet for recurrence statistics. At five years, only 25 per cent of patients survived. I strongly opposed her doing this, showed her that it had no meaning, and made her promise not to do it again.

Three months after the end of her treatment, Lucile had a first series of tests. Her friend Marie went with her to see the oncologist. Lucile was going to be able to breathe again; the results were good.

Lucile spent days searching for and gathering together the paperwork required to calculate her pension. She had worked off the books for several years for the handbag manufacturer and had lost some documents. Assembling photocopies, records of moves, and dealing with the pensions department seemed an insurmountable task to her.

Lucile was exhausted. Her back, arms and shoulders were hurting. She was taking stronger and stronger medication for the pain by the day. Her hands and her legs had started to shake again.

Her cancer treatment had ended, but the pain remained, though it was supposed to diminish over time. Lucile had to go for tests every three months.

Distressed by her shaking, Lucile was afraid that she had the early signs of Parkinson's. She asked to have diagnostic tests, which came back negative.

She began her walks around Paris again, signed up as a volunteer for an association that taught literacy courses, followed the beauty programme offered in the hospital by a cosmetics company. Though slowing down, out of breath and depressed, Lucile was trying to invent a new life for herself.

★

One Wednesday, when I was having lunch with the children, she called me.

'My mother's dead,' she announced, not without a certain brutality, which I long ago identified as a major element of her defence system.

And then Lucile, who never cried, began to cry.

She wanted to go to Pierremont at once, but wasn't able to pack her things; she was so tired, she didn't have the strength.

I told her I was coming over. I rang the father of my children to ask if he could come and collect them; he said yes and I left. I found Lucile confused and lost.

Justine and Violette had been staying in Pierremont for several weeks. They had been with Liane to the end, enabling my grandmother to die at home, as she had wished.

Lucile phoned them while I was there. From her protestations I gathered that they were asking her to delay her arrival for a day or two. Lucile hung up and burst into tears again.

I went straight into the kitchen and rang my mother's sisters back. I forget now which of them explained that they were planning to go and fetch Tom from his hostel and break the news to him in a restaurant. Lucile's arrival would complicate things; the timing wasn't good. I said: you don't have the right to do this.

I helped Lucile get her things ready. In pain and breathless, she was incapable of taking the smallest decision. I rang SNCF to find out the train times and then called Pierremont back to tell them when she would be arriving. I think we took a taxi to the Gare de Lyon. There was no time for Lucile to get a ticket. I carried her bag and put her on the train. I looked for money to give her, but didn't have any. I left her in the carriage, pale and trembling.

Liane's funeral took place in early December. The church was icy cold. I read out something I had written about my grandmother. I wasn't the only one. The tributes all shared in the same affectionate impulse, paying homage to her vitality, her gaiety, and using the same words to evoke the bright memory that she left behind, an enduring, luminous trace. Family, friends and neighbours turned out in force.

Back at the house in Pierremont, Lucile scarcely took any part in the meal her sisters had organised. She hid herself away in Tom's room.

After some time, I remember realising that she had disappeared and going upstairs to look for her. I found her lying on the bed. She was very pale and waxy, almost transparent. I felt resentful that she wasn't with us, had cut herself off, wasn't sharing. I had a brief, irritated exchange with her that haunted me for months.

I didn't see her pain. I didn't see her distress. I closed the door abruptly.

I stayed downstairs, in an atmosphere imbued with the emotion and tension which often follows funerals. I laughed, chatted, talked about old memories, saw various people, admired photos of people's children or grandchildren. I ate quiches and drank wine.

For a long time I was obsessed by this thought: I wasn't in the right place.

Back in Paris, Lucile broke her foot, just like that, stepping off the pavement. She took this as proof that her body was done for, falling apart.

I went to visit her several times. I remember going a few days later to buy her an orthopaedic shoe, which was supposed to enable her to walk.

Manon visited Lucile too, and took charge of the shopping. Lucile's list only included cakes, compotes and sweet things. Manon suggested that Lucile should stay with her for a few weeks' rest. Lucile refused.

I was busy with various meetings to do with my book. I was working out the last weeks of my notice period (provoked by my alleged refusal to subscribe to the strategic objectives of the business). I was tidying my office and transferring my files.

Right at the start of January I left my job with mixed feelings of relief and anxiety.

In mid-January Lucile invited Manon and me round with the children one Wednesday, I think, for a kind of mini-Christmas, which we had got into the habit of celebrating late. (For my part, I had given up on the memorable Pierremont

Christmases and all family-inspired Christmases.) Lucile had also invited Sandra, my childhood friend from Yerres, and her family. We exchanged gifts; the children were pleased. The afternoon was both happy and sad. I was unable to see that Lucile was saying her goodbyes. I didn't see anything apart from her tiredness.

At times, Lucile seemed a little nervy to me. I wondered if she was definitely taking her medicine, if she wasn't on the brink of a relapse.

Manon called her up and again suggested that Lucile should come and stay with her for a few weeks. Lucile said she would see.

The following Sunday Lucile suggested going with me to the Saint-Ouen flea market. She was beginning to walk more easily. I had told her that I was looking for vintage enamel advertisements for a friend. She thought I might find some there. I was tired and absorbed in a love affair that was going nowhere. I said no.

On Friday 25 January 2008, Lucile rang me. I was about to go out. I leaned on the edge of the kitchen sink by the window and we chatted about this and that. Lucile was feeling better. She was about to go off to her friend Marie's for the weekend and would be back on Sunday night. I thought this was a good sign; she was picking up the thread of her life, her tone was cheerful, as though she felt liberated. There was an unusual lightness in her voice, a higher, more open tone. I treated this call like any other, of no special significance, a little sign in passing. Lucile rang off mid-sentence. Our telephone conversations often had a weird, disconnected quality, which struck me as part of her, her inner disorder. Lucile had always broached subjects without any apparent logic and would end a conversation abruptly. I supposed then that she had said the essential.

Lucile called me that Friday morning. It was the last time and she knew it.

Over the weekend I didn't think about her. I don't really know what I did; those days elude my memory like useless, idle time, a time of unconsciousness. I didn't call her on the Monday either; I worked on the novel I was rewriting for someone else.

On the Tuesday I rang Lucile around 2 p.m. and left a message on her machine. I called again in the evening at dinner time. She still wasn't there. I tried her mobile. She didn't reply. Later I called Manon. Lucile sometimes spent the night there when she was babysitting Manon's daughters. But not this time. Manon hadn't had any news either. She, like me, had heard from her on Friday. Lucile had told her she was going away for the weekend. Since then, nothing. Lucile was in the habit of keeping us informed of her comings and goings, probably as a way of reassuring us or of marking out her own path. I tried to reach her several times that evening. I imagined several explanations for her silence; none of them struck me as satisfactory. The next morning, Manon rang me at half past six. She hadn't slept all night. She had tried to call Lucile at all hours, but there was no answer from either the land line or the mobile. She was convinced that some-thing had happened. Someone needed to go round.

It was a Wednesday morning. I had a shower and got dressed. I left my son in front of the television. I said to him, Grandma Lucile isn't answering the phone. I'm going to look in on her quickly to make sure everything is all right. As I was responsible for watering her plants when she was away, I had had the key to Lucile's apartment for ages.

In the metro I thought how early it was and that I was going alone. That is exactly what I said to myself: your mother isn't answering the phone and you are going round there on your own. I thought that Lucile had had a relapse, that I would find her in a state of great agita-tion as my sister had done a few years earlier, that I'd have to persuade her to go to the hospital, that she might resist, that the emergency services would have to be called. I thought that being an adult offered no protection against the suffering I was heading towards, that it was no easier than before, when we were children, that even though we had grown up and made our way and built our lives and had our own families, whether we liked it or not, this was where we came from, this woman; we would never be strangers to her pain.

Before I set off, I left one last message in a schoolmarmy, motherly tone: that's quite enough. Manon and I are worried. I'm coming over.

When I left the metro, I took the Sente des Dorées, the straight road that led to her building. I crossed the square. The air was damp and there was little light in the sky.

I rang the bell and waited briefly before slipping the key into the lock. I saw her at once, lying on her bed. The door to her room was open. Lucile had her back to me. In the silence I called out: Mum, Mum. I believe I remained there for a few seconds, waiting for her to answer, and then I went along the passageway. I told myself that she was asleep. I mustered all my strength to tell myself she was sleeping. I went in to her room. The curtains were drawn, the radio was on. That was a sign of life, there was life somewhere. She often went to sleep like that, with her ear against her transistor. I went closer and bent down. I shook her gently, then more firmly. I repeated, Mum, Mum.

The thought could not get through to me. It was unacceptable, it was impossible, it was out of the question. It was no.

Lucile was lying on her side, her arms folded on top of the blanket. I wanted to turn her round but her body was stiff, resistant. I tried to turn off the radio, which was tuned to France Inter, as it had been since time immemorial. I couldn't find the right button. My hands started to shake. I was overcome by a silent, growing panic. I stood up and went to the window. I opened the curtains. I took off my jacket and scarf. I put them on her chair. I put down my bag too at the foot of her desk. This felt like dead time, suspended time, frozen so that things could be different, so that things could resume their normal, acceptable course, to let me wake up. But nothing had moved, or reversed. I went back over to her and, kneeling on her bed, leaned over to be able to see her. In the daylight her hands were blue as though splashed with paint. Between her fingers and on the knuckles, midnight blue paint. I said aloud: What's she done? What's she done? I thought she had been painting with her hands.

The words were there – what's she done? – but I couldn't understand their meaning. I didn't want to. It was no. It was out of the question. It was impossible. It was unimaginable. It wasn't true. It wasn't reality. It wasn't what I was experiencing. It couldn't end like this.

Then I saw her face. It was swollen and also blue, a paler blue, and there was a trace of mould high on her cheek, beside her eye, covering an inch or two, a circle covered in very fine white hairs like on a cheese that's been forgotten about at the back of the fridge.

I got up suddenly. In the passageway my whole body emitted a cry – it was abrupt and powerful. A cry of terror.

I went back into the bedroom and picked up the phone beside the bed. That was when I became aware of the pungent, revolting smell. I opened the window. I felt as though I was going to faint, as though my legs were sinking into the floor, turning to jelly. Unsteadily I leaned against the back of the chair. I managed to turn round and collapse into it. I had to get out, escape the smell, escape the sight of her, get away as fast as my legs would carry me, but my legs were no longer responding. I was pinned, glued to that chair. I could no longer move. I don't know how long I remained like that. I was shaking. My hands were trembling. I was trying to recompose myself. I told myself: You've got to calm down. You've got to do something. You've got to call someone. That was when I saw the package lying on the desk with the presents she had left us and the letter sticking out of it. I don't think I read it then. I picked it up in my trembling hands. I wanted to get out but I couldn't. I managed to dial the emergency number. I got music. I waited for someone to talk to me. I said: My mother's dead. My mother's been here for five days. Don't leave me alone. They put a doctor on, who told me what to do. I think that was the moment when Manon rang on my mobile to find out what was happening. I saw her name come up on the screen. I believed I had rejected the call, but I pressed the wrong button. Manon heard the end of my conversation with the doctor before I managed to hang up properly. I called her back immediately. Manon had understood. Manon shouted, No, no, no. She can't be. I realised it was Wednesday and her daughters would be with her, that her daughters would now be listening to Manon shouting. I don't know what else she said. I tried to explain: the letter, Lucile in her bed, the medication, I was crying and shaking. I told Manon I loved her. She didn't hear. She asked me to say it again. She asked where I was. She said, Get out of there, get out.

With her voice in my ear, I managed to get out of the bedroom. Manon's voice got me as far as the kitchen.

I read Lucile's letter out to Manon; it was a love letter and an expression of exhaustion.

I called the father of my children and in a shrill, suffocated voice asked him to go to my flat and pick up our son.

Later Manon called me back to say she was coming.

Later the police came. There were five of them. They closed the door on Lucile.

Later Manon arrived with Antoine.

★

We went into the living room. I sat in a wicker chair and Manon sat on the sofa and said: I wish I could have hugged her. I looked at Manon's devastated face.

On Manon's face I could see what we were going through and that death was irreversible.

Later they removed Lucile's body wrapped in her blankets, because her body had lost a lot of blood.

Later Manon and I went to the police station to make a statement.

Violette, Justine and Barthélémy had to be told. Lisbeth was travelling. Someone left a message for her.

An autopsy report had to be requested and we had to wait for the appropriate paperwork and accept that for twelve days Lucile was stored in a drawer in the Medico-Legal Institute.

Throughout this whole time I was unable to sit down, I mean unable to sit still without being forced to. I had to stand up in order to resist the rushes of terror, to get rid of the adrenalin, I had to stand up in order to fight against the image of my mother, to keep it at bay.

The day of the funeral, Tad and Sandra, my childhood friends, travelled a long way to help us organise things, as did Mélanie, my dear, lifelong friend. We went to the supermarket, we bought roses, we prepared the buffet for after the funeral. Then we met up with Justine, Violette and Tom for lunch in a café near Père-Lachaise cemetery. In less than two months we had lost Liane and Lucile; once again it seemed to me that that was a lot.

It was a cold, sunny February day, infinitely sad and beautiful. The sky was pure blue.

Near the crematorium, we greeted people who had come from all over from all periods of the past, alone or in little groups; as always, I wanted to remain standing, simply keep myself together, but as people streamed up, it became increasingly difficult. I had to breathe deeply, then hold my breath for a few seconds before releasing it. I felt great emotion when I saw the father of my children approaching, with whom things had been so complicated, followed by his parents. I saw Lucile's friends, I saw her colleagues from Avicenne and Lariboisière, I saw my friends and Manon's, I saw cousins, uncles, aunts, I saw my editor, I saw Barthélémy, I saw Marie-Noëlle, I saw Camille and her husband, I saw Gaspard, my beloved little brother, I saw Forrest and Nébo, and then I saw my father coming towards me, and that was when I cracked.

Lucile had left a number of instructions in her apartment concerning gifts and things to be given back. Her Pléiade edition of Rimbaud was destined for Manon's husband, Antoine.

On her paperback copy of Baudelaire's *Prose Poems*, 'L'Invitation au voyage' was marked with a Post-It note. I think Lucile loved Baudelaire's poetry more than anything.

In front of fifty or so stunned faces, I read out this text which resembled her so well:

Do you know that feverish malady that seizes hold of us in our cold miseries; that nostalgia for a land unknown; that anguish of curiosity? It is a land which resembles you, where all is beautiful, rich, tranquil and honest, where fantasy has built and decorated an occidental China, where life is sweet to breathe, and happiness married to silence. It is there that one would live; there that one would die.

Lucile's little world was before me, a whole life of different periods and worlds all mixed together, and nothing else mattered any more, not the defeats nor the pain nor the regrets.

In the corridor which led back outside, just as I was crossing the threshold, in an absurd gesture as though I were the hostess, I turned around to make sure that everyone had gone out, to make sure we hadn't left any stragglers behind. That was when I saw Nébo's face, distorted with tears. Nébo was weeping openly.

When we got outside, my father realised he had left his wallet with all his documents in the taxi that had brought him to the crematorium. Through this marvellous subconscious act, Gabriel had turned up bereft of himself, his identity.

L ucile had left a dozen little presents for our children, each labelled with their names.

The letter had been slipped inside a grey cardboard bag, in which we found two other packages for Manon and me, each containing a Lalique crystal pendant in the shape of a heart, attached to a fabric cord.

My darling girls,

The time has come. I've reached the end of the page and I'm done. Scans are all very well but you also have to listen to your body. I never tell anyone all the things I have wrong with me. I tell one person about one thing and another about something else.

I'm very tired. My life is hard and can only get worse.

Since I took this decision I have felt serene, even if I'm afraid of the transition.

You two are the people I have loved most in the world and I have done the very best I could, believe me.

Give your beautiful children a big hug.

Lucile

PS: They're better on a chain. You can change the colour, but do it quickly before the end of the sales, both at the same time if necessary because there's only one gift receipt.

I know that this will hurt you but it's inevitable at some point and I would prefer to die while I'm still alive.

★

I reread this letter dozens of times, looking for a clue, a detail, a message beyond the message, something I had missed. I read and reread Lucile's sense of propriety, the elegance of mixing the prosaic with her pain, and the incidental and the essential. This letter resembles her and I now know how much she passed on to both of us her capacity to take hold of the ridiculous, the trivial, to try to rise above the fog.

In the days that followed the discovery of her body, when I felt that mine had not yet expelled the terror (the terror was in my blood, in my hands, in my eyes, in the irregular beating of my heart), I thought that Lucile had not spared me. She knew that we would eventually get worried. She knew that I lived much closer than Manon, who now lived outside Paris. She knew I had a key. She knew that I would go round on my own. In spite of myself, this realisation left me with a bitter taste.

One morning more than a fortnight after her death, the caretaker of her building called me. She had just found a letter Lucile had written, which had been returned to sender.

This letter was addressed to me and had been written on the day of her death.

In this short message, which I should have received on the Monday, Lucile in her way informed me of her death: she enclosed a cheque for €8,000 'for [her] costs', hoped that there would be enough left to buy ourselves a lasting gift, added in a PS that she had put money in her account to cover all her bills up to the end of March.

If I had received this letter, I would have had the choice of going round to her apartment or sending the emergency services.

In her confusion before she committed the act, Lucile had got the street number wrong.

For weeks, I kept going over the details, words, situations, remarks, silences which should have alerted me. For weeks, I tried to grade the causes of Lucile's suicide, the despair, her illness, her exhaustion, Liane's death, her inactivity, her delirium, and then I dismissed them all. For weeks, I went back to the start and then approached it from the other direction. For weeks, I asked myself the same questions over and over, and asked them of other people: why had she put an end to her life when her test results were good? Why hadn't she waited for the scan which was scheduled for a few days later? Why, right to the end, did she continue to smoke half a cigarette when she was cracking, instead of taking up smoking properly, if she was going to end up like this?

Why?

I was sure of one thing: it was in the moment of emptiness and exhaustion that followed her treatment that I should have been there. That was when I took my eye off the ball.

I went to see Lucile's psychiatrist with Manon. I wanted explanations. According to him, the question was not determining why

Lucile had chosen that particular moment, but how she had held on all that time, for all those years. He told us that she often talked about us, that she was proud of us; we were her reason for living.

I used Lucile's travel card for several weeks (the payment went through before her account was closed) with a strange satisfaction: in the eyes of the Paris transport authority, which records journeys made, Lucile was taking the metro, travelling all over Paris, continuing to exist.

Every night the image of my mother in bed came back to me: I saw her blonde hair and black cardigan, her body turned to the wall. As soon as I lay down on my side, the position in which I found her, the image came back to me, preventing me breathing. I saw her blue hands, the carafe and the water glass. Every night I could not stop myself imagining Lucile, on Friday 25 January, wrapped in her blankets, alone in her little apartment. I imagined the long minutes which came before she lost consciousness, without anyone to stroke her hair, hold her hand. I cried silently, tears that tasted of childhood, tears without goodbyes. I tossed and turned, unable to get to sleep.

Lucile had kept everything: photos, letters, drawings, milk teeth, Mother's Day presents, books, clothes, trinkets, gadgets, documents, newspapers, notebooks, typewritten texts.

When we had finished sorting through the unlikely bric-a-brac that her apartment contained, we organised an open day so that everyone could come and collect an object, a piece of jewellery, a trinket to remember Lucile by. The rest would go to charity.

My children came along with everyone else. They were pleased to see Lucile's green refuge for the last time. I wanted them to be able to choose as a souvenir some toys from the wooden box that she had put together for them over the years.

They left with my friend Mélanie, who put the boxes I couldn't take on the metro in her car. They went to her house to store some of them in the cellar (I didn't have room for them), before bringing home the photos, plants and some other things I wanted to keep.

I met them outside my building. I opened the boot of the car. In pride of place on top of the bags and boxes was the 'Keep off the grass' sign from Lucile's building, its spike still covered in soil. At the children's request, Mélanie, who is not one to flinch at the thought of transgression, had uprooted it.

My daughter explained to me, as though it were the most natural thing in the world, the nature of their homage: 'Grandma Lucile used to want to nick it, so we did.'

A few months after her death, when I had to fill in Lucile's tax return, I discovered that her monthly pension, after appeal and re-evaluation, came to €615.50.

Lucile paid €272 in rent; the sums were easy enough to do.

She would have preferred to die rather than ask us for anything, I said to myself, and then I thought that that was exactly what she did and I cried a lot.

It's an idea that often comes back to me.

When we had emptied Lucile's apartment, I kept the radio that she fell asleep on, a little transistor that I had given her a few years previously. I hesitated before I took it; Lucile's right cheek and ear had been resting on it when I found her. In the end, I cleaned it and put it in a corner of my living room, while I made my mind up about its fate.

For weeks, Lucile's radio would come on of its own accord at different times. At first I was terrified and then I told myself that Lucile was sending me a sign, and then I looked unsuccessfully for the mysterious function that turned it on.

On a narrow, confined area around one of the buttons, I discovered a fine, brown film which was impossible to identify but which might have been food residue. I was surprised that it had escaped my first clean with a cotton bud and alcohol. I rubbed it again.

The brown stain returned.

I cleaned it ten, twenty times, but the brown stain came back as though something invisible to the naked eye had been deposited which was going mouldy or oxydising.

One morning, in a fit of panic, I threw the transistor away.

At more or less the same time, the idea came to me to write about Lucile, which I immediately dismissed.

And then the idea, like the stain, came back.

A few months ago, when I had begun writing this book, my son was in the living room doing his homework as he often is. He had to answer comprehension questions on 'L'Arlésienne', a short story by Alphonse Daudet in *Letters from my Windmill*.

On page 99 of *Living Letters*, the French textbook for the second year of high school, he was asked the following questions: 'What details prove that Jan's mother suspected that her son had not recovered from his love affair? Is she nonetheless able to prevent the suicide from taking place? Why?'

My son thought for a moment and carefully wrote down the first part of his answer in his exercise book. Then, speaking aloud in a categorical, completely detached voice, as though none of this had anything to do with any of us, didn't concern us in any way, my son answered slowly as he wrote: 'No. No one can prevent a suicide.'

Did I need to write a book imbued with love and guilt to come to the same conclusion?

Among the photos of Lucile we found in her house, I came across a tiny image of my mother on a black and white contact sheet, taken round the family dinner table at Pierremont or Versailles. On the same sheet you can see Liane, Georges, Gabriel, Lisbeth and others.

Lucile appears in profile. She's wearing a black polo neck and holding a cigarette in her left hand. She seems to be looking at someone or something, but she's probably not looking at anything. Her smile has an elusive sweetness.

Lucile's black is like the painter Pierre Soulages's. Lucile's black is an *ultra-black*, whose reflections, intense highlights and mysterious light point to an elsewhere.

Today, I am no longer searching. I am sticking to the letter that Lucile left. I am taking Lucile as she liked to be taken: literally.

She knew and felt that her illness would eventually get the better of her. She was suffering. She was tired. The battles she had fought throughout her life hadn't left her the strength for this one.

Lucile died at the age of sixty-one before she became an old lady.

Lucile died the way she wanted to: while still alive.

Today I'm able to admire her courage.

ACKNOWLEDGEMENTS

The title of this book comes from the song 'Osez Joséphine' by Alain Bashung and Jean Faque, whose dark, bold beauty accompanied me all through the writing of this book.

I would like to thank my sister, my mother's siblings, my father's sisters and everyone who gave me their trust and their time.

A NOTE ON THE AUTHOR

DELPHINE DE VIGAN is the author of *No and Me*, which was a bestseller in France, where it was awarded the Prix des Libraires (The Booksellers' Prize) in 2008, and in Britain, where it was a Richard and Judy selection. *Underground Time* was shortlisted for the prestigious Goncourt Prize in 2009. Her books have been translated into twenty-five languages. She lives in Paris.

A NOTE ON THE TRANSLATOR

GEORGE MILLER is the translator of *No and Me* and *Underground Time* by Delphine de Vigan. He is also a regular translator for *Le Monde diplomatique*'s English-language edition and the translator of *Disordered World* by Amin Maalouf.

MORE FROM DELPHINE DE VIGAN

UNDERGROUND TIME
A Novel

An *Elle* Readers' Prize Pick

"The book isn't just about [two] strangers and what they have in common, it is about what all of us have in common, strangers or not."
—*Bust*

"De Vigan has beautifully captured the behind-the-scenes agendas of personal and professional lives . . . An engrossing, well-paced story that takes us into a world most of us know but rarely discuss."
—*Booklist*

"[An] elegantly constructed, sympathetic, compelling, enjoyable novel."
—*The Guardian*

Available everywhere in paperback and as an e-book.

ISBN: 978-1-60819-712-5
eISBN: 978-1-60819-739-2

www.bloomsbury.com